PROPHECY OF EDEN:
A SUPERNATURAL PSYCHIC THRILLER

WRAITH HUNTER CHRONICLES: BOOK 5

By John R. Monteith

I0640304

PROPHECY OF EDEN:
A SUPERNATURAL PSYCHIC THRILLER

WRAITH HUNTER CHRONICLES: BOOK 5

By John R. Monteith

Prologue

Diane dreamt of a humanoid figure burning on a cross, blood pouring from the blurry apparition's chest. Time stopped, accelerated, and slowed again as the surreal nightmare unfolded.

An unseen wind flapped a milky gown over a spirit of feminine form who spoke like a young woman. "Heed my warning."

In her vision, Diane responded with her human voice. "No."

Unfazed by the resistance, the ghost stepped down from the crucifix, and her wounds instantly healed. She stood straight in misty white perfection. "You must."

Even while dreaming, Diane was adamant. "That's only true if I get involved in whatever you're selling, which I won't."

Round eyes narrowed under a cloudy brow. "I must warn you."

"I've helped your kind enough already." Guided by the ghosts of murder victims, Diane had used her psychic skills while hunting immortals, seeking supernatural combat, and risking her life for strangers. "I quit."

"You cannot quit."

"Why not?"

"You are an empath. You know."

"I've had enough close calls with death in the last year to last a lifetime. I'm getting married tomorrow, and I'm starting my life over. You got it? I'm done."

A thin smile formed on the apparition's face. "You can pretend to lie to me, but you know your fate."

The suggestion begot introspective glimpses into Diane's future, and terrible visions of mutilated bodies flashed through her mind. "I hate this."

"I know the horrors you see. You must face them."

"Face who? I killed the last wraith. I broke the line. Me, my sisters, and the hunters. We broke the line!"

"Who broke the line?"

Diane recalled her prior confrontation during which she vanquished a monster. Her brother had channeled a being of green light during an exorcism. "Josh helped."

"Yes. And who helped Josh?"

"An angel."

"You needed the angel because you faced a demon."

"Okay. So, I helped defeat a demon. Isn't that enough?"

The specter tilted her head. "Your victory over a demon and his puppet wraiths was a trial, but you've only begun. There are many evil spirits requiring your attention."

"Oh, great. Now I'm the evil spirit police?"

The ghost's black orbs narrowed. "You are an empath. You know."

Diane feared the apparition's tone. "Whose job is this normally, anyway? I didn't ask for this."

"You have been called."

"Who called me?"

"I cannot tell you."

"This sucks."

"You have allies, and you will find new ones."

"I'm not getting out of this, am I?"

The ghost's voice became icy. "It will start at your wedding."

"What will? I can't fight demons at my wedding!"

"Not demons, but dangerous. Deadly."

"What do I do?"

"Prepare for combat against wild animals."

"What sort of animals?"

Ignoring Diane, the apparition continued her advising. "Remember the enchanted daggers."

The empath's blessed blade had saved her life, allowed her to hunt wicked men, and had given her superhuman combat abilities. "They're designed to defeat wraiths, not animals."

"They will still serve you and your sister empaths against all enemies, not just the wraiths you've defeated. Trust them."

"If you say so."

The ghost whispered as she became translucent. "Prepare for battle. Enemies may appear from anywhere, and they are always ready to strike. Even on holy ground."

"You mean, like the church where I'm getting married?"
Without answering, the apparition vanished.

CHAPTER 1

Looking over her shoulder as her train caught the carpet, Diane stumbled and rolled her ankle. The dagger in her garter belt pinched her thigh as her legs crossed. "Oh!"

Beside her, Connor demonstrated remarkable reflexes for his seventy-six years as he caught her forearm and reached behind her backless dress to stabilize her. "Are you okay?"

She regained her balance, wiggled her foot, and glanced at concerned faces standing in the church pews. "I'm fine. Thanks."

"What did you trip–"

"Myself. I tripped over myself."

"I imagine it was inevitable, given your horrific dexterity. I fear for my grandchildren." His smirk relaxed her.

And she needed relaxing.

Six months earlier, she'd been working two jobs to support herself. Then came a whirlwind discovery of her psychic and enchanted abilities with immersion into mortal combat against immortal powers. Her head spun as she internalized her new reality, but her desire for Liam as her husband kept her grounded.

Despite her confidence, nuptial nerves twisted her stomach as she walked down the small church's aisle. She was getting married in County Cork, Ireland, an ocean from home, with less than twenty familiar faces attending, and an inner voice teased her with the absurdity of marrying an Irish hunter of supernatural beings.

Worse, she sensed a sentient force beyond her reckoning preparing to destroy her, but she refused to let that stop her. "Your grandchildren will be athletes thanks to Liam's genes, if we can get married before the storm hits."

The elder Irishman glanced at the dark stained glass window. "By the looks of it, the storm's already here. The rain's been beating down for half an hour, or perhaps you were too nervous to notice?"

She drew strength from her entourage. Her bridesmaids carried daggers, and the groomsmen were armed huntsmen. Among the guests, a half dozen Knights of the Order watched over the entrances and windows. "I was talking about a different storm."

He gave a knowing smile. "Indeed. I was trying to get your mind off your premonition."

A foreboding fear constricted her chest, and she knew something wicked was coming. "I'm a mess. This isn't fair."

Connor looked ahead to the bridesmaids. "Don't forget to count the upside to your mess. You have found your psychic sisters. Let's join them. You're stronger together."

Diane shrugged and stepped forward. "Yeah. I got it. People here are supporting me, but we still need to sprint through my wedding so that we don't all get killed."

"I'm afraid that abnormal powers come with abnormal responsibilities."

"I don't like it."

"Let's keep our wits about us and make sure it's a happy day worth remembering, whatever perils challenge us."

She found his assurance soothing. "Thanks, Connor."

"Come. Let's get you married to my son."

Wary of her stiletto-heeled handicap, she balanced herself against Connor's arm with each step. For magical moments, she met the smiling faces of friends and family standing in the pews, and her anxious anticipation lifted. She was a bride.

The largest smile she'd seen on her fiancé cut the rugged lines of his handsome face as he flushed with excitement. When his blue eyes met hers, she knew marrying him was her destiny, but a loud thunderclap made him look away.

Nature's strobing lights pulsed through the colored windows, illuminating the wedding party with multiple hues. Startled,

Diane released Connor's arm and climbed towards the altar in hopes of hurrying through the ceremony before the anticipated evil arrived. She glanced at her future husband, and then stared at the presider. "*Yulla.* Let's go."

Wearing a white robe with an eight-pointed cross, Friar Lucio nodded and then pulled two printouts from his Order of Celebrating Matrimony book. He handed the folded papers to Connor, who'd taken a detour behind the bridesmaids to reach the officiant's side.

Connor accepted the papers. "Thank you, Friar Lucio."

"My pleasure, my old friend. You must be proud to assist in your son's wedding."

"I am quite so. But to Diane's point, we must make haste."

"Right." The Friar projected his voice. "Welcome, friends of Diane and Liam, friends of the Order, friends of the Church. As most of you know, this is a special wedding with unusual circumstances. Given Miss Yousif's recent premonition, I will make efficient use of our time. We begin the liturgy with a reading from the Gospel of Mark."

Connor lifted his pamphlet and read aloud. "Jesus said 'From the beginning of creation, God made them male and female. For this reason, a man shall leave his father–" A loud bang on the building's main door hushed the Irishman.

Diane snapped her jaw towards the attacking danger but hoped the doors would hold. "Keep going!"

Connor returned his face to the reading. "For this reason, a man shall leave his father and mother and be joined to his wife, and the two shall become one flesh." A second bang interrupted him.

The would-be bride glared at her future father-in-law. "Don't stop unless you want to deal with Psychic Bridezilla."

"Right. I'm sure that's worse than whatever's trying to break in and kill us." Connor raised his eyes to the rear pews and then pointed. Two friars slipped away to investigate the disturbance, and the Irishman continued his reading. "So, they are no longer two but one flesh. Therefore, what God has joined together, no human being must separate.' The Gospel of the Lord."

A third bang rang throughout the church, and despite nervous glances from the congregation, the friar urged the ceremony forward. "Continue to a reading from the Gospel of John."

Connor flipped papers and then read. "Jesus said to his disciples 'As the Father loves me, so I also love you. Remain in my love. If you keep my commandments, you will–".

The next echoing bang included the harsh crack of shattering oak. Unaccustomed to paranormal attacks, the groomsmen cringed, and a nervous usher called from the entrance. "The door's breaking. Whatever's out there is getting in!"

Diane's future father-in-law stepped forward.

She stopped him. "Connor!"

"I'm sorry, young lady. Your nuptials must wait. The enemy is here." He turned his head towards the groom. "Grab your gear, lad. We have work to do."

Caressing her dagger's lines through her dress, Diane accepted the interruption and looked at her bridesmaids. "I guess this is really happening. You girls ready?"

Lacking supernatural powers, her childhood friend and maid of honor, Mary, stared at her in terrified silence. But the next two ladies in line furrowed their brows and withdrew their enchanted bronze daggers.

Diane shook her head. "Hide those until you need them."

The empaths returned their blades to sheaths under their gowns.

Retracing his steps up the aisle, Connor marched beside his son behind their riot shields while shouting. "Brothers of the Order, prepare your arms and shields. Protect the unarmed guests. Everyone else get down!"

Diane called out to her fiancé. "Be careful!"

Liam glanced behind the shotgun he grasped with a white glove, rolled his eyes, and then looked towards the entrance.

The world slowed, and Diane questioned if her enemy tampered with the temporal realm. But she realized that reality unfolded at its natural speed and that shocked disbelief caused her skewed sense of time.

In slow motion, splintering shards shot from the shattering door, and the front two ushers, Knights of the Order who'd volunteered to protect the congregation, dropped their riot shields and collapsed.

Two ushers stepped forward to replace the fallen, but the beast bursting into the foyer overwhelmed them with its acceleration down the aisle. Antlers knocking their shields, the second pair of ushers staggered backwards.

Diane counted more than a dozen tines protruding from the stag's head. Larger than she imagined a male of its species could grow, the deer sprinted down the aisle towards Connor and Liam.

The Irish hunters crouched, lowered their shotguns, and aimed. As the beast lunged towards them, each man sent a slug into its brain, and the animal collapsed.

Realizing she'd withdrawn her dagger and had raised it to her ear, Diane glanced around the sanctuary. Time became normal, but an eerie quietness suggested a calm before a storm.

Connor broke the silence. "You two, check those fallen men and see what else is out there. Liam, reload."

Pandemonium crashed through the busted door. Dark forms emerged in the foyer and pounced on the two closest ushers. More beasts entered and trotted into the sanctuary's light.

Diane called out to her empathic bridesmaids. "We've handled wolves before, girls! Get your daggers!"

The blonde psychic called out in a German accent and pointed towards the ceiling. "Look!"

Motion caught Diane's eye overhead as broad wings whipped around the space above her veil. "What is it?"

Emma covered her blonde strands and ducked as the bird spread its six-foot-long wings over her head. "Not friendly!"

Beside the crouched empath, Layla whipped out her blade and shooed away the raptor.

Diane stepped towards her sisters but stopped and reconsidered her plan under the assumption that two armed empaths could handle an angry eagle. "You two deal with the bird. I'll handle the wolves."

Layla's dark hair cast shadows over her face as lightening strobed. "All of them?"

"Sort of." Diane trusted her instincts. She kicked off her heels, stepped from the altar, and strode up the aisle towards her fiancé and his father, each of whom held a snapping wolf back with a shield while striking with military blades. "You're using knives?"

Liam glanced at her with cynicism, whipped his steel around his shield, and embedded the blade between furry ribs. The canine whimpered but kept pressing, knocking back the young hunter.

Holding ground with his own beast, Connor capitalized on the gap between his attackers and kicked his son's assailant in its wound, stunning the canine. "It's faster than reloading."

Strobes of light pulsed through the windows and then thunder shook the room.

Liam thrust his knife into the dazed animal's neck and then jabbed it into the ribs of the black beast snapping over the top of his father's shield. The cut angered the wolf, and it sank its teeth into the young hunter's tuxedo sleeve. Liam yanked his arm free at the expense of torn fabric.

As the angered animal redoubled its thrust at Connor, a new beast replaced the fallen one beside it, challenging Liam.

Behind the frontline wolves, the largest canine's silhouette lurked in the foyer's shadows. Empathic insight identified it as Diane's target, and she pointed her dagger at its snarling fangs. "That's the alpha! Kill the alpha!"

"I'm trying to get to him, young lady. Keep pushing, Liam!"

Imbued with divine awareness, the bronze blade shifted Diane's attention. It compelled her to snap her arm over her head. She obeyed, twisting and turning.

The angry eagle's extended claws scraped the knife but released it as the bird angled from the sharp metal.

Diane stared at her psychic friends. "What the hell?"

Layla yelled with her Persian accent. "We're trying, but it's flying like it's possessed."

Diane replied under her breath. "I'm sure it is." From the corner of her eye, she saw Liam's groomsmen trotting up an outer aisle with firearms. As she looked back towards the wolves, she considered hurling her dagger at the alpha. But she sensed a malevolent force negating her blade's offensive abilities, and she sought a more mundane solution. She snatched the shotgun from her fiancé's back, aimed it at the beast, and pulled the trigger.

Nothing happened.

Surprising her, Liam clamped his bloody knife between his teeth, grabbed his shield with both hands, and pushed back his wolf. Having cleared himself a free moment, he grabbed three shells from his tuxedo pocket and extended them.

Diane grabbed the ammunition. "Got them!" As a trained member of a hunting team, she slid the three slugs into the chamber, aimed the barrel at the alpha, and pulled the trigger. Her ears rang, and the kick sent her sideways.

Connor announced the verdict. "You got him! They're running!"

Scraping claws became staccato clicks against the foyer's hardwood flooring while the wolves fled.

The raptor screeched as it flew out the battered doors and into the pulsating lightning, but the bird stopped, flapped its wings, and hovered outside the church. It turned its beak towards Diane and revealed its angry eyes. The eagle taunted her with the defiant pause in its departure until she raised the shotgun.

Diane unleashed a shot in the dark but missed. As the scent of gunpowder caressed her nose, she studied the darkness beyond the foyer, but the bird was gone.

In the battle's silent aftermath, Connor pressed forward into the foyer. "How are you gentlemen?"

The two ushers who'd met the wolves straightened their riot shields and gathered themselves to their feet.

Connor examined them and uttered commands beyond Diane's hearing. He then returned to the sanctuary and closed its glass doors behind him.

Diane hungered for knowledge. "What just happened?"

"We were attacked, young lady."

"I know that. I mean, why? Who?"

"Your guess is as good as mine. I was hoping since you had the premonition that you might enlighten me."

She shrugged.

"Well then. That leaves us in doubt." Connor lifted his gaze to the altar. "Although I suspect Friar Lucio may have some insights. Let's head back there and finish the wedding."

"What? No! Tell me how the ushers are."

Connor stepped to her and lowered his voice. "We must finish your wedding. Whatever enemy attacked us didn't want you marrying my son. We must complete the ceremony."

"Not until you tell me how they are."

"I'm afraid they didn't make it."

Diane swallowed. "You mean, they're dead."

"I'm sorry. The wooden shards became spears when the stag broke in the door. Two knights fell."

"This is terrible."

"The time for mourning is later. We must continue the wedding."

"Ew. No. There's two dead people and puddles of blood all over. Not to mention dead animals."

Liam lowered his equipment, grabbed a canine carcass by its hind legs, and dragged it into the foyer.

Connor grabbed a second dead beast and hauled it over smeared blood, through the glass doors, and into the foyer. "Your wedding is the victory they died for. We must continue."

Diane lowered her gaze. "We should've done this in the order's inner sanctum."

"You didn't have your premonition until last night. I couldn't have asked you to change your wedding plans."

Men were dead, and Diane blamed herself. "You should have."

"You didn't know it would be this bad. You couldn't have." Connor grabbed the headless stag. "Oh my. This is two hundred kilos if it's a pound. Come on, lad. Help an old man."

Liam brushed his future wife's dress as he helped his father drag away the deer.

Diane frowned as her fiancé exposed the ripped fabric of his tuxedo. "You tore your sleeve."

Liam grunted and rolled his eyes.

Diane squealed. "Well, aren't you going to say anything? It's your wedding, too!"

Lighting struck and painted the altar with the multiple colors of the stained glass windows. Standing under the building's peaceful lighting, Friar Lucio projected his voice. "This is a tragedy, and I know this evil. This is worse than anything you've faced."

Diane called out. "So, what's that mean?"

"It means Connor's correct. I'm sorry for how ugly this is, but tonight must be your wedding. We must continue uniting you and Liam in a divine union before the enemy can regroup."

CHAPTER 2

Nick pumped the eagle's wings, dived, and then angled the raptor above the rectory. With the surviving wolves fleeing the church below him, he flapped for speed to escape the carnage. Furious with the failure, he flew the shortest escape route to the woodlands and then skimmed the treetops.

As the battle's shock receded, Nick realized he'd been cheated of an easy victory. He'd expected an unprepared opponent, but the dangerous bride and her colleagues had been ready, and the stag and alpha wolf were among the dead.

"Damn it." As his curse echoed in the eagle's head, the bird became confused and wandered off course. "I mean... back to nest" Nick calmed himself, trusted the raptor to get home, and released it to its own volition.

He extracted his consciousness from his eagle-puppet and returned to his body within the makeshift control center. Seven miles from the church, he awoke and blinked. The stale cloth scent of his meditation cot and his wafting body odor confirmed his return to his human self.

From his reclined position, he lifted the soft helmet that sensed and magnified his brainwaves, and then he rolled his to knees. He turned his head towards his boss. "What the hell happened?"

Seated in the glow of multiple laptop computers, Seth Canter looked up and scowled. "Failure."

"No kidding, but how'd you know?"

The answer came from the shadows across the room. A bulk of muscle groaned as his muscular middle brother, Jake, rolled to all fours and lowered his head.

"I know it was bad." Canter nodded at Jake. "He's been back for two minutes, and he's hardly been able to talk. Joey came back about a minute ago."

Nick glanced at his youngest brother. Next to Jake's folding bed, Joey lay motionless, except for his breathing. "Are they okay?"

"Yeah. At least physically. Their vitals soared in battle but are normal now." To emphasize his point, Canter wiggled his finger at a computer screen.

Nick's pulse still raced from having escaped the empaths' whirling coppery blades, and the backlash his brothers suffered from their animals' deaths concerned him. "Jake? Are you okay?"

"I think so." The muscular middle brother lifted a leg, hesitated, and returned to all fours, begetting a groan.

"Maybe you should lay down again."

"Give me a minute. Check on the asshole."

Nick hated how his younger brothers feuded, but he'd endured and refereed them for decades. "Don't call him that."

Unmoving on his back, Joe defended himself. "This asshole's still alive. Thanks for asking, gorilla."

Jake countered. "Don't look here for sympathy. I just got my head blown off."

"So did I, but my alpha wolf was supposed to survive. At least you knew your stag was going to die."

"No, I didn't."

"It never had a chance, even if we had surprised them."

"Do we seriously have to argue this?" Jake crawled back onto his cot and lay down. "I feel hungover."

Behind the breakfast nook's dining table, Canter stood, displaying his average stature. He folded the laptop he'd used for tracking the three brothers' vital signs. "Enough whining, boys. If you guys can still wiggle your fingers and toes as fast as your mouths, start using them to get out of here."

The firstborn brother tested his first step. "I'm good, but I didn't die out there." Careful to avoid damaging its tiny, concealed wires, he jammed his soft helmet into his duffel bag.

"How are you guys?"

Jake rubbed his eyes, lowered his hands, and revealed a dazed look. "Alive. How fast do we need to bust out of here?"

His face aimed at a side monitor, Canter answered in his authoritative voice. "I've still got the drone over the church. There's no reaction yet. I think they're going to finish the ceremony."

Hearing the prediction, Nick's heart sank. "That's what we needed to stop, the bond between the witches and the warriors."

Canter nodded. "You want to parry punches early, before they gain strength, but we can't stop this punch. This marriage is going to hit us hard, but I'm not going to sit around waiting for it."

Slowly, Joe risked standing and letting the blood course through his veins. "Wait for what?"

"The next step. Their counter. Retaliation."

As his younger brothers groaned, Nick challenged their boss. "Retaliate how? You never mentioned anything about this."

Canter waved his palm. "I don't mean psychically. I mean those religious fanatics around her. We just tried to kill them on their home field, and I'm sure they know we're nearby. What would you do if you were them?"

The firstborn swallowed. He'd faced mortal danger before, in the animals he controlled and within his human hide, but the wedding party's alertness had unsettled him. "I'd hunt us down. I'd try to find us and come after us."

"Right. And this is a small town. They'll recognize anything out of the ordinary. I wouldn't be surprised if they've already got eyes and ears on us."

Butterflies fluttered in Nick's stomach. "Seriously?"

The boss sighed. "Well, I don't know. I didn't dedicate much thought to failing."

Nick watched his brothers gain their balance and pack their equipment. "But you've got an escape plan, don't you?"

Canter shrugged. "Yeah. Pack our stuff and get the hell out of here." He stepped around the desk. "I'll help Jake. You help Joe."

Joey's stench assailed Nick's nose as he took his brother's arm over his shoulder. Thunder cracked, and streaks of white strobed behind the hotel room's pulled curtains. The weight on his shoulders slipped, as his brother fell. He reached across his waist and helped the young sibling to the musty couch.

Jake protested Canter's help. "Put me down, too. I'm dizzy."

The boss lowered the muscular man beside the younger one. "Alright. Nick and I will load your equipment." He turned to the firstborn sibling. "We'll grab the cots, the bags, and anything else that could link us to the dead animals."

While gathering the gear, Nick reflected. Canter had warned him about the daggers, which had behaved as expected in the witches' hands. Even enchanted bronze moved too slowly for the nimble raptor, but the riot shields, shotguns, and the element of surprise had given the defenders the day. With his brothers out of earshot, he whispered. "You still haven't told me what the hell happened."

"We got bad intel."

"You are the intel!"

"I'm not ready to admit a mistake yet, but we were taking a risk with what little I knew about them."

Nick's nerves calmed as his curiosity grew. "Wait. You flew us to the middle of Nowhere, Ireland to attack the most dangerous adversary we've ever faced, made my brothers and me select almost a million dollars' worth of animals, and you had doubts?"

The boss blushed. "Of sorts. These things are never certain."

A man of science, Nick blamed himself for having believed otherwise. "Of course not."

"Okay, I may have oversold it. But I'm still not sure what went wrong. I foresaw the wedding. I foresaw our attack succeeding. It was a clean vision. I know they didn't see me seeing them. I know it, unless I'm losing my edge..."

Flashes of his failed mission flipped through Nick's mind. "But they were ready. They knew we were coming."

"If they knew I was spying on them psychically, they're more dangerous than I feared. They're more dangerous than anyone knew. I was in and out of my reconnaissance mission visions cleanly, like a professional. Hell, I am a professional, but these witches are making me eat humble pie."

Bags over his shoulders, the elder brother stood. An eerie feeling crept over him. "They're witches and psychics, and now they know about us."

Cots in his hands, the boss straightened his back and met Nick's stare. "I've faced witches before. I've faced psychics before. But from what just happened, I'm certain we're facing the most powerful combinations ever. And there's three of them."

Nick followed his boss into the night and then loaded the rented SUV under a steady sheet of rain. He returned into the room and helped escort his groggy brothers into the vehicle's cabin. Sitting in the passenger seat, he interlaced his white knuckles around the drone controller.

Canter drove in silence until the small town drifted into the darkness. "Check the drone."

Looking down, Nick's eyes were glued to the flying spy's camera view showing stillness outside the damaged structure, while the wedding party remained inside the church. "Nothing yet. They're still in there."

For the first time since Nick admitted defeat, his boss sounded confident. "Good. They may have known, or at least suspected we were coming, but they don't have a counter-attack."

"What about the drone?"

"It's useless now. Fly it into the ocean."

The firstborn brother called up stored coordinates and sent the aerial spy on its final flight into the Atlantic abyss. "Done."

"Good. Let's get home and lick our wounds."

As Nick's anger for Canter sending him and his brothers to a slaughter receded, his natural compassion forced him to reach out. "Okay, you got surprised. We all got surprised, but we live to fight another day. Are you okay?"

"I suppose so. The engagement happened so fast. The window

of opportunity was short. I didn't have time to plan every detail. I'm sorry. All of you. I didn't expect this."

Glancing in the backseat, Nick saw his brothers nodding. "Apology accepted. But whoever we were trying to protect needs to be warned."

The boss frowned. "We're still protecting them. We're still on this mission."

"Even though we're running away?"

The youngest brother stirred. "I told you guys to let me go at them straight up without the animals. I could have beaten them with a direct attack."

His jaw tensed, and Nick throttled his frustration. "We already discussed that."

"We did, but I remember you ignoring me."

The firstborn sibling played peacemaker, again. "Nobody ignored you. Psychic assassinations are too dangerous."

"But I can do it! I've done it before!"

Canter grunted. "You've taken on rookies, Joe. I'm sorry to break it to you, but these Brady witches are even more powerful than I'd feared. If you attacked their minds, they'd chew you up and spit you out. We need to stick to our team strengths. Weapons, animals, and military-like discipline."

As the youngest brother fell silent, Nick interjected his concern. "You mean, if we can find them again."

"We will."

"How can you know?"

"Believe me."

With his boss' curt response, Nick realized the three witches wouldn't sit and wait to be attacked again. They'd hunt their assailants.

Diane Yousif, with her fellow witches attending, was marrying into a band of military mercenaries. Before morning, she would be Misses Brady, married into her horde of warriors who were skilled at vengeance against hidden enemies.

Willing and able to crush them, Diane would come.

CHAPTER 3

Liam's head spun.

He was anxious and unsure how a proper husband should behave under the circumstances.

For the first time in his adult life, he appreciated his father taking charge. Connor had canceled the newlywed suite at the airport hotel and had delayed the honeymoon travel arrangements in favor of spending the night in the safest location–their home. Within their kitchen, the elder hunter poured steaming water into his son's cup.

Liam mumbled. "Thanks."

"Cheer up, lad." Connor poured himself a cup of tea, set the kettle on the kitchen table, and sat opposite the young hunter. "You've just married a striking young lady, and I'm overjoyed to have her as my daughter-in-law. You'll see the positives soon enough."

Liam steeped his teabag. "Maybe."

"Oh, there's no doubt about it. The sun will shine through for all of us after this storm."

"Friar Riccardo and Friar Scott would disagree about that, if they were still breathing."

Steam rose as Connor sipped the hot fluid and then returned his beverage to the table. "They died as martyrs. They're enjoying their eternal reward as we speak. We should all be so lucky."

"Lucky? They were torn to pieces by wolves."

"They were honored to risk their lives for your wedding."

Liam raised his voice and glared at his father. "I can still hear them screaming!"

"So can we all, including your new wife, and it's her wedding that was so wickedly... sullied. Yet you don't see her complaining."

The younger hunter snorted. "That's because she can fight back, right now from here. I'm just stuck here like a helpless child waiting for my wife to do my fighting for me."

"She's finding you a target. You're a team, an empath and a hunter. It's natural for her to investigate where you cannot."

Liam sipped his hot and bitter drink. "God help me if I need her to protect me for the rest of my life."

"I swear I must be talking to the walls. Can't you hear me?"

"I hear you alright, but I don't like what you're saying."

"You'll protect each other, as spouses should."

"That's a platitude, and you know it. What if she spends more time in psychic land than with me? She'll end up married to her so-called sisters."

"I don't think that's going to be a problem. I see the way she looks at you. But if it'll make you feel better, we'll check on their psychic session after this cup of tea."

As his emptying cup cooled, Liam's patience ended. He twiddled his thumbs over the handle and waited for his father.

Connor gulped a final sip and plopped the down the cup. "Let's check on the ladies, shall we? They've had enough time."

"I was afraid you'd never ask." Liam sprang from the table, slid back his chair, and strode into the living room. A stone fireplace rose under a high ceiling while the lifeless eyes of wall-mounted animal heads stared at him. Square windows gave a view to a dark, gentle slope leading to the rocky County Cork coastline. Rolling away to the east, the storm winked distant strobes.

Forming a triangle, the three empaths knelt on the carpet, holding their daggers. Diane, their de facto leader, followed her new husband with her eyes. "Hey."

"Anything yet?"

"Nothing on the identity. We've gone in and out a dozen times, and we're about to give up."

Liam felt like a child asking about the ways of the world. "Does that mean we're safe?"

"For the night, yes. Nothing's coming that we can see."

"You're sure?"

His wife frowned. "Yeah. When did you start doubting me?"

"It's not you I doubt. It's the rising pile of unknowns that keeps getting in our way."

"Nothing's in our way." She turned her head and slid her dagger into her jeans, which she'd donned in place of her cumbersome dress. "That's enough searching. Nobody's coming."

While the two other empaths nodded their agreement, Liam raised his voice. "Great. So, we can get out of here. Maybe we can get back our suite at the hotel."

Standing behind him, Connor answered. "It's not a matter of too late. It's a matter of prudence. Just because the empaths can't detect danger doesn't mean that you should invite it."

Diane stood and caressed Liam's shoulder. "We're hanging out with our friends and family. What more could you want?"

The young hunter scowled and whispered into her ear. "I'd like my beautiful newlywed wife and some bloody privacy."

She smirked and smacked his chest. "You've waited all your life, Casanova. Chill out."

Nervous but hopeful about his pending tryst, Liam grunted.

"Oh, don't be a baby."

"I'm trying not to sound like a spoiled brat, but I'd like to find somewhere to be alone with you."

"You'd think you know all the secret spots around here we could hide. It could be fun."

"There's the observatory. It's private and probably useless now. But not very romantic."

She gazed into his eyes, kissed him, and pulled away. "I'm sure you can do better, but that's not our top priority, is it, Mister Brady."

"No, Misses Brady. Sadly, it is not."

Connor interrupted the interlude's planning. "That's enough whispering, you two. What did you ladies find?"

While Diane clutched her husband's hand, the blonde German empath, Emma, responded. "There's nothing dangerous nearby."

In her Persian accent, Layla clarified. "And none of our distant sisters know what happened. We've been reaching out to everyone, but nobody knows who attacked us."

Color rose on Diane's face, and her voice carried the edge of her awoken ire. "But it wasn't a complete loss. We found something that might be useful."

Liam thought she sounded coldly confident, like she was calculating her vengeance against whomever had ruined her wedding. "Something or someone?"

"Something. Traces of movement."

"You mean, in three-dimensions? Like you can see the path someone took to come for you?"

"Sort of. That's accurate enough."

Liam was encouraged. "Okay, then. We follow the path back to them and pay them a rude visit."

"It's not that simple."

"Why not?"

"Don't you think we would've said something if it was possible?"

"Yeah, probably. But it's been a rough night. I'm not sure what anyone's thinking anymore."

"The path becomes blurry when you trace it back in time. The farther back, the more blurry."

Liam tried to envision the empathic void, the timeless world that welcomed only those with the inherent ability to find it. "Like a ship's wake?"

"Yeah. Maybe."

Emma blurted out news. "However you want to picture it, they knew about the trail, and they tried to hide it."

Liam narrowed his eyes at the German empath. "They tried to hide their psychic wake?"

"It's impossible to get rid of them, but there are ways to minimize it. We're all still learning, but we've figured out that if we move closely enough together, we leave the wake of one person instead of three."

"Like ships in formation."

Emma shrugged. "That's how Layla, Diane, and I move when we enter the void separately. The ideal is to enter together from the same spot as one mind, but that's not always possible. We've been practicing for months, but we still leave enough ripples for someone to see that there's more than one of us. It's harder than you'd think to move like that. It slows us down, or at least it feels slower."

Liam turned to his wife. "And that's important?"

Diane nodded. "We had to look really closely, but whoever attacked us tried to leave the wake of one person, but there were at least two. They move tightly together."

"Like professionals."

"They've been operating in this world longer than we have. They knew what they were doing when they tracked us."

Liam considered his wife's safety. "Are you sure they were tracking all three of you together and not seeking just one of you?"

Diane shook her head. "They were seeking all three of us. The tracks disappear a day and a half ago, but I haven't been alone in the void for weeks. I don't like going in there without my sisters."

The young hunters narrowed his eyes. "Why not?"

"It's dangerous. I've told you that. It's like we discovered a new universe, and we're the last ones to show up."

"But nobody's ever threatened you like this before, right?"

"Just verbal threats, and not many of those. But when we encounter bad people in there, we run. The vibes are horrible. It's like being baked alive in pure evil."

"Can you sense the evil on the traces that followed you?"

She sighed. "It doesn't work like that. Their trail doesn't leave evidence of who they were, other than maybe something about their numbers or speed."

"And?"

"And nothing. Two or more people hunted down me, Layla, and Emma at a pretty fast speed, probably moving as fast as they could without revealing their numbers and without getting too close to alert us."

"But still, you got your premonition. That's how we knew to prepare and fight back. Without that, we'd have been... it would have been much worse."

She lowered her gaze. "And it was just me who got the premonition. I don't know why. None of us do."

"Has anyone ever followed you in there before?"

Diane slouched. "I'm tired."

"I'm sorry, honey. I'm trying to solve this."

"Can't we just wind down for the night?"

Liam welcomed his father's presence beside him as the final authority. "I'm torn between figuring out who attacked us and trying to enjoy what's left of the evening. Let's ask my father."

"If the empaths believe we're safe, then I only need to check the grounds and set up a patrol before we retire for the evening. I'll take care of that."

"Thanks, Father."

"My pleasure, lad." The elder hunter swept his arm over the coffee table, dining table, and then towards the kitchen. He'd arranged for the food, beverages, flowers, and centerpiece decorations to be relocated from the reception hall to his home. "In the meantime, enjoy the refreshments. I'll make the arrangements and return soon."

As he stepped away, Connor greeted the lingering guests who'd straggled to his home behind the wedding party, and then he departed out the front door.

Diane straightened her back. "You hungry?"

Liam snorted. "Now that you mention it, I'm starved."

"You should appreciate that your wife can tell."

"I'm sure you heard my stomach growling. I must've been the only guy in the room who couldn't."

She pointed at a platter of mini-sandwiches forming a mound of meats and breads next to an arrangement of cheese and crackers. "Go for it. I'm not cooking tonight."

The young hunter raised an eyebrow. "I should hope not. But now that you mention it, can you cook? You haven't cooked for me much that I can remember."

She smirked. "I'm Chaldean. I can whip a few things up, but I'm not lifting a finger tonight. In fact, get me a plate of salad and get me some of that sliced chicken."

"I don't suppose I can say 'no'?"

"Welcome to married life, buddy. Be a good husband and take care of your wife."

Liam navigated through the ad hoc food stations, greeting a few guests and gathering dinner for Diane and himself. Thinking in terms of her needs, her tastes, and her desires was new, and the impact of marriage began to settle upon him. As he balanced sandwiches and salads on two plates, he realized he was no longer one person but two, and they were no longer two, but one.

He also realized his sexual ignorance worried him. As the adrenaline of the animal attack wore off, performance anxiety gripped him. Less than a year ago, he'd been expecting a life of celibacy and hunting nearly uncatchable, life-stealing monsters.

Then, after meeting Diane, he'd retired four wraiths and had opened a loophole in the restrictions on his freedom of marrying. The current of time had then become rolling rapids, sweeping him into a whirlpool of planning the wedding, the honeymoon, the living arrangements, and other life-altering events. But nobody had shared insights about consummating the nuptials.

Carrying the food, the nervous husband strode towards Diane, who'd moved to a couch. She looked up in anticipation, releasing butterflies in Liam's stomach. They were going to be naked in front of each other soon, and every doubt about his manhood clawed at him.

Was he attractive enough for her? Did she desire him as much as he wanted her? Would they achieve the right chemistry and desired bond of ideal spouses? Would she respond to his touch? Did he know what to do, beyond textbook instruction? Would they make too much noise?

He extended her dinner and sat next to her. "Here you go."

"Thanks. Oh, you forgot the cucumbers."

He was already getting up again.

She grabbed his arm. "Don't bother. It's fine. Just remember for next time."

"Huh. I hate cucumbers."

"You like pickles."

"That's different. They become completely different things after you pickle them."

"I guess so. But you'll have to remember that I like cucumbers."

"Easy enough, since I don't like them. Opposites attract, you know."

Connor entered the house through the front door, escorting one of Liam's hunting friends. The younger man was a neighbor who joined the Bradys on periodic hunting trips, and he appeared wearing the old shirt and bloodstained coveralls he used when cleaning their catches.

Liam stiffened his back and studied them. "Anything?"

Connor pursed his lips. "I'll say. Shocking. He found this still embedded in what's left of the stag's head." The elder hunter lifted a crown of flexible electronic boards.

Lowering his plate to the coffee table, Liam stood and walked to his father. "What the hell's that?"

"I was hoping you could tell me. Technology isn't my forte."

The young hunter took the crown and examined it. A third of it had been blown away, but enough remained to estimate its purpose. "I think it's a bunch of antennas."

Connor frowned. "What could it be for?"

"This chip here looks like a wireless communications module." Liam examined the contraption further. "The way the antennas are spread around, I'd guess it's for communicating directly with the animal's brain."

"Communicating? Like reading its mind?"

"Probably. We know that the brain creates electrical impulses and that electrical impulses generate electromagnetic fields. That's what antennas sense. But it's also what they create and send out. It could be two-way communication."

The elder hunter folded his arms. "So, they weren't under psychic control but radio control?"

Frustrated, Liam held his breath while thinking. "I can't tell. Maybe someone with more technical skill would know."

"You have technical skill, lad. Use it. Don't let doubt bother you. You're holding the answer in your hand."

"I don't know, Father."

"Make a guess."

"Okay." Liam glared at the device. "I'm going to say, both."

"Both, as in psychic and radio control?"

"Yeah. Let's go with that. We have two pieces of evidence, the electronics and the psychic trail. So, let's say they're working in both realms to control the animals."

"So, be it." Connor turned to the hunting friend. "You found something like that electronic radio controller in the head of a wolf, too, but not the other bodies?"

The young man nodded. "The alpha wolf, to be specific. The other two dead wolves didn't have one."

Liam voiced his opinion. "The alpha, the stag, and probably the eagle had electronic controls in their brains. And if I had to keep guessing, I'd say there are three psychics controlling them."

Connor squinted in thought. "I can't wait to get Friar Lucio's opinion when he returns from his patrol of the grounds with Nana. This will make quite a challenging riddle to unravel."

The young hunter had reached his breaking point for informational download. "It's been a wild night, but I think it's time to sleep on it."

Connor sighed. "Very well. We've all been through enough tonight. You're free to focus your attentions on your wife."

"Thanks, Father. In fact, I'm getting ready to say goodnight to everyone."

The elder hunter stepped forward and lowered his voice. "I wish I could give you advice, but you're about to enjoy a life experience that I never will."

"Did I do the right thing after the attack? Was it right to continue with the wedding? People died. The screams. The blood."

"Absolutely. Whoever attacked may have been trying to stop the wedding. That means you had to continue, to thwart whatever goal our new enemy had in mind."

"We need to know what that goal is. Why did they attack? And who are they? But that can wait until tomorrow."

"Indeed, lad. Huh."

"Huh, what?"

"I just realized, now that you're married, I may yet enjoy grandchildren. The more I think of it, the more I realize that I'm truly blessed by this wedding, but not if you keep standing there. Why don't you take your wife upstairs and start your new life?"

CHAPTER 4

Diane awoke the next morning beside her gently snoring husband. Refreshed, she gave thanks for the relative quietness. Unlike his worst nights, during which he shook the earth's foundations, Liam had kept his noise subdued enough for her to sleep, even while she adjusted to her unfamiliar surroundings. She'd rarely been in his bedroom, and consummating her nuptials in her new groom's childhood chambers had been weird.

Despite yesterday's distractions, she'd connected with Liam. As her awareness slipped from her evaporating dreams to reality, she remembered a prior evening of admirable sexual chemistry. They'd hastened past the awkwardness of matrimonial discovery and had found an easy gifting of each other's bodies. While she faced her first full day as a hunter's wife, a warm confidence billowed within her as the new Misses Brady.

As she slid from the bed and crept into the upstairs hallway, a smile curled her lips. Entering the bathroom, she embraced cautious optimism about having a happy life, despite the prior evening's unexpected violence. She had a soulmate husband, a great family, good friends, and supernatural powers, making her wonder who wouldn't be content under such circumstances.

Then came an unwanted thought, the unpleasant reminder. A team of professional psychics wanted her dead.

She'd faced mortal enemies before last night, including crazed animal attacks. But other than being abducted once, she'd always selected her adversary and had taken the fight to him. This time, an unknown force had surprised her.

On her wedding night.

Her inner bridezilla craved revenge.

After her morning routine, she tiptoed down the stairs. The

ground floor was quiet except for the clinking and sizzling of the Brady's housekeeper making breakfast. Diane greeted the stocky woman. "Good morning, Agnes."

Agnes rotated from a pan of grilling bacon, and a genuine smile issued from her face. "Good morning, Misses Brady."

"Wow. I'm still getting used to hearing 'Misses Brady'."

"It will take time. Did you sleep well?"

Diane noticed a pistol sheathed in a holster strapped around the woman's thick waist. "Yes. Thanks. Forgive me, but I have to ask. When's the last time you brought a firearm to work?"

Agnes smirked as she looked to the sizzling meat. "The Bradys showed me how to use this long ago. I wear it whenever Mister Connor says I could become a target. He's worried about his enemies kidnapping me to use as leverage."

"How many times has that happened?"

"To be honest, last night was the first time he made me carry this."

Diane sat at the kitchen table. "Oh. Sorry. That's my fault."

"It's not your fault. Your wedding was your right, after all you've been through."

"You know... everything I've been through?"

"I know enough to take care of the men, and you're a huge part of their lives now. I'm like a sister and mother to them. I know when they come and go, I can read their moods, and I hear things."

"Well, I guess I'm in their lives to stay now."

"I hope that you and Mister Liam will be happy."

Diane picked an apple from a fruit basket and cut into it with a knife. "If we're going to be happy, we've got work to do."

"I know. It's hardly fair, but this is the life you've chosen with Mister Liam. I trust you'll figure out what to do next."

"Maybe the others will figure it out. I have no clue." Diane bit into a tangy wedge.

Agnes laid out a breakfast of bacon, sausages, black pudding, poached eggs, fried potato wedges, and brown bread. She then poured brown tea into steaming cup. "I'm sure Mister Connor will know what to do."

Twenty minutes later, Connor was sitting beside Diane, washing down meats and potatoes with tea. "I'm sorry, young lady. I've no idea what to do. Perhaps Liam or the other empaths will have some insight."

Buttering toast across the table, Emma responded with her German accent. "I don't know what to do, either."

"It means we dust off our wounds and defend ourselves."

Diane looked over her shoulder at Liam wearing jeans and a tee shirt under his matted wet hair. She smiled and kissed him as he leaned into her.

Silence compelled the young hunter to continue. "I mean it. We all want to know who attacked us, and we all want to go after them. But that's the wrong approach. It dawned on me last night while I was staring at the ceiling."

"When were you staring at the ceiling?"

"While you were asleep. Around three o'clock. I was trying to figure out how to track them when it came to me. We can't. We don't know enough about them."

Connor frowned. "So, we do what we must to change that."

"No, Father. I doubt we will. The girls can't find them in the empathic void, and we don't even have a starting point for searching in the real world."

The elder hunter grunted. "No, I suppose we don't."

"But they'll come to us."

"Maybe they will, lad. But we can't say when, and we can't remain on high alert waiting for them twenty-four hours a day."

Liam accepted a full plate from Agnes and sank into the chair next to Diane. "No. But we can lure them in."

"And how do you expect to do that?"

"Give them what they want. Until we accomplish whatever it is they were trying to stop us from doing, they'll keep coming."

Connor tipped back tea and returned the cup to the table. "They were trying to stop your wedding. You're now proposing that our new enemy will strike us again, somewhere predictable?"

"Something like that."

"Do share."

Diane shot her husband an inquisitive glance. "Do you think they're trying to stop us from doing something specific?"

Her husband shrugged. "Yeah. Sure. Why not?"

"What if they just hate empaths? For all we know, we could have natural enemies."

"I guess it's possible, but it doesn't change what I'm trying to say." He jammed a sausage into his mouth and elaborated while chewing. "In fact, it supports my point. I say we set a trap."

Diane thought he sounded overconfident. "A trap requires bait."

"I know. We're the bait."

A chill shot up Diane's spine. "What?"

"Someone's trying to kill us. That makes us bait already. We may as well draw them out on our terms."

"You want to give them another chance to kill us?"

Liam swallowed and shrugged. "Well... yeah. You got a better idea?" He looked at her and then at the other faces around the table. "Does anyone have a better idea?"

After heads shook in silence, the bride sipped orange juice. "I don't like this."

Again with his mouth full of meat, Liam responded. "None of us likes this, but here we are."

Her husband's confidence eased her edginess, and she appreciated his mettle. "Okay, buddy. What's your plan?"

"We keep doing what we're doing."

"But your dad already canceled our honeymoon."

"I'm talking about what we planned to do after our honeymoon."

Diane recognized his intent. "That's three weeks away."

"Not if we move up the schedule."

Diane recalled the plan.

She was supposed to marry Liam, whom she loved, but the union was also to carry symbolic weight. Under the Magisterium of the Order that ruled the Bradys, the betrothal ushered in an age of partnership between the line of hunters and the line of empaths.

No longer was the relationship one of protector and victim. It had evolved to one of hunter and empathic hunter, based upon the synergies of merging the men's military and tracking experience with the women's metaphysical abilities.

After Diane had helped Liam and Connor save Layla's son from becoming a serial-killing wraith, everyone recognized their abilities as a team. With her grandmother's logistical help and her brother serving as a radio transceiver for angels whenever the species was needed, the seven companions formed a unique party for hunting the world's worst evils.

The team's first mission after retiring wraiths, originally scheduled to occur after the return of the couple from their honeymoon, was to stop a different type of beast.

With the wraiths removed and the marriage of Liam and Diane pending, Friar Lucio had approached Connor with an offer. The Order watched evils deeper and older than wraiths, and Lucio had wanted the special team that had proven itself against wraiths. If Connor agreed, the Order would fund the Brady's extended family in the hunting of supernatural monsters.

After conferring with the stakeholders, including an enthusiastic Diane with her new powers, new sisters, and new fiancé, Connor had agreed.

A serial killer roamed the United States taking the lives of religious sisters. One witness had survived to recount the tale of horror to her pastor. With superhuman power, the killer had used one hand to snap a bystander's neck while throwing the witness across the room with his other hand.

Word of the attack had reached Friar Lucio, and he'd offered Connor Brady's hunters and empaths as a solution to the supernaturally-fueled serial murdering.

With her lackluster romance and cash problems solved by her marriage, Diane embraced her new role as a supernatural crime fighter. She knew the serial killer chased his targets through psychic means because she'd seen the evidence. And since he left a trail, she also knew she and her sisters could track him. "We've seen the killer moving through the void, but we don't control when he attacks."

Liam spoke like he refused to accept defeat. "No. But we can gather clues about his movement and get ahead of him."

"We never know where he's attacking next."

"Sure, we do. Two weeks ago, you said he's focusing his psychic energy on Washington. Has that changed?"

Feelings, visions, and impressions governed the void, and translating her interpretation of that world into dates, times, and places grated Diane's nerves. "No. Not really."

"Okay, then. It's sketchy, but it's all we've got. I say we head to D.C. now."

Diane recalled her latest ethereal tracking session. Sloppy, the murderer had left the disheveled trail of a careless mind, and per her mapping of the void to reality, he was tightening his viewing around America's capital city. "No. We can see his anger. Emotions leave trails, and they also leave the strongest paths. When they're really strong, they can also point ahead to where someone's looking, but he could be looking for a random reason."

"Like what?"

She flicked her wrist. "I don't know. I'm learning as I go."

"But you've given us a destination, and that's D.C."

"Yeah, but his anger is rough, like it's shaking out of control. It's a guess if he's really going there."

"I understand, but your guess is good enough for me."

Diane challenged her husband's hasty conclusions with misdirection. "What about the bunch of wild animals that tried to kill us?"

"We'll get close enough and use them all as bait."

"I thought we were the bait."

Liam dropped a piece of buttered toast to his plate and frowned at his wife. "No, silly. We're bait for the... what the hell are we going to call them?"

Looking up from his forkful of potatoes, Connor replied. "The enemy?"

"Yes. You know, the ones who attacked us last night."

The elder hunter shrugged. "Why not just call them 'the enemy'?"

"That's too vague, Father."

"Alright, then. The 'beast masters'."

"Better. We're bait for the beast masters. The nuns will be bait for the serial killer."

Again, the empath challenged her husband. "You want to use nuns as bait?"

"We need them to lure in the serial killer."

Diane disliked the idea. "Even if you can do that, what about the beast masters?"

"You and your sisters will be watching, and we'll all be preparing for them."

"Preparing how? Are you going to set bear traps all over the nation's capital? How can you be sure they'll come?"

"You tell me. You're an empath. You know."

She smacked his husky shoulder. "Don't use that on me, or I won't share my visions with you again."

He smirked. "Hey, careful. You're stronger than you look."

"No, I'm not. And I look scrawny. Quit complaining."

"I'm not complaining." He looked around the table. "If you guys all like what I'm saying, I have no complaints."

Silent eye contact confirmed it, and Connor announced the outcome. "It makes perfect sense, lad, but the devil's in the details."

"I'm ready to explain it. I haven't thought it all out, but I think you'll find it a sound approach."

"I assume so. So be it. You'll review the details with all of us today, and we'll head to Washington tomorrow."

The accelerated timeline reminded Diane of her rescheduled celebration. "I still want my honeymoon."

Liam nodded while chewing. "Of course. When we're done."

As Diane excused herself and pushed her chair from the table, she glimpsed her future. She was an empath. She knew.

Evil would continue lurking everywhere, waiting for those called to justice to rise against it.

Waiting for her.

Always.

CHAPTER 5

The next day, Nick Slate propelled his consciousness through the void. His brothers tucked against his flanks, he glanced over his ethereal shoulders to check their trail, and their deliberate triangular formation left a tight wake. But he noticed a ripple. "Watch it, Jake. You're drifting wide."

Behind his right side, his husky middle brother was obedient. "Sorry. I'm adjusting my course."

The ripple subsided, and Nick looked forward again. Confident in his siblings' disciplined movement, he turned his attention outward, seeking the psychic witches.

But among the countless starry entities dotting the void's horizons, the Yousif—now Brady—woman and her colleagues eluded him. Like a whisper, he sent his thoughts to his fraternal companions. "You guys see anything?"

Jake sounded deflated. "Nothing."

"Roger that, Jake. Keep looking. What about you, Joe?"

His youngest brother responded from his left. "Don't you think I'd speak up if I saw something?"

Nick left the flippant comment unanswered and guided his brothers into a powered ascent for a better view. As he pushed upward through the nothingness, the twinkling dots of the groundless spherical canopy drifted farther apart. "Keep your eyes peeled. Look for any unusual movement, whether you think it's them or not."

Joe protested. "They're not going to let themselves be seen now that they know about us. We're wasting our time."

Ahead, a glowing purple orb represented the spiritual energy of a haunted home outside Philadelphia which served as a geographical marker. Gauging his position to the beacon, Nick estimated himself off the eastern coast of the United States. Again, he ignored his complaining brother and corrected his course. "We're too far to the west. Let's get back over land. Follow me left ten degrees."

Jake acknowledged. "Roger left ten degrees. Ready."

Even Joe honored the risk of unwanted exposure from a disheveled trail, and the young renegade followed communications protocols during the maneuver. "Roger left ten degrees. Ready."

The firstborn brother tilted his awareness sideways and eased through the turn. After steadying, he checked the wake. Tight. He then gazed over the vastness above the infinite water at the azure auras of psychic beings who maneuvered throughout the ether. "We're steady on course. Keep looking."

Carrying impatience, Joe's thought-formed words abraded his firstborn brother's mind. "It's pointless, Nick. Admit it."

The firstborn sibling wanted to silence his youngest brother, but Joe had a good point. The witches he sought, those who'd left tight but traceable trails of eager curiosity during the past year as they'd sought their victims, were unseen. "I don't want to quit. They can't avoid us if they don't who we are."

Joe injected more doubt. "Oh, yeah? Then, where are they? They're afraid of the void all of sudden?"

Crediting his animal attack at the Irish church for having cast a disturbing anxiety over the psychic realm, Nick noticed an eerie calmness. Usually, entities moved about the ether like pedestrians on busy sidewalks, following repeated patterns, but today's activity was a subdued fraction of normalcy.

From his right, Jake supported the firstborn brother. "Nick's right that they don't know who we are, but I feel a creepy paranoia all around us. Don't you guys sense it?"

As he examined the ether's tranquility, Nick agreed. "Yeah. I do. And I'm sure those witches are alerted and being careful, but they can't avoid the ether forever."

"But they're not here now. The asshole has a point. We're wasting our time looking for them in here."

"His name's Joe."

Joe sounded angrier than normal. "I can defend myself, but I'm not going to bother since the gorilla actually agrees with me."

Nick sensed his brothers' frustration challenging his abilities to lead them. As he considered giving up the search, he noticed a steady light against the dark backdrop. Studying it, he placed it in the sky above Baltimore. "You guys see that? On our right, around two o'clock, about thirty degrees below us?"

"I see it. You're right. That's not normal, but it looks familiar. Or not. A lot of stuff looks the same in here." Jake lowered his telepathic voice's volume. "You want to check it out?"

Nick shook his ethereal head. "We don't want to attract attention. Stick to our normal patrol pattern. But I'm going to ask Canter for a scout bird at our next checkpoint."

Jake challenged the task. "You're sure it's worth the effort?"

"Sure. Why not?"

"Because the Brady witch is from Michigan. She's probably heading home."

The firstborn brother rejected the theory. Having sprung onto his psychic radar last year, the Brady witch had revealed herself as the most violent player in the void, blazing through it while leaving corpses in Turkey, Greece, and Italy. "If she's stupid enough to head home, she'll be found. But she's smart enough to hide behind lights in the void and wait until nobody's looking to make her next move. I need to take a closer look."

Jake agreed. "Okay. Let's do it."

Moments later, after quantum slices of the void's unmeasurable time marched forward, Nick saw a patch of pure black. He drifted, stopped, and aimed his voice across its event horizon. "Canter?"

His boss' garbled, computerized voice echoed from the real word into the firstborn brother's mind. "Canter here. Can you hear me?"

"Good enough. I saw something, a bright azure light over Baltimore. I want to check it out."

"You need the grid for coordinates?"

"Yeah. Light it up."

"Here it comes."

Lines of green formed a sphere around Nick's awareness, and he glanced over his conceptual shoulder at the glowing orb above Maryland's largest city. He tightened his focus, mentally zoomed in, and estimated its proximity to the nearest crossing lines. "I've eyeballed the coordinates. Are you ready for them?"

Though garbled, Canter's words were discernable. "Go ahead."

Nick uttered the coordinates.

"Got it. We've got a peregrine falcon staged in Patapsco Valley State Park. I'm checking on it now."

"Cool."

"I've established a radio link to your falcon, and I'm pulling up its file. It's a male bird, surgically altered three years ago, and it's been used twice for reconnaissance missions without problems. No combat experience, though."

"Combat or not, it's a reliable bird. I'll take him."

"Yeah. He looks solid. You'll want to fly on bearing one-one-four for about seven miles to overfly the source of light you found. For reference, the Transamerica Tower will bear about one-two-five from you. Are you ready for a connection?"

"Hold on. Let me dump my brothers." Nick angled his voice towards his flanks. "Are you guys going to behave while I'm gone?"

"As long as the gorilla doesn't talk."

"I'll stay quiet if the asshole does."

Ready to escape his brothers' bickering, Nick shifted his attention back towards the black patch. "Go ahead, Canter. I'm ready."

His awareness collapsed and then materialized within a falcon perched on the branch of a white pine. After a quick check of his host's health, he set the bird into flight and climbed. As the city became clear through the raptor's powerful eyes, Nick placed its tallest building to the right and flapped his wings.

Though the falcon's body flooded Nick with visual stimulation over the sunny cityscape, he tuned his mind to psychic energy. As he sensed a source of vibrant power ahead of him, he angled the raptor towards it.

A building with a grassy yard and brick sidewalks appeared below him. Its colonnade façade suggested a government edifice, but the twin spires rising in front of a huge dome identified the structure as a church. "Down."

The bird obeyed and glided to the crucifix atop a spire where it perched and looked over the Baltimore Basilica.

Sensing the energy source below him, Nick leapt from the summit, swooped towards the main entrance, and landed in front of huge oak door. He took the bird airborne into the sanctuary, drifting over the pews. A handful of faithful patrons prayed, but one devotee caught the raptor's eye.

Wearing a tunic covered by a scapular and cowl, a woman religious knelt in the front row. Praying fervently, she oozed the aura Nick sought.

Curious, he landed the bird a row behind her and then walked it along the aisle. When he reached his target, he flapped wings, extended talons, and perched the falcon above a wooden pocket holding a Bible and a worship aid.

The nun faced the bird, revealing an unexpected image of beauty and youth as she continued praying.

From his distant youth in Catholic formation, Nick recognized the prayer as the Nicene Creed. The familiar recitation represented nothing suspicious, but the firstborn brother's psychic antenna bristled with excitement. He found the nun special. Lacking a voice to speak, he cocked the falcon's head and stared.

Seeming to grasp the greeting, the nun fell silent, angled her head parallel to the bird's, and stretched out her arm. She stopped her hand at the raptor's beak and extended her index finger.

Reciprocating the gesture of trust, Nick hopped onto her digit and clasped it with his talons.

The nun pulled the falcon to her nose. Her voice was sweet. "Hello, little one. I'm Marcy."

Nick ignored the protocols Canter had taught him about concealing his presence within the raptor. Instead, he extended its wings, bowed its head, and then looked up in anticipation of his examiner's next move.

The woman religious rewarded him by remaining calm. "You're a friendly one." She stared in inquisitive silence. "Very friendly. Is there someone in there besides a bird's soul, perhaps?"

The inquiry's directness surprised Nick, and he felt adrenaline flowing throughout his disembodied spirit within the falcon. He allowed a moment for his emotions to settle, and then he continued revealing as much truth as he dared. He made the bird nod–twice.

"Is that a 'yes'?"

Nick nodded the raptor's head twice again.

"Really? Well, if you'll be patient, please let me pray for discernment. You can stay on my finger if you'd like." She looked towards the altar and mouthed a custom prayer asking about knowing the truth of the falcon. "I don't know. God isn't answering me, but you seem harmless."

Again, Nick nodded twice.

"May I pet you?"

Hoping to gain her confidence, Nick nodded twice, and then he felt her gracile fingers stroking the plumes on the raptor's head.

"Are you sent by an angel of God?"

Unsure how to answer, Nick cocked the bird's head.

"Never mind. I suppose God's angel wouldn't make it so obvious–not for me, anyway, and a demon would just lie about it. So, you could be holy, or you could be evil. But here you are, on my finger while I pray for protection from the darkness of doubt."

"What doubt?" Nick's curiosity sent his verbalized question into the falcon's puny mind, overwhelming it. Rookie mistake.

As the question about the abstract concept shut down the raptor's mind, the bird toppled from the woman's finger.

But she caught it, and the raptor's brain rebooted within her warm hands. "Oh, I'm glad you're okay. You didn't like me mentioning the darkness, did you?"

Nick shrugged, as best a falcon could within a human's grasp.

"I mean the darkness around my doubts of faith. Maybe you're here to make sure I don't leave my convent? If you're an angel or a demon, you'd know that's the darkness I'm struggling with."

For reasons unknown, Nick wanted her to remain in her vocation, at least until he killed the Brady witch. He nodded twice.

"You want me to stay with my faith, do you? So, either you're the Lord's angel reminding me that I do belong, or I'm deluding myself about my god. Can you can prove that you're an angel?"

His curiosity sated, Nick pecked the bird's beak against her finger until she loosened her grip. He then shot away and ordered the raptor back to its nest. Withdrawing from the beast, he reappeared in the void with his brothers.

Jake welcomed him. "How'd it go?"

"No witches, but I met a strange nun who suspected that my bird was possessed by an angel or a demon."

"Really? How'd she figure it out? You didn't scratch your name onto a wall with its beak, did you?"

"No. I wasn't too obvious. She just... knew."

"So, she has power? She was the source of the light?"

"Yeah. It was her."

"But this nun's not new to the area?"

"I guess not. She said she was in a convent, and I assumed it was local. To be sure, I'll check her clothes against Baltimore convents when we get back. But why did we see her today but never before?"

"Maybe she just became psychic."

Nick doubted it. "I don't think so. I didn't get that newbie vibe."

"Then what?"

The firstborn brother had a theory. "You were right when you said there's a paranoia in the void. It's gotten so quiet that the background noise of people's thoughts, visions, and movements has fallen, and we were able to see this nun's aura for the first time."

"You don't think there's anything special about her then?"

A warning pricked at Nick's mind, and he'd need to investigate the nun when he returned to reality. "I'm not sure. Maybe. But for the moment, we're still striking out looking for that Brady witch."

"Yeah. Let's finish our patrol."

Canter's garbled voice rose from the conduit. "Never mind that, boys. I'm cutting your patrol short. Come on back."

Nick questioned the decision. "Why?"

"Because I just got a nibble in the real world."

Excitement rose within the firstborn sibling. "No way!"

"An alias from the witch's posse just showed up boarding a flight from Dublin bound for–get this–Washington. Get your asses back here, and we'll make the preparations. They're coming."

CHAPTER 6

Liam awoke to a coppery taste. "Where are we?"

Seated beside him, his new bride smirked. "You slept through half the flight."

The young hunter glanced around the plush cabin. The chartered jet held leather couches, first-class seats, and a crystal coffee table, as well as himself, his father, the three empaths, his new brother-in-law, and his new grandmother-in-law.

From two rows back, the snarky old woman shared her opinion. "You snore too loud. How's Diane ever going to sleep for the rest of her life?"

Liam was embarrassed. "Sorry, Nana. I didn't know I was so tired."

His wife defended him. "He's not always that loud." She turned and faced him. "I hope. For my sake."

The young hunter watched the flight attendant open the door, and Washington's early spring air wafted over him. "I'll buy you some nice earplugs."

Smacking his shoulder as she stood, Diane grabbed her luggage. Her small rolling bag impressed Liam with its efficiency. "You'll sleep in the guest room before I wear earplugs to bed."

Liam grabbed his canvas equipment bag, joined his team on the tarmac, and then followed his father to Immigration.

As the group approached the terminal, Connor leaned into his son's ear. "I don't know if the Order inserted moles to help us through Customs and Immigration. So, get the young ladies ready to control the mind of our agent."

"Right." Liam slowed and waited for Diane to catch up. He then whispered to her. "Your daggers are on your persons, right?"

She shrugged. "Mine's in my purse. The girls usually carry theirs, too. What's up?"

"Father's not sure if the Immigration officer is one of our men."

"Oh. We have to do that, even in the private jet terminal?"

"It's the law."

She frowned at her husband's bag. "You've got enough assault weapons in there for a SWAT team."

"Yeah. So does Father. We came prepared."

"So, you need me to... what?"

"Turn the Immigration officer into a puppet until we're past his station."

"Okay. That's easy."

"All three of you, if possible, to be sure."

"I don't need help against a normal guy."

"Have you ever convinced an Immigration officer to let a horde of armed hunters and empaths enter the country?"

"Of course, not."

"Then if this goes down, I want you to team up. I'm not letting us fail because we held back any firepower."

She sighed. "Fine."

"Give me your passport." Liam reconsidered the task and raised his voice. "Everyone, give me your passports. I'll hand them to the agent." He collected a pile of documents and then joined his father at a red line where he saw the uniformed man behind a window. "You don't recognize him?"

Connor gave a slow head shake.

"Bloody hell. Alright." Liam looked over his shoulder and was relieved to see his wife, Emma, and Layla hiding their held hands under their outer garments. A coppery glimmer under Diane's coat revealed the presence of at least one dagger. The young hunter nodded.

She returned the gesture.

Liam looked back towards the Immigration officer, who gestured him forward. The young hunter walked to the agent and slid the passports onto the counter.

Straining, the officer seemed to fight himself while under the empaths' control. His mechanical stamp squeaked and clicked as he thumped it into each passport, and then his words were robotic. "Welcome to the United States. Enjoy your visit."

The young hunter turned towards the empaths huddled behind him. They were lowering their arms while sliding concealed bronze daggers back into their purses.

Catching his gaze, Diane winked.

Liam followed his father's silent example by marching away from the still-dazed Immigration official.

Once beyond the officer's sight, Connor stopped at a turn in the passageway and addressed his team. "I assume our success there was thanks to our young ladies?"

Diane answered. "I'm glad you warned us. It's a lot easier to control someone's head before they have unanswered questions rattling around it."

"Right, young lady. Sometimes, the Order can simplify this for us with recruits in key places, but it looks like we're dealing with true and loyal employees of the United States today. Get ready to do this again with Customs."

At Customs, Liam stepped forward with a form he'd filled out for his group. The agent was frighteningly old for the job, and the young hunter assumed he was approaching a century of life. He checked the badge, which said "Eleazar".

Holding hands and grasping concealed daggers, the empaths huddled behind the hunters.

Liam waited for a compliant senior citizen to take his Custom form, ask no questions, and wave him through.

But the officer resisted. "I... what's happening?"

Liam's adrenaline spiked, and he feared incarceration and mission failure if the agent discovered the daggers. "Officer Eleazar?"

Straining for words, the old man trembled. "Yes?"

"Are you okay?"

"At my age, being vertical and above ground is okay. But I sense something very strange."

Liam looked over his shoulder.

United by held hands and their enchanted daggers, the empaths were frozen in their unified trance, supposedly invading the mind of the elderly Customs agent. They gave no visible sign of struggle.

Unsure why the empaths were stalled in controlling their victim, the young hunter returned his focus to Officer Eleazar and tried to buy time by extending the conversation. "I'll have to trust you about something being strange. I just got here."

The agent's words came slowly as he engaged the empaths, and his voice revealed the strength of a much younger man. "Something isn't quite right. Not wrong. Just different. Almost... welcomed."

Liam tried to force the segue. "Well then, perhaps you'd be happy to welcome us to the United States."

"Let's review your declarations."

"We have nothing to declare. We're traveling light."

"No. I believe that you do have something to declare."

Unsure why the empaths struggled to control their quarry, Liam tried flattery. "I declare that you're a remarkable example of a senior citizen staying active within the workforce. I must ask your age."

"I'm ninety."

The young hunter continued his verbal tap dance, seeking time for the empaths to get the upper hand. "Wow! And you don't look a day over seventy-five. I should know. I have to look at a seventy-six-year-old face every day." Liam nodded towards his father.

Officer Eleazar ignored the flattery. "You possess something I should like to hold."

"You're holding us as your captive audience, but if you could just usher us along, we'd be most appreciative."

"It's... it's a dagger. Three of them."

Liam followed the man's stare beyond him and to the psychic sisters, who remained entranced. "Three daggers, huh? What makes you think we have daggers?"

The old man's eyes narrowed. "Because I see them. Through all the clothing and subterfuge, I can see them. They have great power, especially in the hands of these lovely ladies. Bring them to me."

Liam glared into the man's eyes and hoped Diane was paying attention while she paraded through his mind. "I'll ask my wife to bring you hers, but the other two ladies will stay right where they are. And I mean right where they are. Unmoving. I believe we can all agree to that."

Taking the hint, Diane broke free from the trance and walked to her husband's side. "I don't get it."

"Neither do I, but this man thinks we have three daggers. I believe he's confused. We have this little relic from the museum that you carry around. Why don't you let him touch it?"

She frowned. "You're sure?"

From Liam's experience, nothing short of hurricane forces could rip his wife's blade from her fingers. "Keep a tight grip on the handle. Don't let him take it."

She extended the blade over the counter.

The officer's eyes grew wide as he caressed the blade. "It's holy."

Diane slowly withdrew the weapon. "He's not wrong."

"You're absolutely correct, Officer Eleazar. It's just an old museum piece, but it was blessed long ago. You have a good eye."

"Not my eye, son. My heart. I know what I just felt. God's work is in that thing. You're on a holy mission."

Seeking signs of an angel within, Liam studied the officer's eyes but remained confused about the man's behavior. "Yes. I'd like to think so."

Officer Eleazar's face became ashen. "If I let you pass into the country, it will be my doom."

"What? Why?"

The old man buried a cold stare into the young hunter. "It is my cross to bear, and I will bear it. Go, before I change my mind."

Liam knew when to stop talking. He darted from the window and towards the exit. "Everyone, follow me. Let's go."

The team followed the young hunter out of the secure area.

With the doors to Customs shut behind the group, Diane collapsed to the worn carpet and wept.

The young hunter dashed to her side. "What's wrong?"

"He's right. He's going to die."

Although he would have preferred leeway in challenging her conclusion, Liam acknowledged the folly of telling his wife she was fooling herself. She was an empath. She knew. "Do you see it?"

As tears streamed down her face, she nodded. "It's horrible. He's going to be killed for this."

"No, honey. He was being melodramatic. He was struggling for a grip on reality with you all controlling him. Right?"

Inconsolable, she shook her head.

Liam stood and addressed the other empaths. "What's going on?"

In her German accent, Emma clarified. "We got into Agent Eleazar's head without any resistance. We normally have to deal with some sort of fight, usually a very weak one, but he was almost welcoming."

"That's weird, but do you know what Diane's seeing?"

"Enough. We caught glimpses. Diane's right. He just signed his own death warrant."

"For making what will amount to a mistake? I wasn't aware that America executed its Customs agents."

Before Emma could answer, Diane stood, wiped her tears, and responded. "No, Liam! Someone told him to hold us so that we could be arrested. But he disobeyed his orders to help us."

Liam saw the insight as a warning. "Shit. That means people are coming for us. We need to get out of here. Father?"

"A car is waiting at the curb. Let's make haste."

"Awesome. And great job, ladies. It looks like you came through, even if you didn't know it."

Diane protested. "No! Officer Eleazar did this on his own. He learned about our mission while we were inside his head, but we never took control."

Liam swallowed the enormity of the sacrifice. "Wow."

"I heard him talking in my head, but he's stopped now."

"Was he threatening you?"

"No. He was telling me it's okay and not to cry for him, but that's impossible. I feel his fate."

"Tell me what he said."

She looked up at him. "I remember it so clearly."

"That happens in your trances. Tell me what he said."

"And so, I will bequeath an example of fortitude to youths, if, with a ready soul and constancy, I carry out an honest death, for the sake of the most serious and most holy laws."

Although the man was running out of years, the young hunter considered the gesture epic. "Maybe we can do something for him. Through backchannels, or through the order."

Diane grabbed his arm with impossible strength. "No! He wants this. He wants to be a martyr. He needs it."

"Okay." Liam stepped to his father. "I could use some advice here. What's our next move?"

Connor hoisted his canvas bag to his shoulder and stepped away. "Come, lad. We have much to consider, but before we do anything, we must flee. We must escape before whoever wanted to arrest us catches up."

CHAPTER 7

Seated in a cloth-lined chair between her sister empaths, Diane watched her husband creep along the conference room's walls. "What are you doing?"

Liam kept his eyes on his handheld gadget. "Sweeping for bugs."

"You already swept everything in the room."

"True pros would embed a listening device behind the drywall."

"Nobody even knows we're here. You're making everyone nervous."

The unit squawked in the hunter's hands as he turned it off and lowered it into his canvas equipment bag. "No bugs, which means you're right about me being paranoid. Guilty as charged, and no apologies. As for being nervous, that's appropriate given what we're up against here."

She flicked her wrist at him and turned her nose towards her father-in-law.

With his daughter-in-law's attention, Connor began the lecture at the whiteboard. "Very well. We have our privacy. Shall we begin?"

As her husband became a statue at the whiteboard's far end, Diane nodded. "Yeah."

Connor tapped a dry erase marker against the board. "Alright. Let's recap." The elder hunter listed names in the order the victims had died. "Five nuns murdered in five months. All abducted from church sanctuaries, all taken somewhere private for torture and mutilation, all burned to death."

Diane recalled the sickening cases. Each lady had suffered her tongue being cut out, her head scalped, and her hands and feet severed. Then, while still alive, each woman religious had been burned to death. "We felt it when they died. They all cried out. It was horrible."

Connor softened his voice. "I know this must be difficult to relive, but I want to verify. All three of you heard the victims crying out, each victim, each murder?"

The empaths nodded.

"And you were all in different places during each of the five murders. Specifically, nobody was in the void."

Again, the psychic sisters nodded.

"But you all felt it, independently?"

Diane verbalized the experience. "After it happened the first time, we got together and entered the void. We saw a trail from an evil source that had moved to the victim's location before the murder. By the time the third victim was attacked, we knew we had a pattern, but you never get used to someone dying."

"Indeed, you do not, young lady. And we shall put an end to this suffering. The FBI has shared a good deal of information with the Vatican, and when we became involved, the Vatican shared with the Order, and the Order shared with us. In addition to our own psychic insights, we are privy to confidential information."

The lingering pain of five slain innocents receded from Diane's body as she engaged in her father-in-law's discourse. She hoped his plan would work. Otherwise, she feared failure, shame, and continued violence.

Connor lifted the marker again and jotted down the states of the crimes. "The locations of the attacks don't yield any clues. They appear random. The first attack was in Kansas, the second in Florida, followed by Texas, Oregon, and Virginia. Liam and I have completed our own analysis, and we agree with the authorities that there is no discernable geographical pattern."

Standing at the whiteboard's far end, Liam agreed. "I ran every pattern recognition program I know, and there's nothing. If there's a clue in the locations, it's subtle."

Connor cleared his throat and raised the marker again. Next

to each victim's name and location, he wrote the name of her religious order. Then he stepped back and examined his work. "Looking for patterns, I see nothing in their names, locations, or convents."

Liam clarified. "They're all from Catholic communities in communion with Rome, but other than a religious devotion to a cloistered life, they have nothing in common."

The elder hunter canted his head. "Not exactly. From my perspective, they were all young women. Aged late twenties to mid-thirties. From your perspective, that's a wide spread, but from my perspective, they share the quality of youth. That's a commonality worth remembering."

Liam added his insights. "I can accept that, but you can't shoehorn them into a single demographic based upon their physical characteristics. For example, they were different races. Two White, one Asian, one Hispanic, and one Black. So, there's no racial hatred issue."

Connor jotted the ethnicities next to each victim. "That's a simplification of their races, but it's good enough to support your point. Let's remember then to keep in mind their youth. We must remember the commonalities we notice, since there are so few."

"I'll buy that, Father. But their ages say more about the killer than a pattern between the victims. He selects pretty young women who've committed to a consecrate life."

Connor frowned. "They were pretty?"

Diane rotated her head towards her husband and let him squirm.

Liam blushed while answering under his wife's scrutiny. "I admit to noticing that none of them were hard on the eyes, based upon their photos in the case file."

Connor grunted. "The killer may prefer attractive women to satiate whatever craving his crimes serve, but this isn't sexual predation. Brutal torture and murders, yes, but there's been no sexual assault."

"Then what the hell's this all about?"

"I'm not sure, lad. Let's jump into the profiling and see if that sheds light." Connor started a new list. "The FBI says he's a man in his thirties or forties, and he's physically strong."

Diane doubted the age. "Hold on."

"What's wrong?"

"He could be older than that."

Connor gave a coy smile. "Well, young lady, when men age into their fifties, they lose muscle mass and strength. It would be difficult for this killer to manhandle his victims without real strength."

"But you're seventy-six, and you could do it."

"Yes, but for my vocation, I've been divinely blessed."

Unflinching, she held his gaze.

"I see that you're not ruling out an unseen source of strength for our killer."

She shook her head. "No, I'm not. There are plenty of supernatural sources of strength."

"I stand corrected." Connor etched a question mark next to the killer's expected age range. "Do you accept the gender as male?"

What little she'd sensed of the killer from his trails within the void left her ignorant. Along with her empathic sisters, she shrugged. "We don't know enough to question that."

"Alright, then. We'll trust the FBI that our killer is male. I'll move quickly over the character traits, which are obvious. He's disciplined, patient, and meticulous because he sticks to a complex and rigorous modus operandi. Now, let's discuss his motivations. Why's he doing this? What need is he serving by killing?"

Liam volunteered ideas. "Hatred of women, hatred of religious people, hatred of youth?"

"Why so sure of the hatred, lad?"

"He leaves behind clothing, scalps, tongues, and everything else he cuts from his victims. A lack of trophies means he's not reliving the murders. He's not playing God, and killing isn't a part of his identity. He's probably killing and trying to forget about it when he's done. It's more like a necessity, like scratching an itch. He may even know it's wrong and feel ashamed."

Connor nodded. "That agrees with the FBI's assessment, but if we add the supernatural element, does anything change?"

Liam looked away in thought, faced his father, and then shrugged. "Demonic influence can vary from subtle to full-blown possession. If it's subtle, we may never know, but if it's a possession, that can turn someone into a puppet. At that point, the hatred is the demon's."

"We have ways to determine that and address it if needed."

"Sure, but we're still groping in the dark. We've got nothing better than the empaths tracking the killer in the void, and that's probably going to keep us one step behind him."

Connor dropped the marker onto a tray. "Indeed. We have a man torturing and killing innocent women. That's not much to go on, but it's familiar territory for us." He faced his daughter-in-law and her sisters. "Ladies, how about a psychic update?"

Diane stood and walked to a corner of the room, and Emma and Layla followed. Forming a triangle, the empaths clasped hands and held their blades upward. "Ready, girls?"

The German and Persian empaths nodded.

Sensing Emma and Layla, Diane brought the trio into a transcendent link in which emotions stamped meanings into their unified mind with understanding beyond words. The conference room, their team, and Connor's scribbling on the whiteboard receded into a lethargic near-timelessness and then yielded to the immaterial psychic world.

As a symbiotic, triune super-empath, Diane floated with her sisters in the center of a blackness backlit by stars of ghostly energy sources. With an unspoken impetus, the Diane-Emma-Layla creature moved towards a reddish-purplish star with an evil, sanguine aura.

Diane's consciousness remained hers, but she shared a mind within the empath entity, which willed itself closer to the energy source. As she recognized the ugly light as the killer they'd tracked, she willed a halting, her sisters agreed, and the triune psychic drifted to a standstill.

Nearby, a bright azure glow marked the location of the Basilica of the National Shrine of the Immaculate Conception. Because the killer had remained inactive since leaving a trail to the Washington area a week ago, Diane concluded he was lurking in the area, studying his future prey.

He wasn't going anywhere, and there was no evidence pointing to a possible victim. Diane had gathered all she could from the void and urged herself and her sisters back to reality. The starry darkness receded, and the conference room materialized. "Nothing new. The killer's still nearby, but we can't get any closer without making it obvious we're watching."

Connor scowled. "Heavens, no. Don't risk that."

"We've been careful. Still no sign of a victim, though. We've never had a premonition or any idea about who he's going to attack next."

"Darn it. I'd half hoped that being in-country would help you young ladies find him. Perhaps I was dim-witted to hope."

Liam folded his arms. "We'll do it the old-fashioned way."

Diane appreciated her husband's confidence and hoped it was contagious for a mission that lacked clues. "What way is that?"

"Old-fashioned police detective work. I was afraid we'd end up here, spinning our wheels. Well, we're no smarter than we were a week ago about the killer, and we also know some psychic beast master is trying to kill us, too. So, we go undercover—sort of."

Diane's curiosity was piqued. "Sort of?"

"Yeah. Our secret Order is buried within a recognized religious group, or did you forget that we've got three knights and four dames of the Order of Malta in the room?"

Diane shot a glance at her brother, Josh, and her grandmother, who rounded out the seven-person team with the two hunters and the three empaths. "So?"

"So, all the attacks have been within a Catholic church. I say that we insert ourselves into the local diocese as worshipping pilgrims and follow every nun under the age of forty who walks into any Catholic church in the Washington area."

"Dear God, lad. We don't have the manpower for that."

"No, Father. But the FBI and local police do."

"You know from the killer's trail in the void that there's a supernatural element to this, yet you want to partner with people who reject even the possibility of such a truth?"

"We don't need them to believe, Father. Only to observe and share the movements of the potential victims."

"It's not perfect. In fact, it sounds like a desperate and incomplete tasking."

"You have a better idea?"

"No, lad. No, I don't." Connor pulled his phone from his pocket. "But I see no better options. I'll call Friar Lucio and have him connect me with the archbishop, who can introduce us to the FBI lead."

CHAPTER 8

Inside a surgically-altered falcon's mind, Nick stared through the conference room's window. The raptor's predatory eyes were useless for penetrating the drawn curtain, but his psychic ability revealed auras rising from the seven occupants.

Powerful azure hues bloomed from the three witches and their henchmen, while a weaker, violet glow surrounded a shape reminiscent of Brady's grandmother. The final rising light, a blazing and bright regal violet, came from the autistic brother.

Nick mulled over the righteous colors coming from the witch-assassins and their entourage. Encountering the psychic opposite of the expected reds, bruise-like purples, and sanguine blotches of evil souls, he suspected deception. "Clever girls. I'm not falling for it, but I'm getting a second opinion."

He ordered the bird to stay on the windowsill, withdrew from his avian spy, and receded to the void.

From his right shoulder, his husky middle brother greeted him. "What'd you see?"

"I picked up the falcon northwest of the airport and got to the terminal in time to see them getting into a Black Jeep Grand Cherokee. Maryland License plate J, R, H, seven-three-seven. They were easy to follow since they drove straight to the Tabard Inn. Right now, they're all together in a conference room. They're hiding behind curtains, but I can see their auras. It's weird. They're all glowing azure, violet, or blue."

"What? Those are virtuous colors."

"I was surprised, too."

Jake continued his challenge. "It's not only weird. It's wrong. And why didn't you notice it earlier?"

Nick knew from years of avian-based spying that auras faded over distance. "I must've been blind to it from far away, but I'm sure of what I just saw. I came back to tell you guys."

Tucked against the firstborn brother's left flank, Joe protested. "It's a trick to throw us off."

Canter's garbled voice issued from the pure darkness of the communications conduit connecting the psychic brothers to reality. "I don't know how they're doing it, but I'm making note of it. Learning how to camouflage ourselves like that could be useful."

Nick's ethereal vocal chords issued a grunt. "Learn from the enemy, huh?"

"Why not?"

Nick suspected a deceptive spell but trusted Canter, a veteran psychic warrior, to exercise caution and judgment. "Makes sense."

"By the way, I heard your report on the vehicle and the hotel. That's good work. Now get ready to track their next move. Are you ready to go back in?"

His boss' calmness with the witches' unexpected aura colors emboldened Nick to return to the falcon, but his words sounded hesitant as he shared them. "Sure. I guess."

Canter was assuring. "I admit that I haven't seen anything like this, but it's hardly worth panicking over. Get back in there. I'm also getting two eagles ready for Jake and Joe, just in case we need to attack. I've found a few birds nearby with good track records."

Nick preferred falcons for reconnaissance thanks to their extreme speeds, smaller size, and incredible eyesight. But their larger cousins trumped them in combat, and eagles were also satisfactory second choices for tracking, trailing, and spying. "Okay. I'll head back in."

Canter affirmed his decision. "Go. You're still connected."

Jake encouraged his older brother. "We'll wait here and watch your back."

Nick pushed his consciousness into the falcon. An initial

kinesthetic check informed him of the bird's hunger. "Wait for food." As the raptor accepted the command, the firstborn brother rotated its head to the window.

The curtains were opened to an empty conference room.

Nick flapped the wings and circled the bird above the building. Seeing the enemy's parked Grand Cherokee in the tiny lot behind the establishment quelled his rising anxiety about losing contact, and he lowered the falcon to the top floor's height. During a slow flight around the hotel's irregular perimeter, he looked inside each window but failed to locate the witches.

Within its small mind, the feathered spy complained about its growing hunger.

"Wait for food." Nick commanded the bird to glide downward to the next floor and scan the visible guest chambers, but he saw only one maid conducting her mid-morning cleaning of a corner suite. "Where the hell are they staying?"

Movement caught the raptor's eye, and its mind focused on four people on the dining patio. The first young lady carried laminated brunch menus towards an empty table. Following her were Brady and her witch sisters.

Nick's adrenaline spiked, and he flapped the raptor's wings. Momentum and effort lifted the bird to the hotel's roof where the firstborn sibling perched it overlooking the patio.

He ordered the bird to wait, and then he withdrew into the void.

Jake challenged him. "Back already?"

"The falcon's on the roof looking down over the three witches. They're on the dining patio ordering brunch." Even within the void's unnatural time flow, Nick sensed a prolonged silence while his siblings and Canter digested his report.

His husky middle brother's observation was an odd one. "No one orders brunch."

Nick aimed his mind's eye over his right shoulder. "What?"

"Nobody orders brunch. Brunches are buffets."

"That's not the point. I–"

Canter's watery words spilled over the communication conduit's event horizon. "Kill her."

After another uncomfortable silence, Nick verified the order. "I'm willing to do it. I was thinking about it."

"Kill the head, and the body dies. Without the Brady witch, the others will founder. They may even give up and go home."

Nick agreed but weighed the cost. "I need to remind you that a falcon costs a hundred grand all-in, counting brain surgery and training. If you want me to kamikaze it, it's your call."

"Do it. Don't hesitate. Don't think about it, because you'll overthink it. If you can't kill her, kill one of her cronies. Jake will take an eagle and assume reconnaissance duties after you sacrifice your falcon. Joe, you're not getting an eagle anymore. You'll have to stay in the void and guard Jake's back after Nick gets ejected. Everyone got it?"

The three brothers affirmed the orders.

"Good. Get it done. Attack!"

Nick returned to the falcon and looked down to verify his prey.

The Brady witch was accepting a mimosa from a waiter.

"Perfect." Nick ordered the bird into flight over the hotel, out of his target's line of sight. Pumping its wings, he took it high enough to see the Atlantic shoreline and to achieve a gravity-driven boost for the raptor's hunting dive. He then focused its vision on Brady's head. "Hunt!"

Fed with amazing visual acuity, the falcon assessed its potential meal as being oversized. Its instincts forced its passive protest, and the bird's body became a limp rock falling towards a concrete jungle.

Having expected the resistance, Nick adjusted. "Flap wings."

The order spurred the airborne predator's awareness of its predicament, and the falcon recovered into its powered decent. In its hunting stoop, the small animal achieved its top speed.

Nick estimated the dive at two hundred and twenty miles an hour as he gazed through protective membranes rolling over the avian eyes. The ground approached, and witch's head grew larger. "Snap neck."

Again, the falcon protested and became a limp, falling object.

Again, Nick countered by imposing his will on the bird. "Tuck wings. Hunt."

The bird obeyed but trembled with its instinctive understanding of a flawed attack. Air friction transformed the light trembling into violent shaking, but the falcon angled its head and curved its wings to compensate.

"Good stoop. Talons out. Snap neck. Tear flesh. Snap and tear!"

Having relinquished its will, the raptor slowed to the speed of a landing jetliner and transformed itself into a rigid, aerodynamic structure. It extended its wings and withstood deadly accelerations.

Nick released his part-electrically stimulated, part-psychic grip on his assassin and let nature complete the unnatural attack. His rising eagerness merged with the bird's heightened awareness and slowed time.

As the raptor angled its momentum towards its target, its eyes zeroed in on exposed flesh above Brady's shirt's collar.

Mentally, Nick gasped as seconds separated him from a mammoth step towards victory, and even a possible outright win over the Brady coven. He couldn't believe he was ending her witchcraft here and now, without further loss of innocent life.

And he was right to disbelieve.

The two companion witches stiffened their arms, reached below the table, and then whipped their hands into the falcon's path. Crossing the bronze daggers of their white-knuckled grips, they created a barrier.

With superhuman reaction time, Brady also defended herself by clanking her swift dagger's flat end against the crossed-swords formation.

In the milliseconds before the falcon reached its fatal collision, Nick saw the targeted witch's eyes. They seemed calm and knowing, lacking the instinctive startle response.

The bird passed out, sparing it awareness of its demise and ejecting Nick to reality.

He awoke on the padded recliner of his team's primary lab. A cursory examination showed mild sweat and the inception of body odor, but he'd had insufficient time to drench himself in fear-sweat. "Oh, shit."

Behind a wall of Plexiglas, Canter looked up from monitors and sounded hopeful in the open microphone circuit. "I've got one dead falcon and one psychic returned to his body. Tell me the Brady witch is dead."

Nick slid off his helmet, glanced at his reclined and unconscious younger brothers, and bowed his head. "Not exactly. I don't know if it was psychic power or witchcraft, but they just won this round."

CHAPTER 9

Liam slipped his head through the tunic and checked the mirror. The cloth covering his body was dyed deep black except for a white collar and cuffs and the eight-pointed cross printed on his chest. Seeing himself garbed as a religious knight stirred his emotions.

He whispered. "I don't recognize myself."

The glinting wedding ring, a simple but elegant casting of gold, steel, and titanium, reminded him of the whirlwind his last year had been. A lifetime of training to hunt one wraith had exploded into the violent extinguishing of an entire wraith line, freeing him from generational bonds to marry.

Diane Yousif had broken into his life as the captive of the first wraith, and she'd changed everything. Evasive wraiths had been exposed. Failures measured in centuries had become successes measured in months. Combat between humans had escalated into angelic and demonic exchanges. And he was married to now-Diane-Brady, an inspiring person with intimidating power.

He darted to the door, walked the hallway to his father's room, and knocked. Wearing a similar black and white choir dress but with a red-bordered black scapular distinguishing him from his son's attire, the elder hunter opened the door. "Ah. Come in, lad."

Liam entered a space which was a reverse mirror image of his hotel room. "I still can't believe you packed these cloaks."

"I packed even more. Here." Connor extended a gold pendant with an eight-pointed cross and pinned it on the young hunter's robe below his chin. "Now, you're fully dressed as a Knight of Honour and Devotion. My son!"

Liam snorted. "Sounds cool. What's it really mean?"

"It's an honor which you've earned by your lifetime's training and by the execution of your duties."

"Duties? Bloody hell, Father. Forgive me if I sound arrogant, but I think we're heroes."

Connor's tone was stern. "You performed your duties admirably, as did I, but remember that you did God's work and that His intercession made your successes possible. Beware the sin of pride."

Liam traversed the worn carpet and sat in an armchair. "My brain just tripped offline."

"Excuse me?"

"My brain. It's fried. I can't think straight."

"That's understandable given the rapidity of changes you've experienced recently."

"Yeah. No kidding."

"Well, at least you've got a few blessings. A history of unparalleled success, a strong wife, and a great team."

"Yeah." Liam's voice tapered off as his mind rebooted. "What are we, again? Knights of Honour and Duty?"

"You're a Knight of Honour and Devotion, which is a third-level ranking. I am a second-level Knight in Obedience. I'm also an ordained Catholic priest, like all my fathers before me. You would've pursued that vocation, including the exorcist training, had you not earned a different path."

Liam felt pride. "You just said I earned a different path."

"Indeed. Retiring the complete line of wraiths wasn't just considered impossible, it was beyond conception until we did it. And you did your part."

"But you said to avoid pride. After everything, I can't help be proud for my part in it."

"The praise goes to God. You owe him for your abilities, for the opportunity, and for the support you received."

After fighting alongside an entity of green light that he believed had been an angel, Liam enjoyed a renewed faith. The Catholic Church had literally written the book on angelic and demonic warfare, and his father's exorcising of a demon had been awesome to witness. But the allocation of praise seemed murky. People he loved faced mortal danger and underwent hardships while their omnipotent Lord risked nothing. "Um. Sure. I guess."

Connor sat. "What are you uncertain about?"

Liam snapped. "Come on, Father! It feels like only yesterday that we were in combat with an angel and a demon, and we're moving on like that was normal."

"Of course, it was shocking, but it's all within the paradigms of our beliefs."

"Well, how about me getting married? It sounds so simple, but it's leaps and bounds outside the paradigms of... what you just said. Most people grow up thinking about who they want to marry and how they want to raise families, but I only had a couple months to consider the concept before committing to it."

"Yet you made the right choice."

Liam shrugged. "No doubt. She's great. But I don't know what to do. We barely made it past the engagement when she started sensing the serial killer in the void and our entire focus shifted to him. Then, the premonition and the attack at our wedding..."

"Yes, lad. That was indeed tragic. You deserved better. You both did. I'm sorry it happened that way."

Sinking in the chair, Liam sighed. "I'm trying to queue up a temper tantrum, but you won't fight me."

"Why would I?"

"To make me get over it and move on."

"You'd have me spank you and trust that you'll be better for it? No, lad. It's quite the opposite. I, more than anyone, can see the difficulties you face. Nobody cares what you did yesterday, and everyone expects you to be a hero and to humbly praise God for your heroism. And Diane needs you to be a strong husband, which requires a different type of heroism in its own right. This is a good deal of pressure."

Liam tried to picture himself as a husband, and perhaps even a father, and his mind froze. He lacked vision for a married life and found comfort in concentrating on the immediate need of protecting innocent murder victims. He lifted the fabric of his tunic. "And what of this? What expectations does wearing this add?"

"Nothing more than the body armor and weaponry you're wearing below it. A uniform is just another piece of equipment, and you'll use it as such. Outside of Rome or Malta, you're unlikely to encounter anyone who expects anything from it except piety."

The young hunter recalled the order's long history. "It's an order born from hospital and welfare work, but I'm hardly a hospitaller."

"It started as a hospitaller order, but it added military defense of the sick, pilgrims, and captured territories during the Middle Ages. Then as nations grew strong enough to defend themselves, it reverted back to its emphasis on assisting the disadvantaged and those in need of disaster relief."

"And supposedly, I fit in?"

"There's still a military corps, if that helps you envision a connection. But you're overthinking this."

"Maybe."

Connor eyed him. "You're not having a crisis of faith, are you?"

Liam sat straight. "No, Father. In fact, it's the other way around. I've seen enough supernatural phenomena to know that I can't ignore it. There are supernatural beings, both good and bad, and they are superior to humanity. I don't know how anyone who believes that can be an atheist."

"I guess it depends on your definition of atheism and what constitutes a god. In theory, you could believe in spiritual beings who are not deities. In fact, I think many people do."

"But that leaves you with angels and demons running amok, fighting each other for control, like humans. Come to think of it, spiritual beings with unfathomable power are a terrifying concept without something or someone of infinite power setting their boundaries."

"Indeed, lad. There are many arguments to arrive at faith in God, and I believe you've stumbled upon the beginning of one, but none of them are foolproof. If just one was as airtight as a mathematical proof, everyone would see it. But a leap of faith is required at some point to cross the gap between the limits of evidence and the beginning of truth."

The young hunter believed. He'd always wanted to believe, but his witness of demonic possessions erased his lingering objections. "You don't have to worry about me. I'm good."

"Remember now, you're worshiping for two. Do you question Diane's faith?"

Liam was too busy assessing his own perspective that he'd failed to consider his wife's. "She grew up Catholic. She said she's Catholic. We got married in a Catholic church."

"Careful about your assumptions."

Unsure of his wife's philosophy, Liam accepted his doubts. "It's hard for her. Can you imagine what she sees in the void? What happens when she's controlling someone's mind? When her dagger takes on a mind of its own? I'm grateful that she found Emma and Layla so that she has understanding friends, but her abilities might make it harder for her to believe in any god."

"And I thank God that you recognize it."

Liam squinted at him. "What do you mean? I'm aware of my need to bring her to God if she falters. That's a husband's duty."

"I'm sure you will, but that's not what I meant. I meant, you were so enamored with her that you never considered the source of her powers."

"Okay. That's a fair point."

"For your protection, I tested her, and Emma and Layla, too."

Reflecting upon their last mission to Irbil, Liam understood. "Holy water. All the time we were in Iraq, we were drinking holy water."

"Indeed. I wanted to be sure they weren't subject to demonic influences as the source of their powers."

"Bloody hell, Father. Subconsciously, I knew that was a risk, but I never tested it. I was a fool."

"A fool in love. Be careful with the next psychic you meet. Make sure to rule out demonic intervention as the source of power so that you know it's instead a charism of the Holy Spirit."

"Yeah. I won't make that mistake again, especially when we meet those beast masters who tried to ruin my wedding."

"If they come."

"They'll come, Father. I know it."

Connor looked at a desk clock and then stood. "Right then. It's time to go. The FBI is awaiting two knights of the order, and we don't want to be late."

CHAPTER 10

In the archbishop's waiting area inside the Cathedral of St. Matthew the Apostle, Liam lifted his phone and counted parishes within the Archdiocese of Washington. "Forty churches."

Seated beside him, Connor grunted. "That sounds about right. But we may not need to watch them all if we can reach an agreement with the archbishop and Agent Stiles."

"Even if we can rule out most of them, that's still a lot of ground to cover."

"Before you despair further, let's see what they say."

Liam doubted his pending allies could help cover an impossible amount of real estate. He feared that the serial killer would elude him to mutilate and murder another nun. "God help us."

"That's the plan, lad. Given your wife's gifts and those of Emma and Layla, I'd say He already is helping us."

Liam remembered the wrench in his defense of innocent nuns. "Should we bring up the subject of the beast masters?"

"No. Let's consider that a separate issue until we can prove otherwise."

Liam considered the issues related but lacked evidence. "Fine."

Five minutes later, a middle-aged man in a dark suit walked into the waiting room and stopped at the reception desk. He then turned and addressed the seated knights. "Are you gentlemen Connor and Liam Brady?"

Connor stood and extended his hand. "Indeed. I'm Connor, and this is my son, Liam."

Liam rose to his feet and accepted the FBI man's strong grip. "Liam."

Stiles' tone was methodical. "Please to meet you. Agent Tom Stiles."

Connor gestured towards an empty armchair. "Please, sit." As the trio sat, the elder hunter expressed his gratitude. "I must thank you for joining us, Agent Stiles. It's not every day that we earn an audience with the FBI based upon divine revelation."

Stiles gave a wry smile. "I'm Christian. So, when the archbishop said a couple of devoted religious men had clues revealed by divine intervention, I was less skeptical than the average FBI agent."

Connor responded. "That's wonderful. Perhaps God's hand is at work already by uniting us."

Stiles kept his businesslike tone. "I've been following this killer since the first murder, and he's always been two steps ahead of me. If God's help is required to catch him, I'll gladly accept it. So, what information did you receive divinely?"

Enjoying the chance to brag about his marriage, Liam blurted his answer. "My wife. Her and a couple of her friends. They have the gift of prophecy."

Stiles raised his eyebrows. "Fascinating. What'd they see?"

"They can't see the killer well enough to identify him, but they can sense his presence, even his geographical location with blunt precision. They're sure he's in the D.C. area."

A secretary with her graying hair in a tight bun announced the archbishop's readiness to receive his guests.

Following his two companions through an oaken doorway into an ornate office, Liam saw a white-haired man in a red choir dress stepping around his mahogany desk.

The archbishop gave a thin smile. "Welcome, friends. Welcome." He returned behind his desk. "Please sit." As the threesome settled into upholstered walnut armchairs, the archbishop assumed a stern visage. "In all my years, I've never encountered anything like this. Let me summarize the situation, and correct me if I've got something wrong or leave something out."

Liam watched his companions' heads nod and took the queue

to remain silent.

The archbishop continued. "A serial killer has murdered five nuns across the country. He abducts them from churches, and that's the last we see of our departed sister alive. Of course, this is tragic, but it had nothing to do with me until two knights from the Order of Malta arranged this meeting with Agent Stiles. Now, we're all gathered to share evidence that the killer will attack next within this archdiocese. Am I correct so far?"

Three heads nodded.

"Then comes the tricky part. The Bradys claim that they've learned of the next attack within the archdiocese from divine revelation. Of course, I believe in charisms of the Holy Spirit and in other miracles, but they're rare for a good reason—we need the boundaries and structure of the laws of nature. Without them, we'd live lives of chaos. So, this case is most unusual."

Connor's tone was guarded. "I understand your caution, Your Excellency. If I hadn't seen these charisms working for over a year, I'd share your hesitance. But I've seen enough of our visionaries to trust them, especially my new daughter-in-law, who's been using her gift to fight criminals for the year that I've known her."

"Your new daughter-in-law?" The archbishop faced Liam. "But where are my manners? I forgot to congratulate you. How are you enjoying married life?"

Liam flaunted his wedding ring. "I'm still getting used to it." He paused and then continued. "Well, actually, I'm not getting used to it. We started working on this mission the second we had to fight for our lives at the altar, and ever since then it's consumed our time. We even delayed our honeymoon."

The archbishop faced Connor. "Your father told me about the attack by possessed animals. I verified it with the Ordinary of Cork and Ross Counties. That single, horrible event gave me enough optimism about your team's charisms to approach the FBI. Imagine my relief when I called Agent Stiles and learned of our shared beliefs."

"I'm Christian, but not Catholic, Your Excellency."

The archbishop released a wide smile, his first unguarded gesture of the meeting. "Well, nobody's perfect."

After polite laughter, Stiles shifted to logistics. "I'm willing to believe in divine clues, but I can't get resources from the FBI or the local police based upon them. I've been in this line of work long enough to know that people want to know the evidence before they'll take action in the field, and I don't blame them."

Leaning back in his leather chair, the archbishop tapped his finger against his lips. "Therein lies the rub. The Brady's tell me they can't predict which nun will be attacked from which religious order in which church or when. That leaves us with a lot of ground to cover over an indefinite period of time."

Connor seemed to be forcing an optimistic tone. "He always attacks within a week of arriving in the city of his pending crime. He's here now, and we need to set up our defenses."

"Do you have anything in mind yet?"

"If I may, Your Excellency, I envision three teams, each centered around an empath. We'll want our empaths split up and serving as psychic early warning systems. Then an armed guard with each empath. That allows us to cover three churches."

An idea sprung into Liam's mind. "No. Wait. We can cover four churches. We can count Josh as an empath. If the killer gets anywhere near him, he'll sense it."

Connor eyed his son. "I suppose that's possible, but I admit I hadn't considered it. The young man certainly has abilities like his sister, but his autism limits his participation."

"I would've mentioned it earlier, but I felt a sense of optimism about Josh, just now, under God's roof."

"Are you also counting Nana as his guard?"

Liam shrugged. Using an arthritic grandmother in her mid-seventies as a warrior sounded ludicrous as the idea echoed within his skull, but he remembered Nana's fearlessness and affinity for rifles. "She could do it. We'll want her with Josh, anyway, to help keep him anchored. It's best to have an armed guard with her, to compensate for her lack of strength and quickness."

Connor faced the archbishop. "Do you have anyone within your diocese with a military or law enforcement background whom you'd trust with this?"

"I have a few priests and deacons with military backgrounds."

"Let's call it four teams then."

"What about teams without your... empaths, as you call them? I see no reason to leave churches unguarded."

Connor scowled. "But, Your Excellency, you have forty churches, and I doubt you have that many diocesans with sufficient combat training, belief in the supernatural, and–dare I say–the courage for this tasking."

"You're right, but like you suggested during our phone call, I can get some insight into which churches within the diocese have scheduled nun visitations. In fact, I have a list here of orders who are visiting churches today." The archbishop extended a sheet of paper.

Connor accepted the list, studied it, and smirked. "On the bright side, you have a diocese with an active prayer life."

Liam snatched the paper and read it. "Bloody hell–crap! I didn't mean to swear, Your Excellency."

"I've heard worse, I assure you. But your point's well taken. Twenty-two religious communities have scheduled trips to churches within the diocese today. But I'm sure you noticed that ten of them are to the cathedral, which makes sense since we get the most visits here normally. Plus a few other churches will be receiving multiple groups today. We need to monitor only eleven churches."

Liam shared his dissatisfaction. "Only eleven? That's almost three times what we can cover, and it doesn't account for one-off visits from nuns you don't know about."

Connor shot a corrective glance at his son and then looked across the desk. "Forgive my son's tone, Your Excellency. He gets easily excited about his duties."

Liam was tired of apologizing. "Sorry, again, Your Excellency."

"It's fine. I understand, and I intend to place armed guards in as many churches as possible where your empaths can't be. I strongly suggest you allow them to join whatever communication network you'll be setting up."

After embarrassing himself twice with displays of emotion, Liam guarded his tone. "I'll set up an online meeting where everyone I give access to will be able to send instant messages to each other."

Connor added his desire. "I'd like to meet the guards to explain how to behave if our subject shows up. And, of course, Agent Stiles can inform us of relevant FBI processes and procedures when we're all together."

Stiles kept his businesslike tone. "I'm the only one with the authority to arrest a suspect. However, civilians can intervene to protect human life. It'll be a judgment call, and I'll explain to everyone how to approach the possible situations. I'm sure there'll be questions, and meeting with the guard team is a good idea. Other than the supernatural element, this is business as usual for me."

Liam voiced his concern. "Do we want to share the supernatural element with the diocesan guards?"

The archbishop leaned back in his chair, inhaled, and sighed. "Yes. Full candor. The men I have in mind are ordained–three priests and two deacons. They'll be receptive to the divine nature of your evidence, but you should be prepared to answer the hard question–is it a divine charism, or is it demonic trickery."

Connor answered. "I'm quite ready to answer with a plethora of examples and witnesses from our team. But if you'll pardon the hypocrisy, can you tell me their ages?"

The bishop chuckled. "Young–compared to us. But wise. Give them a chance. I think you'll be impressed."

CHAPTER 11

Wearing jeans, a blouse, and an overcoat, Diane knelt next to her husband. Before her, women religious from six orders populated dozens of pews as they faced the altar under the dome of the Cathedral of St. Matthew the Apostle. "There's so many of them, and they just keep coming."

Liam kept his surveying eyes on the congregation. "That's why we're here. The biggest pool of potential targets means this is the most likely place he'll strike."

Diane had considered it an honor when Connor had declared her and her husband the strongest team and had assigned them to the busiest house of worship, but she struggled to track the flow of visitors. "I'm a good empath, but I suck at people-watching."

Liam continued eyeing the room. "You're an ace at people-watching. You notice everything about everyone, but you suck at military surveillance."

She scowled and glanced at him. "What's the difference?"

He sneered. "If you have to ask, you'll never know."

As she raised her arm to backhand him, she reconsidered the gesture and lowered her hand. She feigned praying while scanning the worshipers for a possible victim, a hidden killer, and beast masters who'd proven their violent resolve with the kamikaze falcon. "No. Seriously, what am I supposed to be doing?"

"You look for someone who's trying to avoid attracting attention, someone who's paranoid."

She slumped her shoulders. "That's great. I'm looking for paranoia while I'm paranoid about people looking for me."

Liam glanced over his far shoulder. "Hold on. I'm checking

our flanks." He revealed his face as he looked over his near shoulder and then pointed his jaw forward again. "Check out the guy who just came in the main entrance."

Diane faced the long wall to her left and saw worshipers gathering. She hadn't noticed the grouping. "What's going on?"

"Those pews are where people wait in line for the sacrament of reconciliation. Confessions just started."

"Oh."

"What about the guy who just came in?"

"I didn't see him."

"Well, look again. He just sat down. He's wearing a blue golf shirt and slacks. Short, dark hair."

She obliged her husband and saw a twenty-something year-old wringing his hands during a silent prayer. She looked forward again, placed her forehead in her hands, and spoke softly. "He looks like he's on death row."

"Then, you know what I mean."

"No, I don't." From her abandoned religious upbringing, she remembered the horror of awaiting her turn in confessionals. "He's not suspicious. He's just afraid to bear his soul to a stranger who's going to pass judgment on him."

Liam's sideways glare was harsh and unsettling.

For the moment Diane locked eyes with him, a pang of fear about having married him shot through her. Assuring herself such doubt was normal for a newlywed, she buried her head back into her feigned praying.

Rechecking his flanks, Liam looked over his shoulders. "You're right and you're wrong. You're right that he looks suspicious, but you're wrong to ignore him. That's exactly where I'd hide, in plain sight with my potential victim pool exposed in front of me."

A man of average build walked up the aisle, stopped, and leaned over Diane's shoulder. His robe's sheen sleeve reflecting the cathedral's myriad light sources, he propped his weight on the back of the pew and spoke in a hushed tone. "Anything yet?"

Recognizing a deacon named Don, Diane shook her head.

"Nothing obvious."

Liam gave their ordained ally a more informative report. "Nothing obvious, but check out the young guy in the blue golf shirt and slacks waiting for confession. He looks suspicious. Stare him down and see if you can make him more nervous."

The deacon nodded and withdrew.

Diane disliked her husband's instructions. "Why'd you send Deacon Don into danger? He's just doing his part to help us."

"It's not danger. If that guy's our killer, he won't expose himself for a deacon."

"I guess not." Diane wearied of the old-school surveillance work and sought her own path. "Can't I look in the void?"

"No. Nobody's entering the void until a suspect's identified. That's Father's orders, that's the plan we agreed upon, and it's warranted caution. After that falcon tried to bore a hole through you, we can't risk exposure to anyone who's hunting us."

"Hunting me. It went for me, not us."

"Yeah. I know. You're the most powerful, and someone evil knows it."

She felt trapped. "This isn't fair. I'm dedicating myself to protecting other people, but I can't use my powers to protect myself. If I use them, I'll attract people who want to kill me."

Liam shrugged. "Not for much longer. We'll find everyone who's threatening you. I won't let anyone hurt you."

"Easy for you to say, but you can't be sure."

"I'll do my best, but no promises. That's life."

This time, she failed to restrain herself, and she backhanded his thick arm. As worshipers in surrounding pews eyed her, she bowed her head again in silent feigned prayer. Her next comment came in soft tones. "How can you say that?"

"Because it's true. It's your life. It's our lives. It's God's will that brought us together to fight evil. If it were easy and risk-free, what would be the point?"

"The point would be saving people. I don't see how you can–"

"Quiet!" Liam shot his arm under his tunic to his pistol and froze.

Diane kept her head pressed against her clasped hands. "What?"

"The priest who just entered through the northwest entrance."

She glanced to her left and saw nobody new.

Liam pursed his lips, inhaled deeply, and then sighed. "Northwest is to the right."

Since childhood, cardinal directions had flustered Diane. She could read tomes in a single sitting with excellent recall, but when understanding her position within cartesian coordinates, she lost her way. After correcting her viewing angle, she watched a sixty-year-old man wearing a green stole over his white vestments. "You're right. He's a priest."

"He might be. Go get Deacon Don."

"What? Why? What are you going to do?"

"Protect the innocent, of course. Go!"

As she stood, genuflected, and turned up the aisle, she stole a glance at the cathedral's new occupant. The suspect priest's clothes were reminiscent of a man leading a Mass, but no upcoming services were planned. She trotted towards the deacon but stopped when she saw him standing in the back of the sanctuary.

Watching over the congregation, Deacon Don stopped his surveying and made eye contact with Diane.

She halted and gestured him down the aisle.

When he reached her side, he reported. "The gentleman your husband informed me of is in the confessional now. I'm no expert in such matters, but I don't think he's our suspect."

"Never mind him anymore." She turned to the new priest. "Liam wanted you to see this guy."

Appearing of holy purpose in his knightly garb, Liam stood between the supposed priest and the closest throng of nuns.

Escorting Deacon Don forward, Diane marched to her husband and overheard him challenge the man.

"Pardon me, brother, but you look familiar. Have we met?"

The seemingly holy man stopped and raised pained, dull eyes towards the challenging knight but said nothing.

Liam stood taller and assumed an assertive tone. "I'm quite certain we've had business together."

Again, the newly arrived priest said nothing.

Liam kept eyes on the suspect while reaching behind his hip and tapping it repeatedly.

Diane recognized her husband's gesture as an order to use the knife to enter the void. She slid her hand under her coat and pressed her fingertips against the handle of the bronze dagger. Concentrating on the nothingness, she stopped and remembered an instruction Connor had left all empaths–inform the group before entering the psychic realm. She addressed the deacon. "Call Connor and let him know I'm going into the void."

Exhilarated to witness pending supernatural events, the deacon revealed wide eyes as he lifted a phone from his cloak's pocket and nodded. "I'll call him now."

Within the void, Diane received an immediate answer. The suspected priest's aura was a deep, purplish red, like a bleeding bruise. In an emptiness that lacked heat or a temperature scale to measure it, the man's glow was dismal thermal sink. Diane felt it swallowing life like a black hole. Her husband had been correct to suspect the new man, and she yanked her consciousness from the psychic realm towards reality.

But something restrained her.

"What the hell?"

She kicked her ethereal legs, but one foot was bound. She glanced around herself and saw a white line of energy stretching into the infinite distance. As she followed it to the fuzzy, subjective outline of her body, she saw the line twist into a lasso around her ankle. Furiously, she kicked again, but the laser-rope held.

A voice startled her. "Going somewhere, witch?"

CHAPTER 12

The rope snapped taut over Nick's ethereal right shoulder. "Hold on, Jake. She's strong."

His husky middle brother demonstrated his physical strength's transference into the void. "I got her. She's not going anywhere."

"Joe, prepare the muzzle."

"Gladly."

Overhearing the orders, the Brady witch protested. "The what?"

"Quick, Joe. Before she casts a spell."

"It's armed. Here we go." Interlaced lines of light blue shot from Joe and onto Brady's face.

Nick watched the muzzle cover his enemy's mouth. "How's that fitting, Misses Brady?"

The witch's mumble provided the desired answer.

"Good. As you can see, we know a few tricks you haven't learned yet. Now, if you'll stop squirming and start cooperating, you might get out of here alive."

Her muffled protest was a high-pitched whimper.

"What's that? You weren't aware that you could die in here? There's so much more going on than you can imagine. In the time we've been watching you, you've hardly scratched the surface of what's possible."

She whined.

"Oh, yeah. Sorry. You don't want a lecture on your shortcomings, do you? That would be unproductive. Let's get down to business."

Joe surprised the firstborn brother with his sadism. "What's the rush. Let's have some fun with her. We can make her feel a lot of pain without leaving any marks."

Nick whispered over his shoulder. "No. Focus." He aimed his unspoken thoughts back towards Brady. "Do you know why we've captured you?"

She shook her ethereal head.

"Let's try an easier question. Are you aware of a series of murders in which five nuns have been taken from churches across the country, and then mutilated and tortured to death?"

Brady's immaterial body stiffened with awareness.

"I'll take that as a 'yes'."

She nodded her affirmation.

"Good. Keep being honest, and you may live. No promises, though, given your violent track record."

She squealed from behind the laser-web-psychic muzzle.

"Oh, don't pretend to be indignant. We've been watching you since Traverse City. Then you left a trail of dead bodies in Istanbul, Lesbos, and Irbil, and that's only the crimes we know of."

She whined again.

Her moaning protest annoyed him. "I advise you to quit whining and only answer my questions. Can you agree to that?"

She nodded.

"Good. Now, is the next attack planned to take place in the Washington diocese?"

She remained silent.

"Are you pretending that you don't know?"

She shook her head.

"Then you do know."

She shrugged, and he sensed her rolling her eyes before nodding her affirmation.

"Good. Theatrics aside, that's good of you to admit. Now we're getting somewhere. Next question, do you know which church is targeted for the next attack?"

Another nod.

"How about the next victim?"

She shook her head.

"So, you're assigning your assassin to a church, but you're letting him randomly pick his victim? What's that about? Keeping the kill at arm's length, so you can tell yourself it's not your fault? That the blood's not on your hands?"

Her fierce head shakes and muffled whines suggested his voiceless words had stung.

"Alright. Let's back up and work with what you've already admitted. Is he attacking in the cathedral next?"

Brady repeated her squirming denial but then relaxed and nodded.

"Specifically, he'll attack next in the Cathedral of St. Matthew the Apostle?"

A nod.

"Good. Your cooperation is noted. I'm not the ultimate judge who's deciding your fate, but I can assure you that your continued cooperation will be considered by those who do. Now, let's–"

Something knocked Jake into Nick's flank.

"What's that? Jake, report!"

"I'm not sure. I'm checking it out now."

"Joe, help him."

From his left, his youngest brother's voice was strained. "I can't! Something's grabbing me."

Nick aimed his consciousness towards the blackness of the communications conduit by which he'd stopped before he'd caught Brady. Months of training scenarios during which Canter had forced him to recite the proper stream of keywords formed from his mind. "Incoming assailants! Minimum two. Jake and Joe engaging."

Canter's garbled voice flowed back. "Stay calm. You're trained for this, and you're the strongest thing in the void."

The words intended comfort, but the attack worried Nick. "Strongest thing that we know of!"

"I said stay calm! Observe. Decide. React. Report. Repeat!"

Nick followed the advice. "Jake and Joe seem okay. We still have the Brady witch."

Jake clarified his status. "I'm fine. Whatever attacked me is fast and tenacious, but it's like a kitten biting my ankles."

Joe's report was equally soothing. "I've got it... stop wiggling, you. There!"

Nick's curiosity was insatiable. "What is it, Joe?"

"Not 'what', but who. It looks like I've got here Miss Layla Jazani, the oldest member of the Brady coven, and an esteemed member of our kill list."

The Arabic accent carried sadness. "Sorry, Diane. We tried to save you."

Extending his attacker in front of his brother for inspection, Jake lifted a fuzzy rendition of the third witch, who invoked thoughts of Smurfette with her aura of blonde hair atop her shifting blues. "And I believe I've caught Miss Emma Zeigler."

The German witch's apology was lamentable. "We tried, Diane."

"Not very well." Nick sighed. "You don't understand the void. You think it's your playground, but you're blind to its true power."

The German empath squawked. "You won't get away with this."

"With what? Stopping you from killing nuns?" Nick reached for the lasso and held it. "Jake, while I hold the rope, see if you can get your hand around her mouth and shut her up."

Slacking the rope, the husky middle brother extended his hand to the witch's shoulder and clasped it–hard. She screamed until Jake's other hand slid from her neck to cover her mouth. "I've got her. I'll take back the rope."

On the other side, Joe silenced the eldest witch.

Nick updated his boss. "We've got all three witches captive and silenced."

Canter sounded elated. "Awesome! I heard your questioning of Brady. See what else you can learn from them."

"Will do." The firstborn brother found the elation contagious until he realized that Canter had no intent of leaving the witches alive, meaning he and his brothers would have to execute them. Even with their crimes, he questioned if he could kill helpless women in cold blood.

Another surprise attack spared him from the decision.

His world became blinding brightness, and he tumbled backwards. The void's dotted canopy raced by like passing stars, and he wiggled and spun to orient himself. Drifting, he willed himself forward, stopped, and assessed himself. All sense of his brothers and his captives vanished, and he was lost.

Around him, the green coordinate grid flashed, calming Nick with knowledge of his boss' awareness of the second attack and providing of an emergency reference frame.

Nick found a known beacon star in his canopy, a basilica in Chicago, and he compared it to the flashing grid. "Impossible." He was a hundred miles west of the Second City. Though alone and in disbelief, he scanned his memory for the nearest communication conduit and sprinted to it. He called out. "Canter!"

"I'm here, Nick. What happened?"

"I was hoping you could tell me. I'm hundreds of miles away."

"Where are Jake and Joe?"

"I can't find them yet, but their bodies are fine. You're all shaken up, but all your vitals are fine. I'm sure they'll report in soon."

"What did you see?"

"It was more like what I heard. It was a loud explosion, like a grenade or a bomb."

"In the void?"

"I know what you're thinking. You're thinking that's weird, and if someone's able to create a bomb, why haven't we developed one?"

"Well, yeah."

"Put that aside for now. It gets even weirder. I thought I heard a man talking."

"You think, or you're sure?"

"I've got a recording. I'm playing it back now. Hold on."

Nick awaited the evidence.

"Here it comes." A soft but assertive voice replaced Canter's.

Nick thought he recognized it, and the message's content

verified his suspicions.

Brady's autistic brother had rescued the coven, sharing his intent while attacking. "Leave my sisters alone."

CHAPTER 13

Liam raised his palm towards the man in priestly vestments. "Stop. Do you hear me? Can you understand me?"

The man moved towards him with a deliberate pace.

"Bloody hell." Liam glanced over his shoulder as he yielded a step backwards. "Stop him, Diane." But his wife was a statue with her hand frozen to her dagger. "Diane? Diane!"

Beside her, the deacon stood in awe. "She's in some sort of trance. What do we do?"

"Clear out all the nuns while I stop him." Liam amped up his request. "Forget that. Clear everyone out of here, nuns, civilians, everyone! Empty the church for their lives!"

Deacon Don stepped behind Liam and addressed kneeling nuns who were observing the ruckus. "Sisters. If you will, please leave from the opposite end of the pews. I'm afraid this newly arrived priest is not in his right mind. He's dangerous."

The sisters hesitated but moved with the deacon's urging.

"Sisters, please. I repeat, this priest is dangerous. For your own safety, evacuate the sanctuary!"

Liam gave up two more steps to the sinister clergyman. "If you can hear me, you need to stop now. I'm about to get physical."

The priest's lifeless eyes glared through the hunter.

"Deacon Don, get everyone out of here, now!" Liam withdrew his pistol and shot a round into the ceiling, spurring gasps, screams, and a mass exodus. He holstered his weapon.

"That worked, Liam. Everyone's leaving."

"Good." Liam forfeited his last step and held his ground as his shoulder brushed his motionless wife. "Now get a real priest! I think we need an exorcism!"

Deacon Don shimmied through the pew and then darted up the outer aisle. "Father Thomas! Father Richard! Any priest who can hear me, please! Leave your confessionals now. You're needed in the sanctuary. It's urgent!"

Liam faced his adversary. Knowing something unnatural worked against him, he kept his first move swift and simple, tackling the man's legs.

Time stopped, and an unseen force pushed the hunter aside.

When he landed, Liam was curled on the aisle's far side with his head resting on a hassock that had supported a praying nun's knees ten seconds earlier. He looked up.

The assailant who'd skirted his tackle with preternatural power passed Chaldean empath and entered the row the deacon had used.

After rising to his feet, Liam withdrew his pistol, aimed it at the suspect's hamstring, and squeezed off a round.

A bullet hole appeared in his robe, but the assailant kept walking.

Liam noticed a lone young nun remaining in the pew behind the suspect and murmuring a prayer in apparent ignorance of the world around her.

The assailant stopped before her, faced her, and extended his arm. His voice was a deep baritone. "Come, my daughter."

Liam screamed. "No!" He aimed at the suspect's buttocks and fired two rounds. Each shot cut holes in the white vestments but left their human target unfazed.

The nun accepted the assailant's arm and stood. In silence, she held him, turned, and walked toward the far aisle with her escort.

Working against the flow of evacuees, Deacon Don worked his way down the aisle with a young priest.

Unsure why his bullets had failed to slow the assailant, Liam assessed possibilities. His target could have a high pain tolerance, he could be drugged, or... he could only think of one more option.

Demonic possession.

Liam screamed. "Rite of Exorcism! Do the Rite of Exorcism!"

Having been briefed to expect a paranormal battle, the deacon grasped the gravity. "I'll tell Father Richard!" He stopped the man beside him and gave him urgent instructions.

The nun and her escort reached the aisle, kept their calm pace, and turned towards the northwest entrance.

Startling him, Diane woke up. "Liam?"

"Diane! Where were you?"

"Caught in the void."

"Caught?"

"Yeah." She looked around. "Josh saved me. I'll explain later. What's going on in here?"

The hunter pointed at the assailant escaping with his prey in a trance on his arm.

"You have to stop him!"

Liam lifted his pistol under her nose. "Don't you think I tried? I put one in his leg and two in his ass. Deacon Don's dragging Father Richard down to try an exorcism."

"What do you mean 'try'?"

"Look at him." Liam watched the young frightened priest who'd been interrupted from hearing confessions. "How many exorcisms do you think he's done?"

"I don't know. Zero?"

"I have no idea either, but zero's a good guess. I'll help him. We need to stop that guy first before he gets away."

"I know what to do." Before her husband could dissuade her, Diane lifted her dagger to her ear and then hurled it.

Imbued with divine accuracy, the knife raced towards its target's back.

The suspect twisted, bent his arm, and parried the weapon to the floor. He turned and continued walking.

"Come on." Liam led his wife past the altar and trotted towards the northwest entrance. He saw the deacon and the priest reach the escaping assailant.

Father Richard stuttered but began the Lord's Prayer.

As Liam locked eyes with the legitimate priest and nodded

his encouragement, he realized he'd seen more exorcisms than the only man in the sanctuary qualified to perform one. "That's right. Keep going. The Lord's Prayer. Louder!"

The young priest found his courage and lifted his voice until it echoed from the cathedral's corners. Deacon Don joined him. "… Thy kingdom come. Thy will be done…"

Slowed for the first time since entering the sanctuary, the suspect halved his pace and seemed to struggle to progress. He twisted his neck slowly towards his exorcists.

"Come on, Diane. It's working!" He looked over his shoulder in time to see her falling onto the altar's steps.

She squealed, extended her hands, and braced herself.

Liam stopped and scanned her surroundings for the reason behind her tumble. "What–"

"Myself! I tripped over myself. Go get him!" She flicked her wrist towards the assailant.

Liam accelerated to a sprint and sprang towards the suspect's legs. Extending his arms, he caught his prize and drove him into the floor while the de facto exorcist and the deacon recited a Hail Mary. He dug his knee into the assailant's back and reached under his knight's tunic into his vest's pocket for handcuffs. He couldn't believe he'd won.

He hadn't.

"Freeze!"

Liam looked up at two uniformed Washington Metropolitan police officers pointing pistols at him. "What?"

"Get off him."

"You don't understand. He's not really a priest. At least, I don't think so."

The larger cop canted his head. "I don't care. Someone's been discharging a firearm in here, and from what I can tell, it's you."

"I had a good reason. Ask them. Ask the deacon and the priest." Liam looked at his companions, but they'd fallen silent with the police force's arrival. "Come on, guys. Tell them what's going on."

Deacon Don and Father Richard had become motionless bystanders.

Liam's bitter failure supplanted his sweet victory, and he controlled the damage. "I won't resist, if you want to arrest me." He rolled his weight off his victim and stood.

The suspect also stood and emerged from his semi-catatonic state. "I'm okay officers, but I thank you for coming." He glanced at the young hunter. "This... holy knight attacked me, but I'm sure it was a mistaken identity. I assure you I'm quite alright. If I may, I'd prefer to keep escorting Sister Jane away from this. It's been quite frightening for her."

The larger cop examined the vestments. "Are those bullet holes?"

The assailant returned to his lifeless walk and uttered his baritone response. "No. Come, Sister Jane. We share a destiny."

Liam shot furtive glances around the sanctuary, but nobody stopped the madness. His target was escaping with the nun he would torture and kill, Father Richard and Deacon Don were paralyzed under the probable influence of the possessing demon, and Diane sat helpless on the altar's stairs nursing a sprained wrist and ankle. Alone, Liam started after the escaping killer.

The cops, under probable demonic influence, each raised a palm and grabbed their pistols. The large one spoke for them again. "No, sir. Not you. You'll be lucky to walk out of here a free man. I suggest you start explaining yourself."

CHAPTER 14

Diane stood like a statue absorbing the police captain's tirade. Her silence required all her restraint because she wanted to scream at the cop to shut up.

But in his office, the captain commanded the world with a power that grew with the volume of his yelling. "What the hell were you thinking unloading a clip inside a church in my precinct? In the cathedral, of all places?"

Liam cleared his throat before answering. "Well, sir. I–"

The captain glared at the hunter with incredulous eyes. "Quiet! That was rhetorical, you idiot. The only person who talks in this office is me, unless I tell you to talk. Is that understood?"

Insulting her husband crossed the line, and Diane reached for the dagger at her hip.

A grim-faced uniformed lieutenant kept his gaze low, but he cast a glance towards Diane's moving hand.

She stopped and scratched her thigh until the cop missed her dagger and looked away. She credited the knife's translucence, which seemed to rise and fall with the weapon's awareness of its need to camouflage itself, for her unchallenged possession of it inside the police station. As her fingers caressed its bronze, she made the blitz hop through the psychic void, found her husband, and entered his mind. "Let me shut this asshole's mouth for you."

With time slowing to its apparent standstill while she commanded the trance, Liam gave a calm response. "How'd I know you'd jump into my head and say that?"

From the corner of her paralyzed eyes, Diane studied the police chief, who was frozen mid-word with a wad of spittle arc-ing from his bottom lip towards the floor. "Because he's wrong! You were arresting the killer when his stupid cops stopped you. That's... that's... disgusting."

"They're not stupid or disgusting. They didn't know what they were doing. They still don't know what's going on. Their captain has no idea."

"If he'd shut up, we could tell him."

"He won't shut up until he's done yelling, and he won't believe us. Do you think a guy like him is willing to listen to anything about psychic surveillance?"

She would have found the situation funny if not for the missing nun who was being tortured, mutilated, and killed. "I think he's going to pass out if he keeps screaming."

"Even if he was the nicest cop in the world, he's not going to believe anything about the void. We got lucky that we found an FBI man who believes us, but the captain won't."

"He's a big jerk."

"Let him finish."

Diane was incredulous. She and her husband had just risked their lives to stop a monster, but the police were ruining their efforts, and the killer had escaped with a nun named Sister Jane. "I don't have to let him finish yelling. I can take control of his mind and make him stop being stupid."

"It would only be temporary, and you'd make an enemy of the local police."

"I'd make him believe in my powers."

"You might, but it'd be a stretch to make him believe you predicted the killer's arrival, and it'd be an even bigger stretch for him to convince all the other cops."

"Then I'll get into the heads of all the other cops! They need to be out in the streets looking for Sister Jane."

"They are!"

Diane questioned the lack of urgency she thought she noted. "Nobody around here looks too worried about her."

"Washington cops deal with murder all the time. Don't expect them to get too worked up."

"So, who's helping? I only see one guy yelling and everyone else trying to avoid him. Even his own cops don't like him."

"His lieutenant sent two cops to her convent to see if she's there."

"Of course, she's not! She's being tortured right now!"

"The cops need to figure that out on their own."

"That's not good enough."

"I know. We'll go after her ourselves once we get out of here."

She appreciated her husband's resolve, but she didn't want him saving the world by himself. "They need to do more."

"Did you see a bunch of cops standing around looking for something to do?"

She considered the question patronizing, but she answered. "No."

"That's because they're all doing something else. Anyone else on the force who could help Sister Jane is probably helping some other would-be victim."

"It's not fair. We had him!"

"I know we had him! I was there, too. He was under my knee and in my hands. Don't you think I know how close we were?"

She realized that she'd been an unsympathetic empath. "Sorry. I know this is horrible for you, too. Plus, that yelling jackass is infuriating."

"Forget him. Let him yell, and let Agent Stiles deal with him."

"Fine. If you say so."

"I say so. Let me go."

She released the link, and time returned to normalcy.

The police captain finished his sentence and then drew a breath. "...out of my office. Except you, Agent Stiles. You're going to stay behind with your tail between your legs and join me in an uncomfortable call to your boss."

Keeping her head down, Diane shuffled behind the hunters through the glass door and away from the loud captain. A beat cop escorted them to a break room where they joined Deacon Don and the young Father Richard by a water cooler and a coffee pot.

The priest shook his head. "It's my fault. I had a chance to exorcise the demon, and I failed."

Connor refused the admission. "Nothing could be further from the truth, young man. Exorcisms are tricky affairs, and from what my son told me, you managed to slow him down."

"But the demoniac got away with our sister. I can't bear to think about what will happen to her."

Connor inhaled through his nostrils and was calming. "Don't think about it, because it's not your fault. It's a misunderstanding, a terrible one for certain, and I hope Agent Stiles is fixing it."

Diane released one of the many protests swirling throughout her head. "Why didn't he tell the police ahead of time?"

"He couldn't have, young lady. What could he have said?"

Diane choked on a new fear–having her psychic gift disbelieved. "Don't police forces use psychics all the time?"

"Very few, and far between. And they rarely admit it."

Diane shot an angry glance towards the police captain's office in reference to his still-thundering voice. "We're trying to save people's lives, and all he's doing is yelling at the FBI agent who's trying to help."

Liam leaned into her ear. "We won't win this argument here. We'll pick it up later."

She grunted.

He continued. "Trust me. We have more important things to do."

"Like what?"

He raised his voice and looked at his father. "We need to go after the killer while Sister Jane's still alive. We're wasting time."

"Agreed. But we're on our own. The police won't..." Connor stepped to his son and whispered the rest of his message.

Liam nodded and then approached his wife with a whisper to her nearest ear. "Father says to give it another ten minutes and see if Agent Stiles can convince the captain to search for Sister Jane."

Diane crossed her arms. "Fine."

Liam leaned into her ear again. "In the captain's office, when you got into my head, weren't you worried about revealing yourself?"

After the animal attack at her wedding, Diane and her sisters had experimented and learned that the even the simplest entrance into a friendly person's mind gets routed through the void, leaving a trail. "Yeah. So, what? I had to risk it."

"No, you didn't."

"The trail from a hop that small is practically invisible. They'd have to be watching closely."

"They are watching closely."

She lacked the patience to explain how the void erased its tracks over time and would render a short-burst trail invisible. "And they'd have to get lucky."

"You mean, like in the cathedral where cops accidentally spared them from me?" He stepped back and raised his voice. "There's plenty of luck to go around, but the bad guys seem to have it all."

"Don't be so dramatic."

"Dramatic?" He pursed his lips while considering a retort, but he chose a wise husband's path of agreement. "Maybe I am a little dramatic. That's because I'm concerned about everyone's safety." Again, he leaned into her ear. "Like your safety in the void. Tell me again, what happened when Josh saved you in the cathedral."

She sighed and then whispered her admission of ignorance and weakness. "Three guys attacked me. They're probably the same three guys who left the trail to the church when we got married. Layla and Emma went into the void to check on me, and then they got captured. We were screwed until Josh rescued us."

"Do you know how he did it?"

She shook her head, leaned away from her husband, and raised her voice. "I haven't had time to ask him, but whatever role he's playing in this is a mystery, like last time."

The captain's distant yelling was a background drone that

became noticeable when it stopped. His door clicked open, and one set of heels clicked against the floor.

From around the corner, Agent Stiles entered the break room and tugged at his suit's lapels. "The next time I conduct an operation based upon a psychic's advice, I'll be sure to spill my guts to the local police chief first."

Still offended by the resistance of those who should be helping, Diane spoke her mind. "Does he get it that we're the real deal?"

Stiles scoffed. "Him? Were you listening to that rant? A guy like him doesn't believe the sun rises unless he wills it and sees it for himself. But I've asked around, and at least his cops have verified that Sister Jane's missing. She's not at the convent, not in any hospitals, and not at the cathedral. He's declared her a person of interest for the unlawful shooting at the cathedral."

"Unlawful? The only guy who fired a gun was Liam."

"It's still unlawful until we can prove that Liam had a reason to believe he was defending someone."

"He was risking his life protecting a nun from a killer. What about him? Is anyone looking for the killer?"

Releasing the first smile from her team since entering the police station, Stiles sounded hopeful. "That could be our first break. A witness caught the tail end of your arrest on video, including the killer. He's been identified as a priest from Nashville."

Diane frowned. "He's a real priest?"

"Yes. And he's been on a leave of absence for almost six months. Coincidence? I think not."

"But we're the only ones who know who he really is."

"That's true, but the police captain has agreed to track him down for questioning. In the meantime, I have his name and the address for a house he rented in Alexandria."

Liam's thick shoulder bumped his wife as he stepped toward the FBI agent. "Good. We'll start there. Let's go."

Stiles raised his palms. "Sorry, Liam. You and Connor need to sit this one out. Police captain's orders, and I suggest you obey while you're on his shit list."

"Bloody hell! No!"

Connor trumped his son. "Yes, Agent Stiles. We don't like it, but we understand and agree."

Liam remained dissatisfied. "Who's going to back up Agent Stiles? This guy's dangerous. Nobody should go alone."

Stiles looked Diane in the eye. "The captain said nothing about other people helping me. I understand that you have some field experience, Misses Brady. If you'll agree to guard my back, we'll pay a visit to Father Jason Solomon."

CHAPTER 15

Diane rode in the passenger seat while Agent Stiles drove his FBI-issued black Chrysler 300. "Shouldn't we go faster?"

Stiles kept his eyes on the interstate highway as he maneuvered the car to the exit ramp. "Relax. I sweet-talked the captain into sweet-talking a couple of Alexandria cops into checking on him."

Her voice wavered. "Okay, I guess."

He reached for the volume knob on the police radio mounted on his dashboard. "If it makes you feel better, we'll listen in."

Electronic static filled the cabin, and then a dispatcher sent a squad car to a liquor mart.

"That's boring. What about our cops?"

"They were pulling up to the house, last I heard. I'm sure they're checking it out now."

Diane feared something would go wrong. She hated being without the hunters. Wiggling, she loosened a constricting strap of the bulletproof vest she'd hurried into upon her husband's urging.

Through the windows, she saw colonial brick buildings rising from the city's old town. A corner coffee shop caught her attention and spurred her desire to relax with a cappuccino, fantasize about being a suburban soccer mom, and pretend that she didn't have to risk her life fighting crime.

Stiles yanked her from her short daydream. "It's only a couple more blocks." He guided the vehicle into residential communities with blockish townhouses two and three stories high.

Diane enjoyed the view. "We don't have neighborhoods like this in Michigan. Not with this history."

He turned down a quiet road and slowed. "I imagine you

don't. Some of these houses are from the revolutionary era."

Her heart raced as the dwelling came into view. The white brick facade of the killer's rented townhouse stood out like a beacon against the brownish red hues of its neighbors.

Stiles parked, got out of the car, and joined his de facto partner on the sidewalk. "Have you ever done an armed entry?"

She remembered storming a tent in Greece's Moria refugee camp. "Yeah. Sort of. I'm usually in the back."

"Right. Stay behind me. Do you have a pistol?"

"I don't plan on shooting anyone."

"But if you need to? You're my backup."

"I'll use my dagger."

He turned his head and checked her out. "I understand you have remarkable skill with it."

After the killer had parried her throw in the cathedral, she questioned her dagger's limits, but she still trusted it to protect her. "I'm not bad."

"Where is it?"

She tapped the knife dangling through her belt loop. "Right here."

After a double take, Stiles frowned. "I didn't notice it until you pointed it out. But now, it's..."

As his voice trailed away, she realized the dagger's translucence was his first direct witnessing of supernatural power. "Obvious?"

"Yeah."

"So obvious you can't believe you missed it?"

Stiles ogled her hip. "Yeah. What's going on?"

"It's got a tricky way of making itself partially invisible for some people, sometimes."

"What people and what times?"

"I haven't figured that all out yet, but my guess is that it uses my mood and sort of reads my heart as a barometer for the people around me."

"And that's why you don't carry it in a sheath?"

"If I have a coat over it, sometimes I'll use a sheath. But the sheath doesn't turn invisible, and I use my jeans when I don't have a coat to cover it."

"As long as it works and you know how to use it. Come on." He marched towards the rented white house's front door.

The door opened, the FBI agent crouched, and two uniformed cops walked through the doorway.

Stiles put away his weapon, reached into his breast pocket, and extended his opened wallet. "Agent Stiles, FBI."

The closer of the cops strode to the agent and scanned the badge. "My lieutenant told me to expect you, but who's your friend?"

Stiles returned his billfold into his pocket. "This is Diane Brady. She's advising me on this case."

The cop tipped back his hat. "Well, sorry you had to waste your time. He's not here."

"He's not, huh? What did you find?"

"A well-kept house. The guy's clean and meticulous. We didn't even see any dust, much less any evidence of a crime."

Diane had expected blood splatter, severed body parts, and a burning victim. "That doesn't make sense."

The closer cop shrugged. "If you want to look around, I'll escort you. You'll need to honor the warrant, though. Don't touch anything without clearing it with me."

Agent Stiles stepped forward. "Sure. We know you've got other things you could be doing, but we'd appreciate if you'd let us take a quick look around."

The entryway smelled like old wood, and the floor creaked under Diane's shoes. She stopped and waited for a clue, a sensation, or a general impression, but the house told her nothing. "I've got a bad feeling about this."

The talkative cop gave her blank stare. "I told you we already checked everything out. There's nothing here."

"That's why I have a bad feeling."

Stiles clarified. "If our suspect's not here, that means he has our victim someplace else. He's... we're concerned that he's tearing her apart as we speak."

The cops shared a glance, and then the senior one spoke. "Our lieutenant said he was a person of interest–not a suspect."

Stiles led the group into the kitchen. "There's a difference of opinion on who he is. But I believe he's our serial killer, and he's at work right now."

"But not here. We checked."

"No. Obviously not." Stiles faced the empath. "Are you getting anything?"

The talkative cop scowled. "What is she, psychic or something?"

Stiles spared the empath from answering. "Like I said, she's my advisor. She's got a knack for cases like this."

As she followed the group into the family room, Diane shot the FBI agent a sideways glance. "Nothing. My so-called knack isn't helping much. This place is too clean."

The senior cop assumed an authoritative tone. "Agreed. We saw no signs of him eating or preparing food. He's got nothing in the fridge or pantry, and his garbage cans are empty. All his personal belongings are gone, too. His lease is good until the end of the month, but it looks like he's not coming back."

Stiles tapped the empath's arm to spur her onward. "Let's finish looking around while I call this in."

Lost, confused, and looking for guidance, Diane followed the FBI agent up the creaking stairs. "Who are you going to call?"

"I promised the police chief in D.C. I'd fill him in, and I'll let your father-in-law know what's going on, too."

"What about the FBI?"

Stiles shook his head. "I'm already on thin ice by being here. My boss won't believe anything until I can show him some hard evidence."

"You mean, like a body? A charred and mutilated corpse? Come on, we need to do something. She's being tortured right now!"

"I know. But where?"

Diane lowered her gaze. "I don't know."

"Until we figure that out, our hands are tied."

She longed for her husband's confidence and affinity for detective work, and she expected guidance from the FBI agent. "What do we do?"

"My boss is skeptical, but I know an analyst who's helping me check on Father Solomon's recent traceable movements. I'll keep shaking that tree. At the moment, she's tracking down his transactions since he landed in the Washington area."

Diane stopped in a second-floor bedroom next to the agent, who made his phone calls. As his voice became a dull drone, she examined her surroundings. The stocked furniture comprised of a bunkbed, a nightstand, and two small desks. Gouges in the stained wood revealed the callous usage of renters but nothing of the serial killer. "I still feel nothing."

Stiles slid his phone into his pocket. "And I still see nothing. There's no clues in here. He probably never set foot in this room."

Diane's helplessness to save Sister Jane creating anxiety. "We're wasting our time here."

"Probably. Do want to leave?"

"I don't want to quit. We can't just leave. Let's figure out why he rented this house."

"I'm willing to try, but we're groping at straws."

Floorboards creaking, Diane followed him into the next bedroom while the silent Alexandria cops watched from the hallway. "He rented this house for privacy, as opposed to a hotel room?"

"I'd agree if there was a shred of evidence that he did anything criminal here, but there's no sign of him having even slept here." Stiles' voice trailed off. "Huh."

"What?"

"He didn't use an alias to rent this house. He used his real name."

"Is that abnormal?"

"It's a lot easier to use aliases for motels. But when you get into an extended stay, like renting property for a month, landlords get touchy about background checks. So, he rented this house consciously, instead of going for something more secretive, knowing full well that anyone who suspected him would start looking for him here."

"Why? That sounds stupid."

Stiles was confident, like he'd seen the tactic from other criminals. "To throw us off. To make us waste time driving out here while he does what he does somewhere else."

Diane's stomach churned. "He's playing with us."

"It's more like he's cashing in an insurance policy, but yeah, we're getting played. We're getting played right damned now."

Following the agent down the stairs, she kept silent while staying on his heels to the sidewalk. After her partner bid farewell to the Alexandria cops, she lamented. "We're screwed. We're so screwed. I can't enter the void without being attacked by beast masters, and you can't ask for help because he's too smart to leave evidence."

Stiles' phone chimed, and he answered it. After a quick chat, he returned the device to his pocket and smirked. "You were pretty much saying we've hit rock bottom and it's hopeless?"

"More or less. Why? Did it just get worse?"

"No. Quite the opposite. We just found our first legitimate hard piece of evidence. My analyst checked, and Father Solomon rented houses at the right times and vicinities to place him at each of the last five murders."

Diane shrugged. "I could've told you that. I did tell you that."

"True, but the credit card trail will make others believe, like the D.C. police captain and my boss. I'll call them now. That's enough to declare him a suspect and cast a bigger search net."

After hitting rock bottom, Diane appreciated the good fortune, ripped off the uncomfortable vest, and lifted her phone to call her husband. She needed to hear his voice.

CHAPTER 16

Nick drifted into the radiating glow of the Cathedral of St. Matthew the Apostle, the brightest anchored star near his location within the void. "Quiet, guys. Listen. Look."

From the right flank, Jake was anxious. "She's hiding. They're all hiding. We're not going to find them."

"We need to look."

From the other flank, Joe protested. "We may have this backwards. They may be looking for us. In case you guys didn't notice, we got our asses kicked."

"Yeah, Nick. I agree with the asshole. We shouldn't be in here until we figure out what her little brother did to us."

"I agree with the gorilla. We got pummeled today, but we're acting like nothing happened. We shouldn't be in here."

Nick countered his brothers. "We're hiding in the cathedral's light specifically because something happened."

Joe's tone became disruptive. "Brady's little brother dropped a flipping bomb on us. We don't know what he did or how he did it, but this changes the rules."

"He's right, Nick. You're in charge, but you're outvoted. We need to get out of here."

Nick recalled his latest debrief with his boss, which happened after Josh had attacked. "I'm not outvoted. Canter agrees that we're safe in here."

Jake protested. "How would he know? He admitted he's never seen anything like that."

"I trust him. He's taught us a lot."

Jake grunted. "He's good, or maybe he was a long time ago, but we've learned half our skills on our own. He's getting old and hasn't been alone in the void in years."

Accepting his husky middle brother's point, Nick sighed. "Let's give this an honest effort, and then we'll withdraw."

"What the heck's an honest effort?"

A streak of azure traced a dying line across a black stretch of nothingness. Nick had seen trails rise, fall, and die as beings of psychic relevance hopped through the void. Such bursts of light left lingering impressions, like contrails, but without his green grid system, he had to guess its location. "Did you guys see movement at two o'clock, up-angle about twenty degrees?"

Joe's search sectors were in the other direction. "Nope."

Jake confirmed the sighting. "I did. It's probably somewhere near the center of the city. Do you want the grid?"

To enhance their positional awareness, Nick agreed. "We're passing a communications conduit." Below and to his right appeared a patch of pure black. Risking a pseudo-shout with respectable volume, he aimed his soundless voice at its event horizon. "Canter?"

His boss' garbled, computerized voice echoed back. "Canter here. Can you hear me?"

"Yes. Jake and I want to check out some movement. Light up the grid for coordinates."

"Here it comes."

Moments later, crisp green lines appeared, their weak glow making the dimmest stars imperceptible.

Nick eyed the dying contrail and marked its location against gridlines. "That's near a Baptist church."

Jake identified the incongruity. "The Brady witch usually hides her team in Catholic churches."

Nick was hungry for information. "Let's look anyway. What does it cost us?"

Jake grunted. "Movement is exposure. We don't know who's watching."

Nick wrestled with the decision but then agreed with his middle brother. "You're probably right. Forget the Baptist church. It's probably a faith healer."

"Yeah, bro. Let's get out of here."

A new aura rose and streaked towards Nick. In a fractional second within the timeless void, the firstborn sibling decided to attack it. "New target sighted, ten o'clock, down angle ten degrees. It's coming from a Catholic church and is going to pass close by us." He timed his tackle. "Collision attack in three... two... one!"

With the new target, the younger brothers silenced their doubts and tightened their formation.

Nick felt their ethereal fists clasp his legs and push him as he shot forward. He extended his metaphysical hands and reached for the moving light. As he collided with his victim, he groped and traced a feminine frame with his fingers.

The woman screamed, but her voice was unfamiliar.

Nick held her. "Who are you?"

Immobilized, she drifted in a random direction and slow speed dictated by the Slate brothers' momentum. She sounded terrified. "Who am I! Who are you?"

Impressed he could compartmentalize his embarrassment by Josh Yousif, Nick assumed himself the law within the void and issued his order with authority. "State your name and your business."

"Sister Agnes Martin. I'm praying to Jesus!"

"You need psychic power to pray?"

She hesitated. "Is that what this is about? My gift of prophecy? Sometimes when I pray, I get premonitions. I can't control when they happen."

"Sorry, ma'am. Mistaken identity." Nick loosened his grip and aimed his voice to his brothers. "Wrong person. Let's get out of here. Extract in three... two... one." He withdrew his consciousness from the void and returned to his body within his team's primary lab. He slid off his helmet and looked at his brothers.

Both younger siblings rolled from their recliners.

Behind the Plexiglas of his control center, Canter greeted his psychic patrol team. "Welcome back, gents. Congratulations on terrifying an innocent person. Who was it?"

Nick defended himself. "I saw an aura rise from a Catholic

church, and I went for it."

Canter's electronically amplified voice shot through overhead speakers. "I'm not second-guessing your decision. It didn't work out, but it was a bold move. I still want to know who it was. I assume it wasn't Brady."

"It was a nun named Sister Agnes Martin. She claimed to be praying and drawn into the void randomly by her gift of prophecy."

"She's probably right, but I'll get some eyes on her."

"We were going to come back anyway. We didn't want to expose ourselves more than necessary."

"Good call. Hold on. I'm coming in." Canter clicked open the door, marched into the lab, and sat on an unused recliner. His voice sounded more familiar without its amplification. "Let's talk about the elephant in the room. I'm afraid I may have sent you back in too soon. That Yousif boy kicked your asses, and I have no idea how."

"Jake and Joe admitted that defeat faster than you and I did, but they were right to be cautious. We need to assess this."

"So, what do you guys think happened when he attacked you?"

Nick glanced at blank stares. "Well, I'll reiterate what we did and see if that spurs some thought."

Canter nodded. "Go ahead."

"When Brady was in the Cathedral, she entered the void and stood in one spot, which means she was probably getting ready to control someone nearby."

"She was definitely getting ready." Canter crossed his ankle over his leg. "I'd say she somehow succeeded in controlling someone, given that Sister Jane got up and walked out willingly with her killer. She must have affected Sister Jane before you caught her in the void."

Still processing the Cathedral attack, Nick appreciated talking it through. "We had Brady pinned down. I was getting answers from her. Then her witch sisters tried to rescue her, but Jake and Joe caught them. Everything was fine. We'd won." His voice trailed off as he tasted failure. "We were that close to saving her."

"Then you guys got blown hundreds of miles across the void. Just like that." Canter snapped his fingers. "And Josh Yousif said to get away from his sisters. You all returned from the void individually, but then I told you to brace up, stop whining, and act like men?"

Embracing the humility, Nick watched his brothers nod. "Yeah. That pretty much sums it up."

"And then I sent you all back in together. Am I right? Did I leave anything out?"

"No, that's about right."

"You did need to get your asses back in there for your confidence, but I sent you in too fast. That's on me."

"Don't beat yourself up. I don't remember complaining about it."

"I'm not making the same mistake. This time, we'll walk it through. We should have time. I think Brady and her posse are just as surprised as us about what happened in there."

Nick inhaled and sighed. "What about Sister Jane? We need to find her."

His boss' slow head shake dashed his hopes. "She's beyond our reach now. You guys didn't see the killer move through the void after he snatched Sister Jane, did you?"

All three heads shook.

"And with Brady licking her wounds on the sideline, what would you hope to find in the void that could lead us to Sister Jane?"

Nick refused to quit. "Nothing. There may not be any psychic trails leading us to her, but we can take control of birds and run our own real-world reconnaissance."

Canter's eyes got big. "Over the whole city?"

"We have to do something!"

"I may let you, but only after we finish this discussion. I don't want you guys even hopping into birds until we've assessed this."

"Fine. Let's start with, I can't explain why an autistic guy would want to help in a series of murders."

Canter raised his eyebrows. "Good point. It's possible that he doesn't know what he's doing. He may not know any better and may be just obeying his sadistic big sister."

"And she knows how powerful he is. His autism must give him a boost, somehow."

"Had you guys seen him in the void before he counter-attacked?"

Nick shook his head. "He's not a frequent flier. If he's been leaving trails, we missed it."

"Yeah, I figured as much. So, he's not in there much, and the only time we've seen him is when you threaten his sister."

"I had Brady in my hands. But based upon his battle cry, he considers all three of them sisters."

Stroking his short graying whiskers, Canter was pensive. "Maybe we learned something valuable. Josh is a big bomb, but he doesn't become a factor until we threaten one of the witches."

"So, we don't attack the witches."

"Speaking of them. You boys handled them well until Josh dropped Little Boy and Fat Man on your heads."

Nick checked his brothers' expressions for confirmation. "Yeah. I'm trying not to sound arrogant, but we were too strong for them."

"I'll brag for you then. That's because you've been exercising your psychic muscles like I told you to. All those hours spent practicing your maneuvers and sparring against each other has paid off. It's not all about raw talent. You have to work at it, and you're stronger than them because you trained yourselves."

Nick recalled another detail. "And they haven't grasped the idea of constructs yet. I saw her face, and she was in shock when Joey shot the muzzle at her. She had no idea it was even possible."

"I'm sure she didn't, but she will soon. She's no idiot. She'll learn from it."

Nick grunted.

"What's wrong?"

"She's always going to learn from us until we kill her. We give away secrets when we fight her."

"And we learned from her, too. Remember how she camouflaged her aura to emanate good colors instead of evil?"

Nick scoffed. "That's still mindboggling. I don't suppose you've made any sense of it?"

Canter shook his head, and then his phone rang. "Hold on, boys." He lifted the device to his ear. "Canter... Yeah... Uh-huh... You've got to be pulling my leg. No? You double-checked... Oh, you triple-checked... Let me stew over this and get back to you."

Nick glared at his boss. "Well?"

"You're not going to believe it."

"It takes a lot to shock us."

"Alright, smartass. That camouflage trick Brady played on you may not have been a trick after all. Her husband was apprehended in the Cathedral trying to arrest the guy who's now the top suspect for the serial killer."

His curiosity piqued, Nick checked his brothers' faces for the same astonishment he felt. "They've identified a suspect? How?"

"The guy Liam Brady tried to arrest has rented houses in the vicinity of every victim of this spree."

Nick considered the evidence damning. "Who is it?"

"A Father Jason Solomon, from Nashville. The Washington police are looking for him now, and the FBI even has an agent involved. Apparently, Brady's working with the FBI."

Nick refused to believe it. "No way. Brady turned on Father..."

"Jason Solomon."

"Father Jason Solomon. She turned on him. That has to be it. She needed him for some killing, but she's done with him and is discarding him. She's got some spell on the FBI agent to help make it look legit. This makes perfect sense. It's the only way she can clean her tracks. I knew she was smart, but she's wicked-shrewd."

"Maybe. There's only one way to find out."

"I'm all ears."

"Parlay. We're going to make contact with Brady's posse, and we're coming in peace. Let's see what they have to say."

CHAPTER 17

Liam slid his tunic over his head and then draped it over his equipment bag. "A lot of good that did."

Connor scolded him. "Don't underestimate its effect. Our uniforms kept people calm and may have enticed the killer to expose himself. Had we been dressed differently, he may have recognized us as law enforcement and turned around."

"Too bad law enforcement didn't recognize us as law enforcement. Otherwise..." He thought of Sister Jane being tortured, mutilated, and burned to death.

"Out with it, lad."

"Otherwise, we'd have Father Solomon in custody, and Sister Jane would still be alive."

Connor disrobed and folded his knight's cloak over his equipment bag. He lifted his gaze and glanced at each person within the room. "She may yet be alive, and any chance she has of remaining so is thanks to us. This feels like a failure, but we identified both the killer and his victim. Tell me how else the authorities might have learned their identities without us?"

Unmotivated to respond, Liam scanned the room for someone else to speak. With his wife and the FBI agent on the road, he looked to the German empath.

Emma shook her head. "No. We came here to save someone, and we're not yet saving her. I want to do something about it."

Connor stood in front of his bag. "The police captain told us to stay out of the way, and he's right. Much as he's an ogre, he appears competent, and he's commissioned a manhunt. We will trust them to do their jobs. If we're going to do anything, we must employ your special skills."

Emma frowned. "But you told us to stay out of the void. It's dangerous, and I agree to stay out. I'm terrified. If it weren't for Josh, I..."

Surprising everyone else into silence, Josh enlightened his colleagues. "Maybe I can protect you."

Liam stepped to his brother-in-law. "That's great, Josh. You already protected them once. Do you know how to do it again?"

The autistic man read his tablet in silence.

The young hunter tried again. "You said you can protect your sister and her friends. Do you know how to do it again?"

Josh looked at a corner of the conference room. "Maybe."

"Josh, when you saved them today, it was amazing. Diane said she was very thankful and proud of you. We're all proud of you. I'm proud of you."

The heartfelt praise sent the autistic man to the room's corner.

Liam gave his brother-in-law space but raised his voice. "We don't understand how you did it, Josh, but we'd like to know."

No answer.

"How did you do it, Josh?"

Again, silence.

Despite his desire to get the empaths back into the void, Liam kept his voice soft, having learned from his wife how to coax his autistic friend. "Can you please explain how you pushed away the evil people who attacked your sister?"

Josh lowered his tablet and howled. "You're so stupid!"

Liam choked back his reactionary indignation and remembered that his brother-in-law's declarations of group incompetence usually preceded his wise insights. "Yes, Josh. Stupid. Me, and maybe the others. Why so stupid, Josh? Tell us."

"I was angry!"

"Because someone was hurting your sister, Emma, and Layla?"

"Yes."

"People have hurt your sister before."

"Not in the void."

"You got angry, and then what did you notice next?"

"I saw the void."

"Diane called for you?"

Josh scrunched his face.

"Did all three sisters call for you?"

"Yes."

"Diane doesn't remember doing that." Liam checked Emma and Layla, who both shook their heads. "None of them remember calling for you. Could they have done it subconsciously?"

"I don't know."

"But they called you for help, you heard their cries, you got very angry, and the next thing you remember, you were in the void?"

Connor stepped to the whiteboard and uncapped a marker. "That's enough, lad. Let Josh have his peace. He said he saw the void. He didn't say he was in it. I think this shapes the situation."

Honoring his father, Liam stepped to a chair and sat.

Connor jotted notes. "If our empaths find themselves in peril in the void, they'll call for Josh, possibly automatically and subconsciously, and I'll speculate that they may give off a distress call. Josh's reaction to such peril is anger. Understandable. But with Josh, his anger becomes a bomb that he's able to launch without exposing himself within the void."

Josh displayed a rare moment of focus. "I never entered. I saw from outside the void, and all I wanted was to protect my sisters."

Connor lowered the marker. "Then we've learned all we can until we reenter and run experiments. We know too little about the factors that turn Josh into a weapon. I'm sorry, but we can't risk reentry while the beast masters are still out there."

The retort burst from Liam's mouth before he could stop it. "But we know Josh can kick their asses!"

"Did he kick their asses? Possibly. But the beast masters may have recovered and have figured out how to counter him. And we won't know for sure that he can do it again until we can experiment."

"We could bluff, Father. Send all three empaths back in like we know Josh is our trump card. Let the beast masters face the hard decision of attacking again."

Connor folded his arms. "Why?"

"Because I want to save Sister Jane."

The elder hunter's voice was steel. "I still ask you why. I say it will bear no fruit."

"Why not?"

"You know, why not. Because Father Solomon only uses the void to find and entice his victims. Once he has them, he has no need for the void until his next victim."

Liam conceded. "Okay, that may be true. But what about rallying more troops? Our empaths could scour the void for local friendly psychics to help look for him. There's a whole network in the psychic realm that we're just starting to tap."

"I don't like it. It seems desperate. But I admit that it improves our chances of finding Sister Jane." Connor turned to Emma. "What do you think?"

Emma shared a glance with her Persian partner. "We'll try it."

"You're certain, young lady? You'd do that without Diane?"

"Yes."

"You understand the risks we just outlined?"

"Yes. Sister Jane's running out of time."

"Alright, then. Your courage speaks volumes. God help us all if this is a poor decision."

A shrill rapping shot from behind a closed curtain.

Liam stood, stepped to the window, and peeked outside. A bird with a white breast and brown wings was perched on the ledge, looking in. "Huh."

"What is it, lad?"

From following birds as hunting targets or as clues for finding other game, Liam knew his species. "A bird. I'd guess a peregrine falcon, if I had to."

"Damn! Like the one that attacked Diane?"

"I'm no bird watcher, but probably."

Connor stormed to the window and flung back the curtain. "Oh, dear. I fear we're being spied upon."

Liam exposed his middle finger. "I'm flipping the bird to a bird. Let's close the curtain before I..." His voice trailed as he watched the bird react.

The raptor shifted its weight, flapped its wings for balance, and lifted a talon. It then curled all its digits except the middle of the front three and lifted its claw.

"I think that bird just flipped me off."

Connor watched the raptor lower its leg and regain its perch. "Its talon was facing the wrong way."

"It's the best it could do without being a contortionist, but I'll give it credit for trying." As a test, Liam locked eyes with the bird and rocked his head back and forth.

The falcon's head swayed in phase with the hunter's.

Liam bobbed his head up and down.

The falcon repeated the gesture.

Ceasing his tests, Liam kept his gaze on the new arrival. "That's a beast master's bird."

"Right you are, lad."

"I want to bring it in for questioning."

Connor scoffed. "You can't expect to catch it."

"I don't, Father. I've a strange feeling that it'll come right in when I open the window."

"Oh. Well, if that's your plan, there's only one way to find out. But remember the time. We've got two empaths who are in a race to save a nun and need to enter the void."

"Let them."

"Even with this new evidence of the beast masters' continued interest?"

"Yes, Father. If this is a stalling tactic to keep us out of the void, let's trump it right now. I'd say it's actually safer this way. There's got to be a pilot for that bird, like a drone pilot, and that's one less beast master to grab an empath."

"I can't argue that. So be it."

Liam scanned the room's occupants. "But not here. Everyone has to clear out. I need to do this alone."

"Why lad?"

"Call me paranoid, but if it were me, I'd jam a nerve agent and explosives up this bird's ass and detonate it once we let it in. So, just me. We're risking only my life."

CHAPTER 18

Diane followed the FBI agent into the hotel lobby. Among the late afternoon's thin guest population, her team sat in silence. She approached her father-in-law. "Where's Liam?"

Connor lowered his tea to a table. "I'll tell you, but you won't believe me. He's in the conference room matching wits with a peregrine falcon."

Diane glanced at her grandmother, her brother, and her empathic sisters, but nobody revealed a clue to the elder hunter's riddle. "Can I see him?"

Connor smirked. "You'd better knock and ask his permission, but I won't stop you."

Diane marched across the lobby and rapped her knuckle against the door. "Liam?"

She heard footsteps, and then the door opened. Her husband restrained the falcon's wings with one hand, his index finger under its beak to prevent its pecking. "Hi, honey. This is Buster."

"What?"

"I named him. Well, I think it's a him. I'm not bothering to check."

Her next two thoughts–in order–were annulment, followed by divorce. "What's wrong with you?"

"Everything's fine. I set up an alphabet grid, and we're having a nice chat, me and Buster."

She looked over his thick shoulder at the whiteboard. Her husband had merged the C and the K into one cell, and every other English letter had a spot in a five-by-five matrix. Scribbled lines above the grid suggested an ongoing inquiry. "We don't have time for this. I need to get back into the void to find Sister Jane."

"Emma and Layla already took care of that. They went into the void to ask for help."

"They went in without me?"

"We all discussed it and decided not to wait for you. You were out with Stiles, and traffic in this town can get nasty."

"How long did that take them?"

"In real-world time, about four minutes. They contacted twenty-nine psychics in the area, and they're all keeping their eyes peeled for Sister Jane and Father Solomon now."

Diane was proud of her sisters' courage and efficiency, but the yield was low. "Twenty-nine people, in a city this big?"

"Seven hundred thousand."

"Whatever, Mister Encyclopedia. That's my point. Twenty-nine people aren't going to help much."

"Maybe not at all. But it's no longer our concern."

She was incredulous. "Not our concern? You're supposed to be a hero. Heroes don't talk like that."

"Like Father was saying while you were out, we've done all we can. We identified Sister Jane as the intended victim, we identified Father Solomon as the killer, and Stiles even found some evidence to make the police believe us."

"So, that's it? We're done? We take your new falcon friend and go home while Solomon rips into a nun?"

"I hate it, but I'm being realistic. We won't do anyone any good if we tie ourselves up in knots."

Her husband's perspective explained her entire team's calm demeanor. They'd conceded defeat. "But you're a man of action. I married a man of action. I'm waiting for you to act."

"Sure, I'll act. Come on. You can help." He carried the falcon to the whiteboard. "Well, come on."

Diane moved to him.

"Grab a marker and write down the letters as Buster answers."

She uncapped the blue marker and read the prior notes. "You've gotten these answers from the... from Buster already?"

"Yeah. Cool, huh?"

"You've asked him if he's under human control, and he said

'yes'. You asked him the purpose of his visit, and he said 'talk'. That's all you've gotten?"

Liam scowled as he moved the raptor before the small grid he'd drawn. "This took time. It's not like Buster flapped in here and started blabbering. I needed three tries to draw this thing small and neat enough for him. We're lucky I thought of it, actually."

"Fine. Whatever. You can color inside the lines. Get on with the questions. Ask him why they tried to kill me in the void."

"Never mind me asking. He's already answering." As the bird pecked the board, Liam called out the letters. "M... I... S... T... mistake? It was a mistake?"

The bird nodded its head several times.

Diane wrote the answer. "I'm not sure that makes me feel any better, coming from a bird."

"I know our next question. Why did you ruin my beautiful bride's wedding?"

As the bird pecked the same letters claiming an error, Diane scribed the question and its answer while venting her anger. "Sure, it was an understandable mistake. You had an oopsie where you dropped Noah's Ark on us and killed two people. I suppose trying to ram your kamikaze cousin through my skull was also a mistake?"

Again, the bird nodded emphatically.

Part of Diane wanted to rip off the bird's head, but she remembered it was only a possessed messenger, and her empathic intuition said the raptor was truthful. "What sort of mistake? You don't attack the same people over and over by mistake."

The bird faced the grid and tapped.

Liam called out the letters. "I... D...E...N...T... Identity?"

The falcon nodded.

Diane felt a chill while she wrote the answer. Three times, the beast masters had attacked her, and they'd sent an expendable falcon as their apologizing lackey. "That's easy to claim, but they can't prove it. Find out who they are and what they want."

"Wait. He's tapping something else." Liam called out the letters. "W... E..."

Diane's hand froze as the door opened. She turned and saw her father-in-law.

"What news, my children?"

"Stay back, Father! We're making progress, but it could all be a ploy for us to assemble around a bomb."

Connor propped a chair under the knob as the rest of the team lined up against the wall. "We'll stay by the door. This gives us an easy escape for a gas attack, and it's far enough to survive any explosive that could fit inside that animal."

Diane scowled at her husband. "You didn't think to mention a bomb when you enslaved me as your scribe?"

"There's no bomb. I'm just being cautious."

"But everyone's lined up against the wall over there except me."

"Til death do we part, right, honey?"

Connor updated the newlyweds. "Agent Stiles has received some unfortunate news. Sadly, Sister Jane was found minutes ago, dead and mutilated, exactly like the others. There's no sign of Father Solomon. I'm sorry."

"Bloody hell."

"I know, lad. But at least it's in the past now. God has surely received her in heaven, and we shall put this behind us, too."

Collapsing under the weight of her psychic life's greatest failure, Diane dropped the marker onto its tray. "Damn it." She recalled having felt the nun cry out hours earlier, but she'd hoped it had been a false alarm.

"Go easy on yourself, young lady. You did all you could. We all did. We must mourn our departed sister, but we must focus on the positive. The authorities know who they're looking for now. We solved that for them."

Diane had seen a lifetime of violence in her year with the hunters, but this crime stung. "I thought we could save her."

"This is personal because it was a chance to salvage the disaster at your wedding. I thought... I imagine we all thought that if we could save her, we'd wipe away that pain. But Sister Jane deserves to be mourned for her own soul, and not for any broader sentiments with which we would burden her."

"Sorry, Connor. You're right. I was being selfish."

Liam consoled his wife. "No, honey. It's normal to feel horrible when the person you're protecting dies."

"I feel like crap."

"And you will, young lady, but not for long. I won't let you."

Fearing that failure would hurt this badly every time, Diane decided to reconsider her career choice. She made a mental note to ask her husband about it in private. "Come on, Connor. You're a great guy, but you're not a magician. This is horrible. I think I'm getting nauseous."

"You'll be fine once you divert your energies to preventing the next victim from becoming a victim."

"There is no next victim, Connor! You said the police are looking for him. He'll be in custody in days or weeks at most."

"Ah, I'm sure the authorities expect to catch their man. I, however, believe otherwise. I believe there's a demon involved and that said demon will keep his possessed priest away from law enforcement officers long enough to find his next victim."

"How's this supposed to make me feel better? All we ended up doing was finding his name. Now you're saying the police won't catch him anyway. So, is everything we did for nothing?"

Connor's tone was reassuring. "I have three daughters who can make some sense of the trail this beast leaves in the void. So, as far as I'm concerned, we're back in business tracking this killer."

Liam sounded hesitant. "Demon tracking?"

"In a roundabout way, that's what we did during our wraith hunting. The final savage revealed the demon."

"But our asses needed saving by the angel who'd hitched a ride on Josh, or did you forget how you peed yourself when the forest started rising out of the ground?"

"I didn't pee... Nevertheless, this is our calling. Father Solomon is on the move now, either towards hiding or towards his next victim. We must regroup."

Liam shrugged. "You're the father. So, I'll trust you, but I don't have to like it. Demons are nasty–"

The falcon squawked and then pecked the board.

Noticing the squirming bird, the scrivening empath refocused her husband. "What's he tapping?"

Facing the board, Liam called out the letters. "Okay. First letter is T. Then we have E... A... M...U...P."

Diane jotted rapid notes. "Team up. That's your plan? You attack us, claim it's a mistake, and then call for team work?"

"You do realize that you're yelling at a bird, honey."

She thought she'd kept her voice to a respectable volume. If her husband considered that yelling, she reckoned he was in for a shock if he forgot their anniversary. "Whatever. There's someone in there listening."

"Yeah. I guess you've got a point. But I'll ask the next question. Why the bloody hell would we want to team up with you?"

The bird tapped, the young hunter called out letters, and Diane wrote the response. "Wear Ecia? Is Ecia a new clothes line?" She glanced around the room.

Her grandmother, Emma, and Layla shrugged.

Diane considered the rest of her audience unqualified to answer a fashion question. "I don't get it."

"Maybe we made a mistake. Tap it again, Buster."

Diane wrote the same letters. "I'm stumped. Anyone?"

All the heads shook except one.

Agent Stiles stepped forward and crouched. "Point him at me."

Liam aimed the raptor's beak at the FBI man.

"I'm Agent Stiles, FBI." He held his badge to the falcon's face. "Send me an email from an official server with a photograph of the agent who'll meet me tomorrow at noon at Union Station. Have the agent come alone. That's noon tomorrow at Union Station, right outside the convenience store in the great hall."

The bird nodded empathically.

"You can let him out the window now, if you're still scared about him blowing us up."

"Not yet. Tell me what those letters mean."

Stiles stood and slid his wallet into his jacket. "If the right person shows up tomorrow, it means a lot. The letters say, 'We are CIA'."

CHAPTER 19

Nick held the falcon steady while Canter pinned the receiver and speaker to its plumes.

His boss tapped the beak and looked into his eyes. "Remember, don't get involved unless I signal for help. Got it?"

Nick bobbed the bird's head.

"That goes for you, too, Jake." Canter looked at the other falcon on the table. "If Brady's legit, this is our one chance to partner up with her. Don't blow it."

As strong fingers encircled his feathers and stuffed him inside his boss' overcoat, Nick doubted Brady's legitimacy. The hope of a good witch could only be a dream.

During the Lyft ride to the station, Nick remained patient but welcomed periodic greetings from his boss.

Canter opened his jacket and looked down. "Can you still breathe?"

Nick bobbed the raptor's head.

"Good. Your brother's doing fine, too. We'll be there soon." When the car stopped, Canter stepped to the sidewalk.

Through the pocket within the overcoat, Nick heard the muffled bustle of foot traffic and the mechanical sounds of the street. He remained patient while his boss carried him in darkness, and the vehicle noise died inside the station.

"Enjoy your freedom, boys." Canter placed Nick's falcon on a bathroom sink, next to a raptor Jake controlled. "But don't get caught, and don't be seen. I know they're expecting you, but try to be stealthy. Get behind me and follow me out. Nick, go left. Jake, go right." The boss walked to the restroom's door and pushed it open.

Nick flew his bird into the great hall and beelined for the

statues mounted in front of an arched window. High above head height, the statues gave a hidden vantage, and the firstborn brother tucked his falcon behind a humanoid sculpture and watched.

Across the hall, his brother revealed similar tactics as he landed his bird behind another elevated statue.

Far from the falcon's perch, but clear to its eyes, the youngest brother was seated alone outside a coffee shop. Thumbing through a magazine, Joe pretended to read but was monitoring his winged brothers and their boss. "This is Joe. Can you hear me, Canter?"

"Yeah, I hear you. I'm about to sit down. Can you see me?"

Wearing sunglasses, Joe cast a glance around the station. "I see you. No sign of the Brady Gang yet."

"Can you see your brothers?"

"Yeah. They found decent positions above you."

"I mean, can you see them now?"

"Jake's hidden from my view. If you can hear me, Jake, step forward and take a bow."

Across the hall, the falcon inched in front of its concealing statue, bobbed its head, and then stepped back.

"I see you, Jake. Now, Nick. Take a bow."

Nick bobbed his raptor's head.

"We're all good, boss. Three minutes to spare. They should already be here, looking for us."

"I'm sure they are." Canter lowered himself into a seat at an empty table. "Remember, guys. This is supposed to be peaceful. Think twice before taking any hostile action."

A minute later, a middle-aged man in a dark suit walked up to the brothers' boss and introduced himself. "Tom Stiles. And if I believe your headshot from the agency, you're Seth Canter."

"I am. Please, sit."

Stiles surveyed his surroundings, pulled out a chair, and sat. "It's good to meet you, CIA officer, Seth Canter. I checked on you."

"And I checked on you, FBI agent, Thomas Stiles."

Stiles snorted. "So, here we are. As I understand it, you tried to kill some good people I've recently come to know, and more than once. Three times, if I count the attack in that psychic sphere."

"Well, don't count it. That was more like an arrest."

"So, you only tried to kill them twice. Once, the premeditated attack during their wedding, and once when Diane Brady presented a target of opportunity to your spying falcon."

"Okay, those two attempts were bona fide. But look at it from my perspective. Me and my boys saw her killing people across the Mediterranean Sea. She left dead bodies in Turkey, Greece, and Iraq, that we know of."

"I had them brief me on it last night, and I see your point."

"See my point? It was cut and dried from where I'm standing. She wasn't approved by any agency of any recognized government to be assassinating anyone, and I'm still waiting for an explanation."

Seeking the FBI agent's support team, Nick swiveled the falcon's head, but his former enemy remained unseen.

Through the receiver pinned to the bird's plumes, Stiles' candor continued. "Connor and Liam are in a religious order that hunts wraiths. They met Diane, who later found the other two empaths when they were targeted as victims of these wraiths. The ladies have psychic power, which makes them targets for the wraiths, but it also allowed them to fight back."

"Against... wraiths?"

"Wraiths, because they steal life from their victims."

"You're telling me those dead bodies were all wraiths?"

"I can't prove anything to you, but I'm prone to believe the Bradys. You can credit them with three wraiths. Four, if you count the one they captured in Irbil. He's in custody but probably appears dead on your radar."

"Missing on my radar, but yes. I counted him among the bodies, and that makes four so-called wraiths. But there were more than twice that many dead in Diane's wake. Are you saying the other victims weren't her doing?"

"That's what they tell me."

"But you don't know them. You just met them when they came to the States."

Stiles interlaced his fingers on the table. "My boss escalated this last night and received confirmation from the Order of Malta. Nobody will reveal the details of the mission, but their top dog friar said the Bradys and the ladies were in their employ during the period of the wraith murders."

"That's hardly a license to kill."

"But it makes you stop and think, doesn't it?"

Canter seemed to relax as he crossed his ankle over his knee. "Look, we're a pair of old law enforcement guys. We know right from wrong. I know that you're wired and that the Bradys are listening, but tell me what you really think."

Stiles cleared his throat. "I think they're the real deal, and I'm not just saying it because they're listening. I took any doubts I had about them and flushed them down the toilet when I saw the results. I spent five months caught two steps behind a brutal monster, but they giftwrapped his identity for me over night."

"Did you see Liam Brady try to apprehend the killer?"

"No. I was in a different church at the time. But the Metro police confirmed it to me, and it's on the arrest report."

"I saw the report, too. Those can be faked, but if you say cops in the precinct corroborate it..."

"They do."

"Fine. So, let's say the Brady Gang was working for the right team yesterday. What guarantee can you give that they were working for the right team all along? What about going forward? How do I know their agenda doesn't blow in the direction of the highest contract-hit bidder of the day?"

"You don't. Neither do I, other than their word and reports from the Order of Malta. But I bet you didn't join the CIA to work on guarantees. You joined to fight the right battles."

Canter chuckled. "Actually, I joined the CIA because they were the only ones who didn't call me a freak. They took me in and trained me. They turned me into a pioneer."

Stiles frowned and fell silent.

"What's wrong?"

"I'm the only person we're talking about who doesn't have special powers. I feel like a human in a world of superheroes."

Canter shrugged. "I'm mostly retired now, if it makes you feel any better. I let the young talent do most of the work. The three boys I manage now are brothers, and they work great together."

"I appreciate the candor. Perhaps it's time to engage in some back and forth until we know enough about each other to determine next steps together, if any."

"Sure. Since I revealed about the three brothers, it's your turn."

"You know the Brady Gang, as you call them. Do you know all of them by name?"

"Yeah, yeah. Connor, Liam, Diane, Emma, Layla, Josh, and Grandma Yousif. Give me something I don't already know. For example, how'd they know about the attack on the church ahead of time? Their defenses were perfect. They must've known."

Stiles shook his head. "They haven't told me. I'll need to get back to you on that."

"Okay, then I get another one. What made you join them? You're real FBI, but they had no real evidence when they approached you."

"They didn't approach me. The archbishop of the Washington diocese did. They had enough spiritual evidence to convince the archbishop, and I had enough faith for him to convince me."

"For a guy without your own psychic power, that's a leap."

"I'm a man of faith, and this time, it's paying off. Your turn again. What's up with the microelectronics inside animal heads? Are you guys doing some sort of hybrid psychic-electronic control?"

Canter raised his eyebrows. "Good guess. That's exactly how I'd describe it."

"I'm a bit of an electronics geek. I'd love to know more."

"Sure. The oldest brother I manage earned his PhD developing an early prototype. We use encrypted radio waves to communicate to a surgically altered animal. It helps amplify their brainwaves and those of our pilots back and forth. After a few months of training after the microsurgery, the animal's ready for the field, and we station them across the globe."

"Fascinating."

"Your turn. Tell me about the daggers."

Stiles blushed. "I… Well, I know a good deal, but… It's time to stop half-assing this."

"Half-assing what?"

Stiles waved his hands over the table. "This. This meeting. My team's hidden around this hall watching for your team, which is also hidden and looking for my team."

"We were mortal enemies two days ago."

"But like you said, it was a mistaken identity. And we're lucky that the only human casualties were two men the Brady Gang hardly knew. We can get past it. We have to. Come on out, everyone."

From his perch, Nick watched hunters and psychics emerge from shops. Wearing inconspicuous travelers' clothing, they'd blended in with the commuting crowd.

Canter grunted. "I guess it's a group hug. Join the party, boys. Come as you are, whatever animal you're wearing, but don't make it obvious to casual observers."

As the teams merged at the table, they exchanged cautious and slow introductions. Nick risked his falcon's feathers and landed on Liam Brady's shoulder.

Petting the bird's plumes, the hunter received the firstborn sibling's gesture well. "Hey, look everyone. I'm a pirate."

Canter eyed the falcon. "Nick, I told you not to be obvious."

The firstborn brother flew from the hunter's neck to the table and shouldered up to his brother's bird. He rubbed his head against Jake's plumes and then looked up for guidance on the new group's direction.

The face staring at him belonged to Diane Brady, formerly Diane Yousif, the violent witch of the void.

Nick wondered how he could be so wrong about someone. Then he wondered if he were wrong about Diane's past, of if he'd been fooled into being wrong about her now.

CHAPTER 20

Liam stuffed a dripping cheeseburger into his mouth and bit into a quarter of it. The meet was juicy and savory, and he wiped his lips and mumbled while swallowing. "What?"

Diane mashed a napkin against his face. "I can't take you anywhere."

"We're at a burger bar. It's supposed to be messy. Hand me those wings, and I'll show you a real mess."

Jake Slate, the middle brother extended a thick arm and lifted the platter. "Here you go, sir."

Liam transferred three wings to his plate. "You don't have to call me 'sir'. We're not a military organization. We're religious 'hospitalers', I believe is the term."

"But you guys fight like commandos, from what we've seen."

"Far from it, but I appreciate the compliment. Anyway, no need to call me 'sir'."

"Force of habit. I used to be in the Navy. Submarines. Let's send these around and see who else wants some." Jake sent the platter on a clockwise journey around the family-style table.

The firstborn sibling, scrawny compared to his middle brother, accepted the plate and passed it on. "We're all breaking bread together, which is great, but we need to get something out in the open. We have a history of violence."

The banter of side conversations ceased.

At the table's head, Connor lowered his ale. "Greater enemies than us have forgiven each other for greater crimes to join in a common cause. Two good men died at my son's wedding, but I trust that we can recover from that."

At the table's other end, the CIA officer agreed. "That's gracious of you, Connor. If we're going to work together, we're going to have to move on from the past. For what it's worth, this was a tragic mistake, and it's on me."

Liam stopped feeding himself like a barnyard animal and watched his father's reaction.

The elder hunter showed admirable composure. "It was indeed tragic, but I speak for my team when I say that we agree to move on. I can't speak for the others about forgiveness at a personal level, but forgetting as a team, at least temporarily, is appropriate."

"You're being a real sport about this, Connor."

"I don't see any other way to behave under these circumstances. However, Agent Stiles will have to speak for the FBI."

Seated opposite Liam, the FBI agent wiped barbeque sauce on a paper napkin. "I got involved after the attack in Ireland. So, from my direct experience, nobody's been hurt. But if we're really moving on, we need to talk about another uncomfortable topic–jurisdiction."

Canter plopped his beer onto the wooden table. "I'll stop you right there. I concede a hundred percent. As soon as the Bradys came off my radar as suspects, this became a domestic issue. The CIA is out, the FBI is in. Period. But I'll stay involved if you'll allow it, if Father Solomon remains at large."

Stiles grabbed a wing. "I'd welcome your support. But let's see where we are at the end of the night. There may not be a mission. God willing, there won't be."

Canter lifted his glass. "I'll drink to that."

Stiles fumbled for his cola and toasted. "Me too, but Connor has me convinced otherwise. I bet Solomon gets away tonight."

Connor sipped and then lowered his ale. "I believe we're facing a demon. That creates a nasty pitfall for unprepared cops or, worse, unbelieving and unsuspecting cops."

"Nick, Jake, and Joe are aces, but they'd get clobbered by a demon. I'm guessing, of course, since demons don't show up on most-wanted lists, and we don't hunt them. I imagine that's best left to the Catholic Church. If I believe what I've read, that's where you go for help with demons. I think I even read something recently about the Vatican ramping up its training for exorcists?"

Proud of his heritage, Liam boasted. "You did read it, because it's true. The Vatican's beefing up its exorcist training to meet a rising global need. And we're part of the Catholic Church. Our order's hidden deep within the Order of Malta, which is in communion with Rome. My father's even an ordained priest and exorcist."

Diane shot him a strange look that confused him.

He whispered to her. "What's wrong?"

"You're taking this Catholic thing pretty seriously."

"Well, yeah. After all we've seen and been through, I believe in the supernatural. I don't see how you can conclude otherwise."

Diane said nothing.

He shrugged. "It's a supernatural religion."

"We'll talk later." Her declaration was an omen.

Connor glanced around the restaurant before responding to his son's latest public comment. "Yes, I am indeed a priest and an exorcist, and that has proven beneficial. We're well equipped for spiritual warfare, but we know little about weaponizing the psychic realm. You seem to have accomplished that in spades."

"I assume you're referring to the muzzle the boys conjured up and threw at Diane?"

"Precisely. That, and the abnormal strength my other daughters noticed when they tried to wrestle Diane free. They said that pulling on Joe and Jake was like trying to shake oak trees from the ground."

Emma and Layla confirmed the statement with silent nods.

Canter illuminated the subject. "That's achievable with training. You can get stronger in the void, and you can teach yourself to create constructs from trace energy. Over time, as we learn to trust each other, we can show you some shortcuts."

"I told my daughters the same thing. Don't be too eager to share secrets. Yesterday, we were enemies. Today, we're aligned. Tomorrow is an unknown."

Canter lifted his beer. "To sharing the right secrets, in light of the unknown future."

After glasses clanked with cautious optimism, Liam broached a subject lurking in his mind. "Mister Canter–"

"Seth, please."

"Okay, Seth. We know it was a case of mistaken identity, but can you explain why you thought we were serial killers?"

Canter cleared his throat. "That's on me. The boys had nothing to do with it. I'm the guy who scouts ahead looking for bad players."

Liam jumped on the discovery. "Wait. You're psychic, too?"

"Psychic, but with a congenital heart condition, which is why I leave the hard work to the boys. I just scout ahead and tell them who to engage. When I saw the corpses piling up during your wraith hunting trips, I started looking for patterns around the dead, and that led me to Diane."

Liam tried to sound neutral, despite his conflicting emotions. Part of him wanted vengeance against the beast masters, but part of him recognized the need to forgive. "What sort of patterns?"

"She kept cutting paths near the victims. She was breaking into the void near them, and I thought she was empowering them. Turns out she was fighting them. But I had to make a decision, and I got it wrong. It didn't help that I kept getting it wrong when I watched her and Emma and Layla doing the same thing with Father Solomon."

"I don't mean to be an ass, but you jumped to a conclusion about my wife pretty quickly."

Canter met Liam's gaze but then lowered his eyes. "I'm not proud of it, but you have to understand how easy it is to get this wrong. Every movement through the void leaves a mark, but the smaller they are, they harder they are to see. Your wife and her friends left a lot of small, quick trails that were hard to see."

Liam was dubious. "Couldn't you see their colors? Our empaths can tell bad from good in the void based upon aura colors."

"I didn't get that close. I saw several actors, both good and bad. Most likely, I was seeing your empaths and the killers they were working against. Unfortunately, I couldn't get any closer to tell them apart without revealing myself."

Under the table, Liam grabbed his wife's hand. "And you launched multiple deadly attacks upon these lovely ladies based upon that?"

"It's my job to make these decisions with partial information. I thought I was saving lives."

"You were pretty damned decisive when you unleashed the zoo on our wedding."

Connor defused the escalation. "That's enough, lad. You've stated your concerns, and Seth has given candid answers. Let the wound heal before you probe further."

"Of course, Father."

During a moment of silence, Stiles lifted his phone and spoke softly into it. After a brief exchange, he updated his colleagues. "That was my boss. He says that Father Solomon's still evading the manhunt. The manhunt's going to continue through the morning, but it'll end tomorrow at noon. Barring a stroke of good luck, we'll be back on the hunt by lunch."

"I'll be so bold as to predict the outcome. Father Solomon's under a demon's influence and getting unnatural help." Connor lifted his glass. "Therefore, I propose a toast… to us working together and bringing a killer to justice."

As he raised his glass, Canter's face flushed. "I appreciate the chance to make this right. I owe you. We all do."

CHAPTER 21

In her hotel room, Diane sought her husband's comfort. "I'm a mess. How can you be so calm?"

Liam stretched out on the bed while thumbing the television's remote controller. "It's a guy thing. I'm probably a bigger mess, but I'm better at fooling myself."

She unbuttoned her blouse, folded it on the dresser, and placed it in her dirty laundry drawer. Dry skin compelled her to scratch under the strap of her tank top undershirt. "I have to agree, emphatically, caveman."

"No need to be rude."

"That wasn't rude. I think I'm jealous."

"Understandable. Emotions can get messy, especially for women."

"Don't be sexist."

"It's true. Women are better communicators thanks to their sensitivity. Men are better hunters thanks to our insensitivity. I'm just going with your caveman comment."

"Whatever."

"And with you being a hypersensitive empath, I can see your emotions affecting you."

"Yeah. I said I was a mess."

"I mean all the time."

She faced him. "What's that supposed to mean?"

"You're an empath, and you're a woman. You're supposed to be sensitive all the time. You can't turn it off, I guess."

"Keep labeling me and see how long your marriage lasts."

"Sorry. I'm trying to be... um... empathetic?"

"At least you're trying, I guess. But you're right. I am very sensitive. That gives you a great opportunity to comfort your wife and talk about what's bothering me."

"Huh? No, there's a basketball game on now."

"Since when do you like basketball?"

"Since I said I'd consider moving to the States with you."

She started pacing in front of the bed. "Okay, let's talk about that."

"Talk about what?"

"Moving to the States."

He grimaced. "No. We agreed to live in Ireland while we figure things out."

"I've got images of a nun being tortured in my head. I'd like to talk about anything else, like where we're going to live."

"Not tonight. We've already agreed to being messes. Let's do something less mentally strenuous."

Fatigued, she backed off. "Okay. Like what?"

"Um, you could watch the game with me."

She wondered if all newlywed husbands were so awkward. "Seriously? Come on! When's the last time I did anything to make you think I liked sports?"

"Well, never. But I figured you never played sports because you've got the dexterity of a pregnant three-legged rhino. I didn't think you really disliked sports."

"What did you just call me? What sort of rhino?"

"I was trying to get your mind off... stuff. Get serious. Do you really not like basketball? It should be a good game."

She stopped walking, faced him, and jabbed her fists into her hips. "I don't like sports, and I don't like TV."

"TV's relaxing, and that's just what you need."

Warming up to the idea of vegetating with him, since a soothing conversation seemed beyond his skill, she started pacing again. "I'd be willing to watch a romantic comedy movie."

"Hell, no!"

"You get a choice. We can keep talking, or we can watch a movie of my choice."

As she'd hoped, the decision weighed on his tightening shoulders. "Um, if we talk, can I watch the game afterwards?"

She shrugged. "Sure."

"But we can't talk all night." He lowered his voice to a deep tone, a trait she normally found sexy, but not tonight. "I mean, we have newlywed affairs to attend to."

She froze and glared at him. "Ew! No! Someone died today."

A pallor of horror consumed him. "You're going to let that ruin our love life?"

"What's wrong with you? It's not ruining anything. I just can't get past it."

"I don't mean to sound like an ass, but people suffer and die every day. There are souls in hell going through unimaginable suffering right now and forever, but we can't stop living for that."

She renewed her walking. "You almost sound like you're addicted to sex. And I'll take it as a compliment, since you spent your entire life before me planning on remaining a virgin."

He shrugged and pursed his lips. "Well, yeah. Forgive me, but I'm kind of addicted to you now."

She shared a reciprocal addiction, but she decided to delay her satisfaction until she could engrain the proper habits into him. And that meant talking when she needed it. "Great! And I'll help you get closer to me by letting you hear my deepest thoughts."

Sarcasm oozed as he clicked off the television. "Every male of the species will be jealous. Please, go on."

"No way, buddy. Not until you put away the sarcasm and act like you care. When you married me, you agreed to listen."

"I don't remember that in our vows."

"It's an assumption behind all your vows!"

"My vows? Aren't they, our vows?"

"We only need to discuss yours because I live up to mine."

He snorted. "We haven't been married long enough to break our vows. And what little time we've had together, we've been busy fighting crime. I'd like to spend more quality time with you."

"That's the sort of sharing I was looking for. This is what husbands and wives should discuss. Time together. A yearning to avoid being apart. Not basketball games."

"Okay."

"Don't you think it's weird that we've been married for less than two weeks, and we've had about ten waking hours alone together?"

"If that much."

"Well?"

He rolled onto his side and propped his head on his hand. "Well, yeah. It sucks."

She slid onto the bed, lay beside him, and looked into his blue eyes. "You've hardly complained. I was afraid... this is going to sound selfish. I was afraid that you weren't as miserable as me."

"I don't know that I'm miserable. I hate that this mission's ruined our honeymoon, and I hate it worse that we couldn't save Sister Jane, but we found the bad guy. We did something good."

"But the police can't bring him in. Your dad says a demon's protecting him. So, he'll get away, and we'll have to find him. That could take all month or longer, and it's dangerous."

"Dangerous, for sure. Demonic combat is tough, really tough. But it only goes so far. We can beat him. It won't be easy, and people may die, but we can beat him."

The answer hit a nerve. "See? This is the problem. I wanted to talk about the impact on our relationship of having to keep hunting Father Solomon. But you thought I wanted a locker room speech."

"That's not what I intended."

"Yeah, it is. You couldn't even conceive of anything other than the mission."

"I guess not, but I don't see your point. Why's that a criticism? Isn't my dedication to protecting others a good thing?"

"Not if it puts our marriage at risk. I knew you'd always want to fight crime first and be a husband second. I just don't like it, now that it's happening so fast after our marriage."

He chuckled. "Technically, it started right before our marriage."

His comment redirected her thoughts. "That's another thing that's bothering me. How can we trust them?"

"The beast masters?"

"Yeah. We went from mortal enemies to dinner dates in a day."

"It's bizarre. But if you think through history, yesterday's enemy is tomorrow's ally. Sides change all the time. Our decision to team up with them was pretty simple, actually. Canter made a huge mistake and apologized. Beyond that, we're lucky that only two men died, and they'll probably earn rewards in heaven for martyrdom."

She pushed up from the bed and started pacing again.

"What's wrong?"

"Your belief in all this religious stuff."

"But you're Catholic."

She visited her church on Christmas and Easter. "It's part of my culture. But I have a mind of my own, and I use it. I don't believe everything the Church tells me."

"Then you're not Catholic."

"Don't be an ass."

"I'm being pragmatic. Catholicism means believing everything the Magisterium teaches as dogma and following everything it teaches as doctrine. To diverge at all is to be something else."

"What the hell's the Magisterium?"

"It's the Church's office for interpreting the Word of God."

"I didn't ask you to spout rules, but you're spouting rules about the world's biggest rule maker."

"You'd prefer anarchy?"

"I said, don't be an ass!"

His tone bordered on patronizing. "I'm not being an ass. I'm saying that without rules, life is chaos. That's a form of hell."

"The Catholic Church has too many rules."

"You'd prefer zero rules and anarchy?"

She wanted to smack him for jumping from "too many" to "zero" in one thought. "People can make laws without the Catholic Church, or even a Christian God, for that matter. Maybe you've heard of the Jewish and Muslim democracies? They're called Israel and Turkey."

He became cold. "You told me you were Catholic before we got married. I'm afraid you didn't understand what you were saying."

"Get over it. I'll be at church every Sunday as the dutiful wife, if that's what you want. Just don't expect me to live and breathe your religion."

"No, I won't expect it. But I'll encourage it and pray for it."

She was used to all levels of preaching from her extended family. "Just don't push it."

"I won't push if you'll allow questions and give honest answers. You just said you wanted to talk more, right?"

"Not about Catholicism."

"Would you prefer basketball?"

She changed her choice. "Catholicism is fine, in small bites. Go ahead."

"Where do you think Sister Jane is now?"

"What's that got to do with Catholicism?"

"Everything. Just answer."

"I don't know. The morgue?"

"I mean her soul, spirit, consciousness... any word you want to describe the concept of her continued awareness. What do you think happened to that?"

Visitations with ghosts were common for Diane, but she'd hardly questions their origins. "I guess she's a ghost or a spirit like the maidens who visit me."

"That means you believe in life after death."

She shrugged.

"That means you believe that Sister Jane is still alive, somewhere, and in some form."

"I guess so."

"Anyone who's even remotely open to the possibility of an afterlife must ask where you go when you die."

"I don't want to talk about death. That's what you're supposed to be getting my mind away from."

"No. I disagree. The way through the fear is to remove it with understanding. Think about it. Study it. Learn that death's not the end, but another beginning. To me, that's the most important truth a human can know, and Catholicism is where I get my answers."

Stopping, she folded her arms. "That's not a terrible perspective, but I don't want to talk about it now. I just got married, and we should be talking about our lives—not dying."

He stood and moved to her. "You're right. I'll let Father know to give us our space tonight. No calls, no texts, no emails. No nothing, unless we need to act tonight."

"You can't act tonight. The police are still on a manhunt. You'd get in the way."

"Right. Then I guess I won't be going out. It'll just be a quiet evening for me in a hotel room with my wife."

She sighed away her tension. "Talking about anything but death."

"Right." He stepped across the room to grab his pants.

"Where are you going? You just said you were staying."

"I'm staying as soon as I get back from buying my wife some flowers. While I'm gone, you get to pick the movie. Romantic comedy is fine."

CHAPTER 22

Nick awoke with a jolt, found his phone, and called his youngest brother. "Come on, Joe. Pick up."

No answer.

He tried his middle brother. "Jake?"

"Yeah. I'm here. What time is it?"

Nick extended his phone, glanced at the hour, and then pressed it back to his cheek. "Just after three."

"What's wrong?"

"I got a feeling about Joey."

"A real one?"

Nick knew that something intentional had woken him up. "Yeah. He's in trouble."

"You think he's at the lab?"

"Probably. Meet me there in half an hour."

After a quick shower and changing of clothes, Nick drove to work. The early morning was chilly, and traffic was negligible as he approached the property. From the parkway, he turned onto the private access road where a guard checked his credentials and then waved him into the intelligence complex. He parked, marched to his building, and swiped himself through a security entrance.

Wearing jeans and sneakers, he jogged through the hallways and into the basement. At a steel door, he waved his access badge over a magnetic reader, and the lock clicked open. He pushed through the entryway and into his lab's control room.

On tables around him, one laptop among half a dozen emitted a dim glow. He recognized the operating computer as the one Canter used to watch Joe during his psychic maneuvers. He looked up, and through the Plexiglas barrier, he saw a silhouette reclining on his youngest brother's bed. "Damn it."

Nick folded his arms and assessed his little brother.

During the sibling's troubled childhood, Joe had been rash and prone to petty crime for cash and cheap thrills. The discovery of his psychic strength had tempted him into years of power abuses until his brothers had convinced him to join the CIA. Together, the threesome became pioneers under Canter's guidance, charting, policing, and discovering ways to exploit the void.

The firstborn sibling assumed Joe was seeking Father Solomon within the void, and he feared for his brother's safety.

He studied the vital signs on the screen. Joe's breathing and pulse were rapid, his skin resistance was low, and his brainwaves were in the cellar. "You stupid ass."

Behind him, the door clicked open, and Jake's huge shoulders filled the entryway. Puffy eyes stared into the darkness beyond the Plexiglas. "Is he in there?"

"Yeah. He's deep in the void."

The husky middle brother bumped into Nick while clearing a line of sight to the computer. "You got that right. Holy cow, he's in deep."

"We should call Canter."

"You don't want to deal with this ourselves? Just try to wake him and bring him back?"

"I would, but I have no idea how he got in that deep."

"Does it matter? We can pump him with adrenaline and bring him home. Come on. What are you worried about?"

"Killing him, for starters. He'd need a fatal dose to come back."

"You think?"

Nick shrugged. "It's just a guess, and that's the problem. We're guessing about how to get him back."

"Canter would only be guessing, too."

"He's got decades of experience to our years. We need him."

"Fine, but is there anything we should do for Joey now?"

Nick wanted to keep his youngest brother untouched until they had a plan. "No. Wait until Canter chimes in."

"Alright then. Call him."

The firstborn sibling lifted his phone, dialed, and heard his boss' groggy voice. "Sorry to bother you."

"What the hell? Do you know what time it is?"

"We've got a problem at the lab. We need you."

Twenty minutes later, Canter entered the control center. "Just when I thought you three idiots had grown up, you let him pull a stunt like this."

Seated next to his middle brother in front of the active laptop, Nick rubbed his eyes and then looked up. "The best we can guess, Joey thought he was doing us a favor by jumping in there alone."

"Move aside." Canter wheeled a chair between the brothers and examined the vital signs. "Are you kidding me? How long's he been like that?"

Nick checked Joe's brainwaves. "You mean in deep theta?"

"Well, yeah. What'd you think I meant? He's hovering a fraction of a hertz above dreamlessness."

For his brother's advanced abilities to control his mind, a twinge of jealousy pricked Nick. "He's been there since I got here twenty-five minutes ago. He's been holding it longer."

"How do you know?"

"I'm giving him credit for getting into theta waves forty minutes ago, when I woke up."

"You got a psychic wake up call?"

"Yeah. I'm sure Joey nudged me from the void."

Canter sounded impressed. "And he's still holding deep theta? Shit. He's damned good."

Jake snorted. "Don't let the asshole hear you say that, or his head'll explode from conceit."

Nick shot his brother a harsh glance. "Let's make sure he isn't killing himself before you insult him again."

Jake sounded hurt. "It wasn't an insult. It's true. He doesn't need any more reasons to think he's the best."

"Pipe down, you two. He is the best. He's better than I ever was. Now let's figure out why he jumped in there without telling us."

The boss' comment gave Nick an insight. "The first clue is that he didn't tell us. He's doing something he knew we'd want to stop if we knew about it."

"No shit, Sherlock? It took you yay-hoos twenty minutes to come up with that?"

Nick had considered Canter beyond reproach as a boss and mentor, but he was worried about his brother and losing patience. "We were both half awake. And if you'll excuse us, we're still adjusting to the rapid changes in our lives."

Canter took his eyes off the screen long enough to give the firstborn brother a sincere look. "Sorry. You got a point. I was just bitching. The real problem is I'm afraid that I know what he's doing. I... uh, I taught him a new trick."

Nick frowned. "You taught him, but not us?"

Canter shrugged. "Sometimes we try out some advanced techniques. Sometimes, they're techniques I've never tried."

Jake interrupted. "Let me get this straight. You and the former inmate of several county prisons are, alone, in secret, and without the protection of his brothers, pioneering new tricks in the most dangerous battleground mankind has discovered since splitting the atom?"

"When you put it that way, you make me sound like an asshole." Canter lowered his gaze. "Well, okay, maybe it was a dick move. But you have to admit, he's got that extra bit of natural skill–you've both seen it. I just wanted to strengthen him and strengthen us."

Jake remained bitter. "It was a dick move. That's about the only thing I agree with."

Nick corrected his brother. "You also have to agree that Joey has more talent than either of us."

"Yeah, okay. Sure. The asshole's the strongest."

The firstborn brother reached his breaking point for dissent. "Jake, shut up, get off Canter's back, and listen to him. Canter, you're the boss, take charge, and tell us to shut up if we get off topic."

Jake groaned and looked away.

Canter nodded his agreement. "You're absolutely right. We need to pull our heads out of our butts and do whatever Joey intended for us to do. Let's figure this out. Did you guys try a communications conduit?"

Nick shook his head. "He's too far away to hear any of them."

"Did you try?"

"We didn't want to draw attention to him. God knows who'd come running if we yelled for him."

"Good call. We've got to get to him, but we need to move cautiously."

Nick leaned back in his chair. "Agreed, but that's as far as we got before you showed up."

Jake stared through the Plexiglas at his entranced sibling. "Look at what the asshole did to himself. What was he thinking?"

Canter defended the youngest brother. "I'm sure he was thinking about catching a murderer. I don't agree with his Lone Ranger style, but he's got the skill and the guts, I'll give him that."

Nick eyed his boss. "What did you teach him?"

"I ought to come clean about that, I imagine."

Nick rolled his chair away and faced his boss. "Come on back here with me, Jake. The boss is going to tell us a story."

Canter swiveled. "Yeah, I am. But not to just you two idiots. I need a bigger audience. I'm calling Connor Brady."

CHAPTER 23

Liam awoke to a kick. "What?"

Lying beside him, Diane was a tuft of disheveled hair. "Go see what your dad wants."

"What are you talking about?"

"He wants to talk to you."

"How did he... how did you know?" Liam sat upright and saw his wife.

After her shining moment of empath work, she stirred under the covers, entered a deep breathing cycle, and fell back asleep.

To avoid waking her, he slid off the bed and crept over the thin carpet to his folded clothes. He put on yesterday's jeans and then skulked into the hallway. He walked to his father's door and knocked gently.

Seconds later, Connor appeared, startled but alert. "What a surprise. What can I do for you at this hour?"

"That's what I was going to ask you."

Connor narrowed his eyes. "Why?"

"Guess who's playing psychic phone operator?"

"Huh. She was awake?"

Liam shrugged. "I don't think so. She kicked me to wake me up, told me to come see you, and fell back asleep."

"Interesting."

"Interesting as in good, you wanted to see me? Or interesting as in false alarm, and I can go back to bed before breakfast?" At the mention of the morning's meal, his stomach growled. "Great. Now I'm too hungry to sleep."

Connor let his son into the room. "Diane was right. Come in."

Liam crossed the floor and then sat in a large arm chair. "What's going on?"

"Our new friends just phoned me. Apparently, they already need our help with some psychic work."

Awake less than ten minutes, Liam's hazy mind choked on the unexpected report. "How can that be? They didn't say anything about going into the void."

"I take it by Diane's reaction that she sensed my surprise. One of the brothers went so deep into the void that they can't get him out. To your point, I suspect they didn't mention it at dinner because the brother's acting on his own."

Alarms chimed in Liam's head. A renegade maverick in the void was the last thing he needed. "Seriously? Which one?"

"The young one. Joe or Joey. They address him both ways."

"Why don't they pull him out?"

"They're afraid it would kill him."

"That is deep."

"Seth said it's deeper than anyone's ever gone, to his knowledge. I asked him what 'deep' means in a world that our empaths describe as an infinite sphere, and he said he'd have to explain it in person."

"But he's sure we can help?"

"Actually, no. He's not sure. I asked him. But it's the only chance they've got."

Liam disliked the proposition. "Not to be an ass, but what if we refuse? I mean, these guys were trying to kill us yesterday. If their team's too stupid to avoid accidental suicide, why's it our problem? Why do we need to place our people in danger?" After speaking, he questioned his hasty and selfish judgment.

"It's not our problem. It's our opportunity. Seth believes that Joe Slate has found the trail of Father Solomon, and I tend to believe him. There's no other reason on God's green earth why the young lad would expose himself to such danger alone."

Liam probed his imagination for a better rationale but found nothing. "I guess not. But I can't conceive of a reason for his behavior, even if he did find a sign of Solomon."

"True. It's a mystery until we know more."

"What's Seth want from us?"

"Three empaths and what he called 'that psychic nuclear bomb'."

"Josh?"

"Indeed."

"So, what now? We race over to CIA headquarters and tell the night watchman that we're there to save them from themselves?"

"Actually, yes. Except that Seth will escort us in."

"Okay. When?"

"The sooner the better, obviously, but I asked him about the urgency. He said it wasn't immediate but to get there before six."

Liam recalled sitting in seven lanes of congestion yesterday. "Six? To beat the horrific traffic?"

"To gain access with guards he knows. I think we'll be violating a protocol or two when he lets us in."

"I'll wake up Misses Morning Monster and grab breakfast sandwiches. You wake up everyone else and get them moving."

An hour later, Liam drove the trailing vehicle behind his father's Jeep Grand Cherokee. While swallowing a bite of a ham and egg sandwich, he watched a guard wave the elder hunter through the gate. "Looks like we're getting through."

In the passenger seat, Diane groaned.

"What's wrong?"

"I should be in bed."

"We all should be, but here we are. Do you sense anything yet?"

"I sense that I should be under the covers."

"You know what I mean."

"It's fine, Liam. This isn't a trap."

The guard waved Liam forward, checked the identifications of his vehicle's occupants, and told him where to drive. He followed his father to two of the many free spaces, parked, and stepped into the morning's crisp air.

Connor gathered the team and led them into the austere

building's closest entrance.

Two guards greeted the arrivals with instructions and a litany of rules, but Canter stood with them and adjusted the weapons policy. "Thanks for coming, everyone. You can bring your daggers, but you'll have to pass them through the scanner." He glanced at the guards. "And I'll have to pass these guys each a bottle of Johnnie Walker Blue for the favor."

After following the CIA supervisor through several checkpoints, Liam's curiosity overcame him as he heard a heavy metal latch click open. "Is this the place?"

As he pushed open the door, Canter gave a wry smile. "Prepare to be impressed."

Liam squeezed into the space with his teammates and scanned the equipment. Other than the speakers, microphones, and controls of an annunciation circuit, everything was portable. He considered challenging the promise of being impressed, but he kept silent.

Canter read his mind. "The impressive part is through the window." He pointed at the Plexiglas.

As heads turned, Liam eyed the silhouettes in the lab for familiar shapes, seeing four recliners that reminded him of hospital beds, one of which held a man. "Joe's in there?"

With a hint of pride, Canter clarified. "Joe, and about thirty million dollars' worth of equipment."

From his university training, Liam had a general idea of technical price tags. Nothing in the lab appeared worth the quoted cost. "Thirty million? Is most of that hidden in research and development? Or maybe in software costs?"

"A little of both. The big software costs were in our communications algorithms. It took a ton of work translating brainwaves into human speech, but we figured it out. That's how we can talk to each other in the void."

"That's really cool. I don't suppose you'd consider–"

"Hell, no. Even if I wanted to, it's not mine to give. Between the need for national security and the protection of intellectual property, I'd be shot for treason."

"Okay. Never mind."

"There's more to the thirty million, by the way. There's also an automated drug injector gun on each recliner. They were custom designed for this and cost a pretty penny."

"What drugs?"

"Serums for helping the boys get in and out of their trances."

Liam glanced at his wife, who shrugged and appeared tired and unwilling to participate. "We don't use serums."

"Yeah. You guys use daggers, and sometimes nothing, if I understand it right. We can do it without serums when we have to, but it's tough."

The young hunter surmised that a serum for entering a trance would complicate extraction. "Did Joe take a dose before going in?"

Canter nodded. "Yeah, he did. That's recorded here on the laptop, and I checked the reservoir on his recliner. He gave himself a maximum dose and then some."

The firstborn sibling raised his voice. "He meant to go in deep, and I think he knew he'd be in there for a while."

Connor pushed the agenda forward. "He may even have predicted that we'd be here to help. So, shall we brief the mission?"

Canter projected his words to the back wall. "Everyone, please sit. I'll tell you what's going on. Again, I thank you all for coming."

The gang milled about the control room and found seats or places to stand.

Canter cleared his throat. "I should probably start with some bad news. You may remember meeting an elderly Customs officer during your entry into the country?"

Liam placed an assuring hand on his wife's shoulder.

The CIA supervisor continued. "Unfortunately, Officer Eleazar was found beaten to death in his apartment."

Diane cried and buried her face in Liam's chest. "We did that!"

Canter corrected her. "No, ma'am. I did that. That's on me. I knew your team was coming to the States, and I tried to have you arrested at the airport. Eleazer never knowingly walked in the void, but he was a psychic researcher back in the day, looking for Russian submarines. The rumor is he found a few, and someone who thought he could resist you called him out of retirement."

Liam remembered the encounter at the airport. "He was able to resist all three of them. He also said it would be his doom to let us pass, but he did anyway."

"There's something happening here beyond our understanding. How he'd know he'd be murdered for it is beyond me, even for a psychic. But it was a quick and dirty job. And here's the kicker. The killer left DNA, and it matches Father Solomon."

Liam narrowed his eyes. "Then we have another good reason to stop him."

"Right. And if you'll all listen up, I'll tell you how we can do that. I think Joey's found him."

CHAPTER 24

Diane yawned as she wedged herself between her sister empaths. "I'm not good with early mornings."

Emma's German accent was thick with her lingering grogginess. "Tell me about it, but these guys know things we never dreamed of."

Diane nodded and then locked her eyes on the CIA supervisor.

Canter addressed his audience. "Joey's got the strongest natural ability I've ever seen, not counting your four psychics."

Diane blurted her answer. "Are you counting Josh? We never include him. You know he's autistic, right?"

All noses rotated towards Josh, who stood in the room's corner with his nose hidden behind his tablet computer. But his alert eyes were looking back at the group. "What? I'm paying attention."

"After that psychic nuclear bomb he dropped on the boys, hell yeah, I count him. But we don't lead with the bomb. We hold him in reserve." Canter looked to Diane's brother. "So, Josh, I'm hoping you won't have to do anything. But if you do, it'll be a request to blow everything up like you did last time against my boys."

Josh stared back at the CIA man.

Diane coached her brother. "Josh, do you think you can do that?"

"I don't know."

"Do you think it's at least possible, Josh?"

"Yeah. I did it when I was afraid you'd get hurt. I guess if I'm afraid again, my reaction will be the same."

Canter shrugged. "We can work with that. Nothing's going to be certain in there. But Josh's bomb looks like a natural defense, meaning he won't have to think about it."

After a moment of silence, Diane prodded her brother. "Josh, does that sound right?"

"Yes."

"Does that mean you'll be ready to help me if I get in trouble?"

"I don't know what I can do, but I'm always ready to help you and Emma and Layla."

Canter raised his eyebrows. "That's the first bit of good news I've heard this morning. I hope that attitude becomes contagious. Now let's move on to the sixty-four-thousand-dollar question. What's Joey up to?"

The firstborn sibling called out from his chair. "And don't spare any details. Jake and I have been dying to hear this all morning."

"Alright. Time for me to fess up. A little background for our new guests."

Nick launched a verbal jab, and Diane noticed rising frustration simmering within the CIA team. "Don't pretend like you've given me or Jake any background. This is brand new for us, too. Our new friends need to know that this is a complete surprise to all of us except you and Joey."

Canter glared at Nick but then softened his features. "What would you have done if I'd told you about his special training? Huh? You would've been angry at both of us, and it would've hurt our team's performance."

Nick verbally bit harder. "Hurt our performance? You mean, like one of us getting stuck in there?"

"I deserve this, but for Joey's sake, can we move on?"

"I said what I needed to. For everyone's sake we can move on."

"Thank you. Now, I was teaching Joey how to improve his search for bad guys, for lack of a better word. The challenge is trying to see void walkers when they're not in the void."

Diane checked her sisters, but they remained still. "Sorry. I think I know the answer, but what's a void walker?"

"Better to ask than to get it wrong. Void walkers are anyone who enters the void on their own power. We've seen plenty of people hitch rides, but we believe that only one hundredth of one percent of the population are void walkers."

Hearing the first statistic of her abilities' rarity, Diane perked up. "Josh can do it. He's a void walker. He just doesn't do it much."

"While he's in reserve, we'll use the other walkers at our disposal. What I suspect happened is that Joey went in there thinking he could find Father Solomon based upon the boundary detection techniques I was teaching him."

The two brothers started a rapid side conversation.

"You boys want to share?"

Nick revealed his growing frustration. "Yeah. What the hell's boundary detection? It's like we don't even know you anymore."

"And you can flog me for that after we get Joey out." Canter scanned his audience's faces. "You all know that you can see some special items reflected in the void, like haunted houses, cathedrals, burial sites, and the like. The most cursed or charmed of those places create glowing lights in the void."

Diane canted her head. "Most lights in there are people–void walkers."

"You're right. Only one in a thousand lights are inanimate objects, but they're valuable. We use them as beacons to map our location to the ground."

Diane was confused. "Don't you just know where you are?"

Canter's eyes widened. "Obviously not as well as you ladies. Me and the boys have always had a good idea, Joey especially, but rarely good enough to take action. So, we came up with a grid system that's oriented to the beacon locations."

Diane liked hearing that she naturally navigated the void better than her former enemy. "Cool."

"It is, but we keep the grid turned off when searching because it makes the dimmer auras harder to see. We probably won't need the grid today because I suspect Joey's near a mapped boundary."

Diane scanned her memories again. "I don't know of a boundary. The void's infinite, or at least it seems that way."

"We see the void conceptually as a sphere that's concentric with the earth. We map downwards to the real world, but when we look upward, it appears infinite to us, too."

Liam interrupted. "We'd love a copy of that map. Can you share?"

"Ninety-nine times out of a hundred I'd say no. But since you're helping us pull our heads out of our asses, I'll concede. It'll be a hardcopy. I can't risk an electronic version leaving this room."

"Understandable. We'll be happy with paper."

"Jake, can you print out a poster-size map for them?"

The husky brother swiveled his face towards a laptop. "I'm on it."

Canter continued his education. "However, every path between the void and reality bends the boundary of reality around it. So, there are conduits connecting the void to ground. I taught Joey to camp out near one of those."

Nick countered the explanation. "You taught us all to do that."

"I taught you to hide near bright conduits so that your auras are drowned out. But that's when you're looking within the void. I was teaching Joey to look the other way–towards the ground."

Doubt seemed to compound Nick's frustration. "No way. We've all looked groundward near the conduits out of curiosity, and we've never seen anything but pitch black."

"It takes a dark conduit, one with almost no light, to reduce your background lighting enough to see through. But if you get a dark enough conduit, you can make out auras on the ground. It takes practice, and Joey must've thought he was ready to find Solomon."

Diane had glimpsed a conduit when the brothers had ensnared and muzzled her. "I remember seeing something like a conduit when I... met the brothers in the void."

Nick blushed. "Sorry about that. But yeah, that was one of the communications conduits I made."

The comment piqued Diane's curiosity. "How do you make a conduit?"

The firstborn brother snorted. "That one was sloppy and only took me a week. But to do them right and make them permanent takes a ton of work. It's completely tedious. You have to enter and leave the void from the same location a bunch of time times. The one we use the most from this lab took a few months to finally stabilize."

Canter clarified. "We travel separately, which means we get three sweeps every time the boys go in, but it still took months. Any time someone enters the void, they carve a path. But like any path in nature, the wilderness will erode it, and if you ignore a conduit, it'll close up."

The scenario gelled in Diane's mind. "Oh. Um, I hope this doesn't turn into a false accusation if I'm wrong, but it sounds like you had Joey create his own conduit, an especially dark one, and he's there now looking for Father Solomon."

Canter aimed a finger at Diane. "Bingo. And since he's still in there, I believe he's somehow found and tangled with Father Solomon, and he's afraid he'll lose him if he lets go."

Nick revealed his anxiety. "Or he's stuck in extended one-on-one combat waiting for backup. Either way, it's time to help him."

Canter nodded. "Right. You'll go in first with Jake on your flank. Locate Joey and assess what he's up against. Since his conduit is new and unstable, don't rely on it for communications. You'll probably have to travel to report back to me, but don't let that stop you from doing the right thing if it's obvious."

"Right."

Canter faced Diane. "You ladies can watch how we operate a bit before you go in. I've already briefed Nick and Jake. I'll brief you after they're in."

Holding his printout, Liam called out. "You didn't map that new conduit, did you?"

Canter shook his head.

"Can you tell me where it is?"

"I could, but you're not going to make heads or tails of that yet."

"I'd like to try, since I'm not helping out otherwise."

"Sure. Okay. It starts here in the lab, obviously, and it shoots up on an angle over Baltimore."

Liam furrowed his brow and studied his map. "There's a conduit nearby called 'Seth's Door Four. Can they use that?"

Canter thought about it and then sounded chipper. "Yeah. You already figured out the map?"

Liam shrugged. "My father trained me in combat skills as long as I can remember. And though we didn't know much about the void until we met Diane, I'm married to her now, and I get a pretty good rundown of what it's like in there. It's fascinating. If I weren't such a muggle, I'd explore it myself."

Diane and several others chuckled at her husband's self-deprecating humor.

"Well, you're right. I sometimes build conduits to help the boys, since my heart condition doesn't matter for that. Seth's Door Four is one of mine. I can talk to the boys through most old conduits, even if they're closing up for lack of use. The boys know where they are, but sometimes they forget, which is why we always have mission briefs before we go in–Joey's present debacle excluded."

Nick stood. "I won't forget. Let's go." He clicked open the Plexiglas door to the lab and entered.

Jake followed him and closed the door.

The group moved towards the forward windows and watched the brothers move as silhouettes. They reclined on their beds, slid on helmets, and then waited for their boss.

Canter spoke into a microphone. "Can you hear me?"

Amplified affirmations came from each brother.

"Are you guys strapped in and ready? Jake, I'm not seeing skin resistance on your left arm."

"Sorry. I forgot to close it." A thick arm cut the darkness as Jake clasped an electrode bracelet around his wrist. "Okay."

"Yep. I see your reading now. Get ready for serum, normal dosage. In three, two, one..." Canter pressed a key on his laptop, and, dragging tubes and electronic wires behind its syringe, two black forms snapped into view beside each bed. The pneumatic injections hissed over the loudspeaker, and then the guns receded.

Nick gave a rote report. "I'm injected, drifting into meditation."

Jake repeated the words. "I'm injected, drifting into meditation."

Diane shared surprised glances with her sisters. Without speaking, she knew her fellow empaths agreed that their CIA counterparts wrapped a ton of military-like formality around steps the ladies considered simple and natural.

Canter fell silent while studying the screen. "Anyone got questions about this? It's just dead air while I watch and wait."

Connor instructed his team. "I'm sure we all do, but I'll ask my family to withhold comments until we've located Joey."

"Fair enough. They're in the void now. Nick's traveling with Jake by his side. They'll be at the Seth's Door Four in a few seconds of our ground time."

As if queued by Canter's introduction, Nick's garbled electronic voice shot from the loudspeaker. But his voice was artificial, like a robot trying to impersonate the firstborn sibling. Diane cringed when she heard it. "We're at Seth's Door Four. No sign of Joey yet."

Canter cast his voice towards the microphone. "You won't see him until you're closer. Nick, go to him alone. Jake, you stay and report back whatever Nick tells you. You'll be close enough to communicate between yourselves."

In the synthesized Nick-emulating voice, the void walker protested. "If I yell to Jake, it'll call attention to us."

"I know. But I can't risk having both of you fall into whatever trap he's in. Let's try having you come back and report if you can."

"Will do." Moments passed in silence, and then Nick's robotic voice brought insights. "You won't believe it. He's stretched out full length with his arms through the boundary."

Canter sounded astonished. "He's reaching through the void?"

"I don't know. You taught him this stuff. I didn't. But that's what it looks and feels like. I ran my hands over him to be sure."

"I never taught him to reach through the boundary, only to look. He invented that maneuver on his own."

"If you say so."

"Did you talk to him?"

"I tried, but he didn't answer. He knows I'm here. At least, I hope he knows it's me. We were reduced to him wiggling his feet and me tapping him to communicate."

"Could you see his face?"

There was a delay in Nick's response. "Um, I didn't mention that his head is through the boundary, too. So's most of his torso."

"So, you were staring at his metaphysical ass?"

"Lucky for him that I recognize it."

"Alright. Good job boys. Stay put, and we'll send in reinforcements."

"You don't think we're strong enough to pull him back?"

"It depends what he's holding. Or what's holding him."

"Yeah. But we can assume it's Father Solomon, can't we?"

Though Nick was beyond his sight, Canter shook his head. "We're so far into uncharted waters, I can't tell you what'll happen next. But what I do know, is there's strength in numbers when you're playing tug-of-war, and we're about to play for Joey's life."

CHAPTER 25

Diane's nose smudged the Plexiglas as she rotated her head towards the CIA supervisor. "What are the helmets for, again?"

"They help the boys communicate, usually with me through a conduit, but also to the animals when they control them."

Getting the insider's tour of the beast masters who murdered two men at her wedding bothered Diane, but her excitement of discovering the CIA's psychic secrets trumped her concerns. "When do we go in?"

"Soon. Let me check." Canter angled his jaw towards the microphone. "You about ready with those constructs, boys?"

The garbled, synthetic Nick-android voice responded. "Jake's got lassos over Joe's ankles. He's making one for his waist now. Okay, done. We're ready."

Diane scowled at the CIA supervisor. "That was fast."

"You're not used to watching from the outside, are you?"

She shook her head.

"The trickiest thing about communicating is the time mismatch. Every second out here is worth twelve seconds in there. Those voices you hear from the boys are slowed by a factor of twelve, and when my voice reaches them, it's accelerated twelve times. That's one reason their voices sound so fake."

"Okay, that makes sense. What about those serums? You're not going to make us use them, are you?"

"You don't need them. This is one area where you ladies have us beat, hands down. You can just get comfortable standing in there, or I'll get you chairs, beds, or whatever you want. But I will ask you to go in separately since I need all three of you in there independently to get a bigger footprint for better traction."

Diane exchanged knowing glances with her sisters. "We can do it from here with our daggers."

"It'll be weird having you standing right behind me, but okay."

Given her experience, an entranced psychic was a docile creature, and Diane noted an anomaly. "Why do you need all this bulletproof glass?"

Canter swiveled towards her. "You've seen Jake's size, right?"

Liam intercepted the question. "Hell, yeah. He's bigger than me by two stones. He's a tank."

"Yeah, he is. And he's a martial arts expert. Liam might be able to stand up to him if push came to shove, but there are few mortals who could. During one session with a stag, he picked up the worst backlash I've ever seen."

Diane interrupted him. "Sorry. Backlash?"

"That's when an animal you're controlling is killed violently or mortally wounded. The pain and fear oscillate out of control. We tried to develop dampeners for that, but the bond between animal and human is too tight. So, the boys may come back to reality with heartbeats and respiration rates in the stratosphere. We even saw some backlash from Josh when he detonated his big bomb."

In the room's corner, Josh smirked. "I'm the bomb."

Canter rolled his eyes. "No doubt about that. But back to Jake. One time, he got kicked out of a stag with backlash so bad that he tried to kill Nick."

Diane gasped.

"Fortunately, Nick was sitting here behind the glass doing my job at the time. But Jake almost broke through. He shattered the door so bad that we had to replace it."

Liam rapped the window. "Shattered this Plexiglas? No way! It's at least a centimeter thick."

Canter shrugged. "Backlash can push your abilities beyond normal human limits temporarily. That's also why we installed a mist system for pumping carfentanil and remifentanil into the room. Knockout gas, in case it happens again."

Diane was getting anxious. "We'll go into the lab so that nobody's worried about backlash. Come on, girls." She clicked open the door, held it for Emma and Layla, and shut the barrier behind her sisters.

Canter's voice was amplified. "Can you hear me, ladies?"

Although she doubted she could wake the entranced brothers, Diane kept her volume at mid-range. "We hear you."

"One at a time. Layla, then Emma, then Diane. Emma and Diane, wait for my signal. Layla, you're going in next. Rendezvous with Nick at Seth's Door Four. Whenever you're ready."

The Persian empath gave a nervous smile. "Should I be scared?"

Diane tapped her sister's arm. "You're an empath. You know."

Layla chuckled. "You're right. Stand back, girls." She closed her eyes, reached for the dagger at her hip, and became a slowly breathing statue.

Diane glanced at the CIA supervisor, who looked back with uncertainty, and then she resolved his confusion. "She's in."

Canter's order was curt. "Thanks. Emma, you're next but wait."

"Okay, I'm waiting."

Nick's computerized voice was becoming familiar. "Layla's with me. I found her."

Canter coordinated the void team. "Nick, put her on the tug line."

"Will do." Time hurried while the firstborn sibling escorted Layla to her post. "She's ready. We've got three lassos on Joey, and their ropes are twisted into one thick tug line. Jake's up front. Layla's behind him. Send in the next void walker."

"Emma, you're up. Whenever you're ready."

"This could be fun." The German empath winked. "See you in there." She shut her eyes, grabbed her dagger, and entered the void.

"Is she in? I'm used to checking the boys' status on the laptop."

Diane nodded.

Canter's order was again curt. "Diane, you're next, but wait."

From a mix of fatigue and nerves, Diane yawned while obeying.

Nick updated the ground crew. "Emma found me, too. I'm taking her up the tug line." Time raced again while the firstborn brother escorted Emma to her post. "Emma's ready, positioned behind Layla. Send in the next void walker."

"Last, but not least, Diane. Whenever you're ready."

Diane closed her eyes, grabbed her dagger, and concentrated. Her awareness shifted into the starry blackness, and as she oriented herself against the familiar canopy, she noticed a companion.

"Welcome."

Unready to befriend her former enemy, she kept her reply short. "Hello, Nick."

"Here. I made you a present." He extended a bronze aura shaped like a blade. "I made one for each of you."

"What's this?"

"It's your dagger, sort of. It's made out of light like every other construct, but it should behave like your real dagger in your hands."

"Sure. Thanks." She slid the glowing construct into the jeans she imagined that she wore over her imagined right hip.

Nick lifted his brother's lasso. "Grab this and follow it until you're halfway between me and Emma, and then get ready."

"Aren't you going to escort me?"

"Nah. You don't have far to go."

"Okay. We're just pulling, right?"

"Right. Of course, you can't dig your feet into any ground in here. So, it's more like dragging. You'll be facing me and trying to move towards me while holding the rope."

"But aren't you and your brothers like ten times stronger than us? I mean, I'm seriously scrawny. Aren't we just in the way?"

"We're stronger in grappling and hand-to-hand, sure. We train for that. But pulling strength's based on your propulsion abilities, and you ladies have above average void-speed. And we need all the help we can get."

Diane voiced her wordless response towards the firstborn sibling as she departed. "I'll do my best." While she followed the lasso, her ethereal hands sensed the line's tautness. "How does this work?"

"All constructs are made of pure light. They behave like particles or waves, depending how you interact with them. You can always see one while it gives off photons, but when you touch it, it comes to life, like matter–particles. The more force you apply to it, the stronger it gets, until it runs out of energy and needs to be remade."

Although she digested half of it, she filed away the lesson as one of many she hoped to learn from the brothers. "Cool."

Nick announced the next steps. "Everyone, turn towards me, grab the rope over your shoulder, and report your readiness from front to rear, starting with Jake."

The firstborn sibling's four accomplices responded.

"Jake ready."

"Layla ready."

"Emma ready."

The Chaldean empath raised the lasso to her neck, looked up at Nick, and tightened her two-handed grip. "Diane ready."

"We're all going to pull on the count of three." Nick counted it down. "One, two, three, pull!"

Diane impelled herself forward, but the taut rope resisted.

Nick prepared the team for the second tug. "Stop. Reset your positions, and report back."

The four accomplices announced their readiness.

"Get ready to pull on the count of three." Nick counted it down. "One, two, three, pull!"

This time, Diane raced forward unexpectedly, and she had to slow herself to avoid flying by Nick and Seth's Door Four. She shouted at her teammates. "What's going on?"

Jake sounded surprised. "He's free. We got him."

Nick seemed dubious. "You can't be serious. That was too easy."

The middle brother's tone was ominous. "Shit! We've got company!"

Diane panicked as she turned towards the danger.

An amorphous entity of light, a blob of shifting dimensions with random hues swirling upon it, spanning the dark red through harsh purple spectrum, loomed over Jake. Dwarfing the middle brother, the newcomer grew a tentacle, lifted it high, and then crashed it down on the husky psychic.

"Ah!" Jake screamed as he lifted his massive ghostly arm and parried the blow.

Before she could process her fight or flight instincts, Diane felt a tug at her shoulder.

Nick yanked her as he passed by her on his way towards the battle. "Come on!"

Diane saw frightening tentacles rising from the unwelcomed beast, and she hesitated as the firstborn brother raced by.

Knocked backwards, Nick howled as he flew over her in the opposite direction, and then he called to her. "Diane, I'm shooting a lasso at you. Grab that rope and Joe's rope, or I'll drift away."

Diane processed the challenge. Her friends stood exposed between her and the worst creature she'd encountered while their de facto leader sailed away.

As an empath, she trusted her instincts. But this danger defied her knowledge, and she gave herself a moment to think.

CHAPTER 26

Diane watched the firstborn sibling speed away.

Green light rose in front of his receding blue aura, blossomed in size and brightness, and then floated past Diane.

Intending to bring the brother back into the battle, she reached for Joey's lasso with her left hand, and then she groped for Nick's new construct. But it evaded her reach. "Damn it."

A loud crack shot from the battle, and Emma cried out. "Ah!" The German empath toppled backwards but recovered her position and then darted back towards the enemy. She updated everyone within earshot. "I'm okay, but I've never seen this before. What is this? It's so strong."

Jake worked behind and body-locked the new beast's formless mass while Joey and the sister empaths punched, kicked, and sliced with bronze daggers.

His lasso drifting in the wrong direction, Nick called out. "Grab my rope, Diane!"

Ignoring her embattled colleagues, she propelled herself towards the green construct and gripped the green rope. She held as Nick's momentum pulled his lasso and her ethereal body away from the battle. But Joe's line snapped, stopping her, like a space-walker holding two tethers.

Nick sounded relieved. "Thank you, Diane. Help them. I'm coming back."

Canter's garbled voice flowed from Seth's Door Four. "Are you guys okay? What's going on?"

Nobody answered, but Diane heard her colleagues screaming in pain as they struggled to dodge and parry blows from the new enemy's growing number of tentacles.

Canter yelled again. "What's going on? Report!"

Diane aimed her awareness toward the door, which served as the closest communications conduit. "This is Diane. Something came into the void behind Joey."

No response.

Nick reached her and stopped beside her. "He can't hear you. You don't have an electronic skull cap."

"Oh, yeah. Damn it. Update him, and I'll join the fight."

"I will. Get in there."

Accepting the firstborn brother's order, she sprang towards her sisters. With proximity, the tentacle-beast revealed its enormity. It towered over Jake, whom it grabbed with two tentacles and flung downwards. Diane called out. "I'm here, jackass!"

The beast repurposed its pair of Jake-tossing appendages into whips it snapped at her, which she dodged.

Diane noticed the beast's difficulty fighting in close quarters. It seemed optimized for cracks of its living whips, which snapped at a distance when adversaries like Nick approached but which flailed slowly near the amorphous body. "Stay close, everyone. It can't strike up close."

While groping the beast's body for stability, Layla slashed with her dagger. The cut left a gash of deep purple. "Got it! Daggers work! I'm hurting it!"

Emma did the same maneuver and stabbed dark holes. "Me, too!"

Adapting, the bleeding beast converted its tentacles into huge hands and then pounded each assailant.

When a purple fist crashed down, Diane pushed herself from the monster, but the blob of light's knuckles scraped her, causing a searing pain she'd considered impossible for the void. She screamed.

Emma called out. "Diane!"

The Chaldean empath was toppling through the nothingness but sensed her sisters' direction and willed herself towards them. As she returned to the battle, she oriented herself and recovered from her spinning. "It hurt, but I'm fine."

Layla shrieked in her native Persian as she launched repeated stabs, but then a fist smacked her, and after she growled in pain, she switched to English and sounded weak, her voice brittle. "My arm's broken."

Diane approached and assessed her sister, whose azure aura and illuminated outline intermingled with the blackish purple bruise on her humerus. "I see your injury."

Layla bent over and grabbed the ethereal wound. "It hurts! I can't use it. I... I can't move!"

The Persian empath's fear chilled Diane. "Why can't you move? What's wrong?"

"I don't know. I..."

As Diane rushed to her sister, she saw the full damage. The blow had broken the empath's arm while using it as a wedge against her ribs. The ghostlike form of her friend showed red blotches over and behind the skin of her human shape. "Your collar bone's broken. A few ribs, too. I think there's internal bleeding, but I've never done first aid in here. We've never been hurt in here!"

Nick reached and examined the injured psychic. "Get her back to the lab."

Diane didn't want to leave the fight. "I don't want to abandon Emma." She almost said 'her friends', but she wasn't ready to grant the brothers friend status.

"I'm stronger than you. Let me stay and fight. Layla will die if you don't get her back." His fuzzy azure face revealed compassion. "It may be too late already. Please get out of here."

Diane accepted the argument. "But I'm not sure I know how to bring someone back with me. Will grabbing her and heading back normally work?"

"Maybe. I don't know. But I want you to drag her back down Seth's Door Four. That's safe, no matter what happens."

As the Chaldean empath considered the tactic, Canter called out. "Vitals are critical for Layla. I need a report!"

Nick's lips remained unmoving as he yelled. "Layla took a nasty hit to her arm and upper torso. She's falling in and out of consciousness. Diane's bringing her back now."

Forced to acquiesce, Diane wrapped her arms around the Persian empath's motionless waist and propelled herself towards the blackness of Seth's Door Four.

Behind her, Jake barked a war cry. "Die, asshole!"

Over her glimmering shoulder, Diane saw the husky brother impersonate Superman by flying up and into the beast, fists extended. She gasped as he impaled the blob like a human-ghost-spear but became embedded within it.

Emma bobbed and parried the nearest fist, but she was helpless to counterattack.

Enraged by whatever ordeal he'd suffered on the boundary, Joey kicked and punched with a vengeance. But even the trained psychic warrior spent more time defending than attacking.

Nick called out. "Jake?"

Emma replied. "He's not breathing! He's trapped inside the monster. He can't move. He looks terrified."

Catching up to Diane at the communication conduit, Nick shouted. "Canter, Jake's caught inside the beast. We're getting pummeled. Get us out of here."

Canter's garbled voice was anxious. "You're sure?"

"Yes. Damn it! We're dying in here!"

"Stand by for the Josh bomb. I hope it works."

As she felt the conduit drawing her towards reality, Diane was confused. "Do I stay or wait for Josh?"

"Go." Nick changed his mind. "No, wait. Stay here in case it doesn't work, but push Layla through now."

Diane braked herself and pushed her sister, who glided towards reality. As she wished Layla a safe return, her leg tried to yank itself from her hip socket. Behind her, a long tentacle extended from the beast and traversed the ether to her foot. For the first time in the void, fear blanked her thoughts, and she stared in unmoving hopelessness at tendril wrapping itself around her ankle.

Canter was furious. "Damn it! Josh says he can't make the bomb go off."

Nick yelled. "Diane, get Josh to help us!"

The firstborn sibling's words echoed in her head.

"Diane! Get your brother to rain down hell on this bastard!"

The Chaldean empath regained her bearings and understood her need to feel mortal terror to light her brother's fuse. She stared at the beast, accelerated towards it, and mimicked Jake's failed attack with a Supergirl impersonation.

The tentacle clasping her ankle slacked as the she charged.

Diane's fists punctured the bruise-colored skin, and her awareness stalled inside the beast. Although the enemy appeared as fuzzy light from a distance, its innards crushed down upon her like the ocean's depths. Her ethereal body began to suffocate.

Terror. Burning. Starving for air.

She told herself the agony was fake, a fabrication her mind swallowed, but the fear of backlash convinced her otherwise and compounded her terror.

She let her fear feed upon itself, surging, spiraling, soaring.

A blinding flash. A deafening howl beyond human lungs. A catapult hurling her through the universe of nothingness.

Diane tumbled backwards as the dotted canopy raced by like a speed-of-light traveler's panorama. She righted herself and struggled against her momentum until she stopped.

She was alone and lost.

But safe.

Canter's distant voice was weak. "If you hear me, follow my voice... If you hear me, follow my voice..."

Diane obeyed and impelled herself towards the blackness of a communications conduit. She hurled herself over its event horizon and dove headfirst towards reality.

The lab surrounded her, and she opened her eyes.

Her blonde hair disheveled with sweat, Emma stood by Diane's side, steadied her shoulders, and examined her. "Are you okay?"

As she held the German empath's shoulders for balance, Diane sniffed her body stench and caught a whiff of the room's mingling fear-driven odors. As she shook the grogginess from her head, she noticed a commotion across the lab. "I'm okay, I think. What's going on?"

"Everyone's back, but Layla wasn't breathing. Liam's performing CPR on her, and Canter's got a medical team coming."

Diane peered at the crowd gathered around the spare recliner and saw glimpses of the Persian empath between the hunters tending to her. "Layla?"

Emma clasped the Chaldean empath's hands. "I don't know what god you know, but if you're open to praying for her, you should."

CHAPTER 27

On his recliner, Nick stripped off his helmet and flipped away his skin sensors. Surreal sensations overwhelmed him, and he lay back to gather his thoughts.

As the firstborn brother assessed the battle, the beast who'd defeated six psychics, and his second tumbling Josh-bomb voyage across the void, Canter cast a shadow over his face. "You okay?"

Nick was surprised to see his boss in the lab. "I'm fine. What's all the commotion?" He feared the answer was the Persian empath.

Canter's face was grim. "Layla's not breathing."

"Shit."

"The medical team's here. Let's hope they can save her."

Nick looked towards the spare recliner and saw medics huddled over the Persian empath. "Seriously? Not breathing?"

"Bad backlash. But she's getting the right attention." His boss tapped his shoulder as he stepped away. "Grab your brothers and debrief the mission before you forget what you saw."

"Okay." Nick rolled off the recliner and strode to the Plexiglas door. Behind him, people tended to Layla while before him, his brothers sat in the control room. He passed through the doorframe, clicked the latch shut, and faced his siblings.

Jake extended him a bottle of water. "You look like dog meat."

After checking himself for stench and sweat stains, Nick agreed. "Yeah. You guys don't look much better." He gulped water.

Jake pursed his lips. "This would've been a great mission if…"

Nick finished the sentence. "We have to trust that Layla will be fine. She's strong. They're all strong."

"They fought like Amazon priestesses, but I've got a bad feeling about this, man."

Joe interrupted his brothers. "No shit. We just got mauled. We thought we we're the baddest asses in the void, but we were that thing's bitches."

Nick counted to three before administering a dose of oldest-brother love. "We got mauled because of you. You've got the benefit of the doubt for now, but it's wearing thin. You've got some explaining to do."

The youngest brother looked up with pained eyes. "I don't know how I got there."

Silence.

Joe elaborated. "I woke up in the void. I mean, I was no kidding asleep and literally woke up on the boundary, right where you found me. I swear."

More silence.

"Don't you guys believe me?"

Nick judged his brother's veracity. "I don't want to, but I'm afraid I have to."

Jake looked up with horror. "It's been over five years, Nick."

"Apparently, our little brother's still a lightning rod for demons."

Shaking his head, Joe raised his voice. "No way! No way! I haven't cast a Wiccan spell since I was exorcised."

Nick shared a knowing glance with his middle brother. "Staying away from Wicca was step one of many. There's a long laundry list of shit you knew to stop doing."

Unable to meet the firstborn sibling's stare, Joe examined the control room's tiles. "It was just a little bit of psychic help."

Nick's heart sank. "Shit! What the hell did you do?"

"I needed cash." Joe looked up pleadingly. "But it was for us. I was doing it for all of us."

Raising his voice, Nick reprimanded his brother. "You've got a steady job now, you idiot! What trouble are you in?"

"Nothing. I'm not in any trouble. I just needed to know how to place a few bets, that's all."

"Why?"

"Because I made some bad ones."

Nick's patience ended. "Spit it out, man! Don't make me pull teeth. We need to understand this and react."

"Fine! I've been seeing a fortune teller to place sporting bets to get us enough money to branch out on our own. Are you happy!"

Jake stormed through the Plexiglas door. "I've got nothing more to say to the asshole. It's in one ear and out the other. See if you can recalibrate him."

Alone with his youngest sibling, Nick pressed for information. "You've been stupid, and Jake and I are going to kick your ass later. But now, I need you to tell me if you were possessed."

"I was careful."

"There's no such thing when you're playing with fire."

Joe shrugged.

"That's it, then. I'm assuming you got possessed. Stay here and wait for Canter to rip you a new one."

Joe yelled. "Screw him! Why do we even bother with him? He's old news. I'm stronger than he ever was."

Devastated by his brother's failure, Nick ignored him, marched into the lab, and found his boss. "Canter?"

"Yeah?"

"We need to talk."

Canter kept his eyes glued on Layla. "Now?"

"Well, it's–"

A tall medic, the evident leader of the three-man response team, lifted a breathing bag from the reclining psychic. "She's breathing! Pulse is weak but steady, but we've got her back."

A fog lifted, and a chorus of relief rang from the onlookers.

Canter stepped forward. "She's breathing, but she's not waking up. What else is wrong?"

The tall medic ran a flashlight into his patient's eyes. "Pupils are unresponsive. Let's get her ready to transport to medical." A stretcher appeared from behind the recliner.

Canter took charge. "Everyone, against the wall. Make way for the medics."

With care and haste, the responders carried the unconscious empath through the control room and angled the stretcher into the main hallway, out of sight.

Nick moved to his boss. "I need to talk to you."

"Okay. Talk."

"Joey tangled with a demon."

"Come again, son."

"I think he got possessed tonight. He's been seeing a fortune teller and…"

His jaw clenched, Canter turned red and stormed into the lab.

Nick caught up to his boss and his little brother and became a witness to the warranted verbal scathing.

Venom was Canter's tone. "Just what the hell were you doing, you dumbass?"

Joe attempted misdirection. "Like you've never wanted a lot of money?"

Canter blew up. "Don't patronize me with bullshit. You know you were high risk for being possessed again, and you had to keep your nose clean."

"I didn't think I'd get possessed."

Caustic sarcasm seeped into Canter's voice. "You thought you were too strong for a demon to trick you, didn't you?"

Joe shrugged. "Maybe."

"You got played, son. This is why we never tangle with demons. They're masters at tricks. Let me guess. You lost you some money and then won you some money, right?"

"I lost the money on my own. I didn't go to the fortune teller until I was deep in a hole."

"Well, I don't know if you placed stupid bets or if a demon made you lose them, but either way, he was watching you and playing a long con game."

Joe lowered his forehead into his hand. "Maybe. I guess so."

Interrupting the interrogation, Connor Brady walked into the lab. "Seth, I appreciate your quick response on Layla's behalf."

Canter's demeanor became compassionate. "She fought like a warrior. I made sure our medical group is going to treat her like a VIP."

"Thank you."

"You're quite welcome." Canter turned back to Joe. "Now, we have this disaster to resolve. Joey was just about to tell us everything he can remember about letting himself become possessed by a demon this morning."

Connor raised his eyebrows. "Oh, dear. That would explain a lot of our recent challenges."

Canter's interest shifted from his misbehaved psychic to the hunter. "You've got recent experience with demons. Irbil, if I remember correctly."

"Indeed, I exorcised one outside of Irbil, although I'm quite certain I had a dose of divine help. You see, Josh channeled a powerful angel to help me."

"That thing the boys and your ladies just fought in the void. You think it was a demon?"

"Based upon what the ladies reported, yes, but it's only a diagnosis of exclusion since I have no other guesses."

"Demons in the void would be news to us, but the CIA doesn't hunt them, and we've never found one by accident before today. But given your track record and what Joey just admitted to, I agree."

"I didn't admit to anything. Why am I the bad guy?"

Canter turned his index finger into a knife pointed at the psychic's heart. "Pipe down and suck it up."

"I don't have to take this shit." Joe stood and headed for the door.

"Get back in here! I need all you boys to talk."

"Get off my back!" Joe departed.

After the youngest brother disappeared, Jake entered the lab. "Where's the asshole?"

"Go get your brother back in here, will you? He just left."

Jake trotted out the door and shut it behind him.

Nick refocused the group. "Jake will bring him back. Let's get everyone in here and catch them up on what we know. Then Joey can fill in the gaps, and we can plan our next steps."

The normal color returned to Canter's face. "Good call, Nick. Gather the troops and we'll debrief in here. The only difference is that Joey gets my seat."

Nick nodded. "I like it. Put him in the hot seat and make him talk."

Canter scoffed. "Damned straight. That beast, or demon, or whatever it is just turned this from a policing mission into a war. We need to be flawless from now on. Let's get together, plan it out, and get it right."

CHAPTER 28

Liam distanced himself from Canter's empty control chair, giving the CIA men space to deal with their wayward son upon his return.

The control room's outer door opened, and Jake appeared with his little brother secured before him in a joint lock. He snapped as he pushed the youngest sibling's back. "Sit down and start talking."

Joe stumbled, recovered, and eyed the room. With accusing glares shaming him, he lowered his head, walked to Canter's chair, and sat.

His arms folded, Canter looked down upon the accused and began the inquisition. "Let's recap. You wanted a ton of cash, you placed bad sports bets, and then you went to a fortune teller for some help to recover your losses. Am I right so far?"

"Yeah."

"Then you made some good bets, with the help of the fortune teller, enough to get back the money you lost?"

"Yeah, and then some."

Canter dripped sarcasm. "Well isn't that wonderful? You made a profit, and it only cost us putting Layla into a coma."

"I'm sorry."

The CIA supervisor seethed. "Sorry doesn't cut it. Start talking. Elaborate. Now!"

"Okay." Joe gazed at a wall as he tapped his memory. "I started going to the fortune teller about six weeks ago."

"What's her name. Or his name?"

"Madame Zoroaster."

Demonstrating his broad repertoire of attitudes, Canter attempted comic relief. "Zoroaster was man. Did you check her private parts to make sure she was a she?"

Joe knew he was in trouble, and he stayed stoic. "No. She just said she attributed her abilities to Zoroaster, whatever that means."

Liam knew the answer. "Zoroastrianism was a pre-Christian monotheistic religion. I think it still has a few hundred thousand followers."

Everyone looked at him like he'd spoken a foreign language.

"Any unnatural abilities the followers of Zoroastrianism might enjoy, like Joe's fortune teller, would come from the devil and his demons. It's a preternatural power as opposed to a supernatural power, which comes only from God."

Canter scrunched his face. "Huh?"

"It may sound like doubletalk, but it's an important distinction."

"You really believe that?"

The question surprised Liam. "It's a dogma of my faith."

Connor expounded. "It's also a foundational belief required in surviving as an exorcist. If you fail to grasp the rules of engagement, you're going to lose the battle."

Canter shook his head and stepped to the back wall. "Shit, Connor. You and Liam know more about demons than the rest of us combined, and I'm about ninety-nine percent sure that's what we're dealing with. Why don't you take over the questioning?"

"Yes. Of course. I'd be happy to oblige." Connor drew close to the seated subject. "Did the demon reveal his name?"

"I didn't ever talk to a demon. If I was possessed—"

Canter snapped. "You were possessed, damn it. Own it!" The CIA supervisor softened his face. "Sorry, Connor. He may be your interview subject, but he's my disobedient child."

"No offense taken, I assure you. In fact, I believe you've motivated the young man to speak."

"Yeah. Okay. I was possessed. I must have become possessed during the night. But I don't remember it last night or ever. Not since..." He looked at his boss.

"Go ahead and tell them."

Joe lowered his face. "About five years ago, I invited a demon to possess me."

Liam swallowed. He'd never met anyone who'd allowed demonic control. "Bloody hell. That's an integration."

"Whatever you call it, I thought my powers came from the demon. I thought all our powers came from him. I was wrong."

Connor sought the beast's identity. "Did he give you a name?"

Joe's pained eyes pleaded. "I can't say it. I won't. I'm sure you know him, if they teach demon names in exorcist school."

"I'm aware of many of such names. Why don't you write it down on a small piece of paper, and then I'll burn the paper immediately after I read it."

Joe shot a glance at his boss.

"Don't look at me. Connor's the expert."

"I suspect the demon from Joe's past integration is the same one behind his fortune telling and is the same one our psychics battled in the void. An integration is the most dangerous relationship one can suffer with such a beast, and even after years of freedom, the demon will be watching you and trying to trap you. In this case, I'm afraid you were taunted and tempted into this."

Joe looked up hopefully. "It wasn't my fault?"

Canter barked again. "I told you to own it. No excuses."

After a moment during which the interviewee seemed to crumble under the weight of judgment, Connor defused the tension. "It's often shared blame, and we'll never know how much belongs to Joe and how much to the beast. But no matter. May I have a flame source and then the name, please?"

Canter extended a lighter. "Here."

Joe accepted a scratch pad from the firstborn brother, tore off a note, and reached for a pencil. His hand shaking, he scribbled letters and then thrust the paper to the elder hunter's chest.

Connor grabbed the paper, read it, and then burned it. He let the smoking cinders float to the floor. "Now I'm absolutely sure this single beast comprises our complete preternatural enemy.

He's tormented Joe since the beginning, he's the one who possessed Joe tonight, and he's the one who hurt Layla..." The elder hunter's voice trailed away.

Liam took a half step forward. "Father?"

"No, I'm fine. It's just... do I dare conclude that it's the same demon who's possessing Father Solomon?"

Canter scowled. "You just said he was possessing Joey. How can one demon possess two people at the same time?"

"He can't. But a demon can possess one person one moment and another person the next. I read about a demon bouncing between two girls while an exorcist pushed him from one girl only to have him enter the other and taunt him. The session required a second priest who exorcised the second girl under instruction while the exorcist handled the first."

As information overloaded him, Canter's face went blank. "Are you saying that every exorcist is a priest? Are you a priest?"

"Indeed, I am. Catholic, in full communion with the Vatican."

"I missed that little detail while I was researching your team."

"I don't imagine it's public knowledge. Liam and I are knights in the Order of Malta, but a minority of us are actually ordained as priests. Case in point, though he's trained as a deacon, Liam will not become a priest now that he's chosen a family life."

Nodding at the wayward psychic, Canter redirected the elder hunter to the interview. "How does that play into his situation?"

"Priesthood is a requisite of performing the Rite of Exorcism. Beyond that, training, apprenticeship, and on-the-job training. I'm far from your most experienced exorcist, but I've had a few battles. More importantly, I'm the only one who's willing and able to shoot his way close enough to a hostile demoniac to do the job."

"You might be getting ahead of yourself with talk of 'SWAT-team-exorcisms'."

Pondering the challenge, Connor grunted. "Perhaps."

"And what's this about priests and rites? I thought anyone could do it with the right words."

"There are many who attempt deliverance through prayer and other means, but not through the rite. Some are successful in their approaches, but nothing equals the rite in terms of efficacy."

"So, what can you do for Joey?"

"I can offer cleansing work while we work together. Specifically, ongoing exorcisms, prayer, and sacramentals, such as holy water or a crucifix, to wear for his defense. In fact, we should all wear sacramentals. I'll see to it that I bless enough of them for everyone."

"What do you mean, 'ongoing exorcisms'?"

"Rarely does one session expunge the demon. There are no public statistics, but it's commonly understood that five to ten sessions are needed over weeks and months. Sometimes it can take years."

Canter stepped forward. "Can you exorcise him today, just to make sure he still isn't possessed?"

Connor looked down upon the miserable psychic. "It's possible, but I doubt it's necessary. I believe the demon is keeping his attention on Father Solomon. With the demon outside of Joe now, I believe a strong defense is all that's required."

Joe met the hunter's stare. "I'm scared."

"That's natural, young man, and it's a good sign. It shows your respect for the demon. However, I'm afraid that you'll be at risk for the rest of your days. You must embrace your defense as permanent and be diligent about it."

"Okay. I guess I can do that."

"I'll spare you the sermon on theology and doctrinal rules, but there's a wonderful deposit of faith within Christianity that offers truth and guidance. For your soul's eternal well-being, I implore you to explore these teachings. But you don't have to become a Christian to evade a demon. Commitment to virtue will serve you well."

Liam chuckled.

Canter frowned. "What's so funny?"

"The looks on your faces when Father brought up Christianity. People can't be bothered to think about Christ until a demon scares them into it, whether they're haunting houses, cursing objects, or ambushing void walkers."

Connor was stern. "Careful where you're going with this, lad."

Despite his father's warning, Liam vented his frustration. "So many people are fascinated by magic and witchcraft but reject Church teachings as absurd for being supernatural. But here we are, fighting a demon, and we're using the Church's playbook."

"That's enough. This is neither the place nor the time."

Liam thought about apologizing to the elder hunter, but he let his points stand. He instead returned the conversation to the interrogation. "Are you going to share the demon's name?"

"It's best that I don't." Connor glanced at the humbled wreck. "In fact, we're done unless there's anything else Joe wishes to share."

Joe shook his head.

Concerned the CIA members may try to retake control of the team, Liam placed leadership into the elder hunter's lap. "Then we know what we know. Lead us on, Father. What now?"

The brothers looked at their boss.

Canter closed his eyes and nodded. "This is Brady Gang territory. I'd be a fool to challenge your expertise." He elevated his voice to signal his commitment to the Slate siblings. "I'll want veto power before we enter the field, but Connor's in charge, and I don't want to hear any bitching or second-guessing about it. Am I clear boys?"

The Slate siblings nodded their agreement.

"Good. It's your show, Connor. I echo Liam's question. What the hell do we do now?"

"We stay out of the void, since we don't understand demonic powers in there yet." Connor eyed Diane and Emma. "In fact, all psychics need to turn off their antennas, so to speak, while we pursue Father Solomon. Staying out of the void means staying out of everyone's heads, staying away from visions of the future, and… well, behave as if you had no psychic powers."

Diane broke her silence. "What if visions come to us?"

Connor shrugged. "I can't ask you to ignore a warning, but don't seek them. The void must remain off limits. We've learned what we needed during this battle. Seth, did you not pinpoint the demon's location while rescuing Joe?"

"I haven't fine-tuned it yet because I was helping with Layla, but it was somewhere in Baltimore."

His eyes sparkling with enthusiasm, Nick blurted out his clue. "When I was controlling a falcon in Baltimore, a young nun was very friendly with me. She could even tell that the bird was under someone's control. You may be on to something."

"I was indeed hoping so. In addition to these preternatural clues, we also have real-world detective resources at our disposal. We know whom we seek, and we can pursue him through normal policing means."

Canter nodded. "We've got CIA and FBI forces on it already. I'm sure we can find him if the search is limited to the Baltimore area."

Connor scowled. "But I urge you to make it very clear that nobody is to engage Father Solomon. He's armed and dangerous, and his weapon is demonic. I'm quite sure that anything other than a coordinated assault by our team will end in disaster."

CHAPTER 29

Diane glared at Liam, but his conversation with Connor and the CIA men consumed her husband. She then thought about invading the young hunter's mind to get his attention, but the recent edict to shun the void precluded it. Instead, she glanced at Emma and tried a different approach to challenging the void-ban. "Come on. Let's find a girl's room."

Embracing the offer, Emma grabbed Diane's wrist and yanked her into the main hallway.

"I guess that's a 'yes'?" Diane followed her sister through the doorway, twisted her ankle, and then stumbled into the German empath's arms. "Dang it!" The sting of another strained tendon rose within her flesh.

"You really are clumsy."

Diane stepped back. "Seriously? You jerk me out of the room and blame me for it?"

Her face reddening, Emma ignored the jab, wiped a tear from the corner of her eye, and swore in German. "*Scheisse!* This is terrible."

Heat billowed up Diane's ankle, but it bore her weight and passed her subconscious test of rolling it through its range of motion. "Yeah. Tell me about it. What the hell's Connor thinking?" As her words hung in the air, she reflected upon her question. "That's what's making you mad, isn't it?"

"Yes. Does he really want us to stay outside the void?"

Diane suspected that her sister shared her thoughts. "You want to get into Layla's head, don't you?"

The German empath's eyes narrowed. "I thought I was crazy to think of it, and then I thought Connor was a fool for preventing it. But if we get inside her mind, we could help her."

"Maybe he didn't think of it."

"Or maybe he's willing to give up on her for the greater good."

Diane couldn't fathom abandoning Layla. "I hope not. Connor's not coldhearted like that."

Emma held her ground in the debate. "He may not be coldhearted, but his job is to make difficult decisions."

The clicking of heels against tiles announced the arrival of two suited men. Fifty-somethings with graying hair and thickening waistlines, they engaged in small talk, but their eyes revealed intense thoughts, like they were holding back tidal waves of sensitive compartmented information while traversing hallways unworthy of their confidential knowledge.

Diane smiled as they passed.

They returned the gesture and then rounded a corner.

"Let's get to the restroom. I bet..." Diane reconsidered. "No. Wait. We're in the middle of CIA headquarters. I'm sure they've got hidden cameras and microphones everywhere."

Emma frowned. "Even in the restrooms?"

Diane shrugged. "Consider where we are. Let's not talk until we're someplace far away and private."

"Okay."

"We need to see Layla now, but no psychic maneuvers like Connor said, until we figure things out."

"How are we going to figure things out?"

Leadership of the sisters weighed on Diane. "I have no idea. I'm not even sure what we're doing next."

"Connor's planning something."

"Yeah. He's got an intense look like I've never seen before."

The laboratory door opened, and Canter led the team from the control room. "I'm glad you're still here, ladies. We're going to the clinic to visit Layla. I don't know if she'll appreciate it, but it can't hurt."

Diane joined the somber gaggle and followed the CIA supervisor down the hallway. After a handful of turns and one security checkpoint, she saw signage with a red cross jutting over a doorway. Her heart broke, and she mindlessly reached for her dagger to comfort Layla.

Emma whipped her hand around the Chaldean empath's wrist and whispered. "No."

Reminded of Connor's edict, Diane relaxed. "Sorry. I already forgot."

The German empath whispered her reply. "Careful."

Diane's intuition was murky about her injured comrade. "I want to know if she's going to be okay, but I can't tell without getting into her mind. Can you?"

Emma's blonde strands caressed her cheeks as she shook her head. "No. But we can't risk using the void."

Fearing an accidental slip into the ethereal realm and becoming the next coma victim, Diane made a mental note to encase her knife. "I'm going to cover my dagger in something so that I don't touch it by mistake."

"Maybe we should give them to the hunters for now?"

Diane's heart sank. Yielding a beloved enchanted dagger was like parting with a child. "Not even my husband gets to hold this. We'll get something to wrap them with in there." She nodded at the infirmary and then marched into its waiting area behind the CIA supervisor, who was explaining his team's presence to a receptionist.

Canter faced his companions. "I'll escort you in there, two at a time. Diane and Emma, I assume you want to go first?"

Springing forward, Diane grabbed Emma's hand, marched past the reception desk, and examined the four-bed clinic. Three beds were empty, but on the nearest one, her comatose sister rested in her perplexing slumber. "Layla…"

Surrounded by two nurses, a technician, and an examining doctor, the Persian empath was a tranquil body, a shell of the warrior Diane knew.

The physician looked up and sent a haughty stare over the guests. "I assume you're all family?"

Diane wasn't turning back. "We were just cleared by your receptionist."

"That's not what I asked."

The attitude grated Diane's nerves, and she pointed at each 'relative' in order. "We're her sisters, and you've got her grandmother, father-in-law, brother, and brother-in-law waiting in the reception area."

Suspicious of the obvious demographic differences, the doctor frowned but said nothing.

Canter reinforced their right to see Layla. "They're legit, doc. I vouch for them."

Apparently unhappy with the crowding, the doctor's face darkened, but the resistant physician's compliance revealed reverence for the CIA supervisor. "Keep everyone out of the way."

Diane made another mental note–Seth Canter carried weight.

"Will do, doc." The CIA supervisor called to Diane and Emma. "Come down here." He then stepped away, yielding space beside Layla's matted and sweaty hair.

Diane led Emma to their sister's bedside, but her mind went blank as she sought comforting thought. The Persian empath appeared entranced, but a chorus of sadness flushed Diane's frame, and she accepted that her sister's eyes may never again open. Strolling tears tickled her cheek.

The doctor examined Layla's unconscious eyes and then looked to the CIA supervisor. "Still unresponsive. What happened?"

"I can't really say."

"I knew you'd say that. The secrets in this building are great for getting people killed."

Displaying a patience and charm Diane hadn't foreseen, Canter withstood the insult with a smile and an Oscar-worthy portrayal of an appreciative man. "But I'll tell you that it wasn't an impact trauma. She was lying down when it happened."

"That doesn't help, but I'll note it."

Canter shrugged and offered a meek smile. "Such is the CIA."

The doctor rewarded the supervisor's tact with a darker scowl. "I need to transport her to Inova Fairfax."

With emotions swirling insider her, sadness wrapped in fear

and colliding with anger, Diane yelped her protest. "Don't take her away."

Perceiving the challenge as a personal affront, the doctor trembled in anger. "I've made my determination."

Diane's patience evaporated, and she reached for her dagger to invade the doctor's mind.

Again, Emma grabbed her wrist and protected the Chaldean empath from herself.

Relaxing her arm, Diane shifted her hands to her hips. "Why does she have to go?"

Uncomfortable silent moments passed as the doctor seemed to struggle with the bewildering concept of a layman's questioning. Unwilling to honor her interrogator with eye contact, the physician looked to the CIA supervisor while answering in a partial growl. "It's the closest level one trauma center."

As a scream billowed within the Chaldean empath's lungs, Canter calmed her with a soft hand on her shoulder. "She got hurt working for the CIA, and we'll take care of her. You have my word."

Diane choked up but squeaked her agreement. "Okay."

The CIA supervisor stepped to the edge of the curtain surrounding Layla's entourage and raised his voice for the hunters' hearing. "I'll make sure she has armed guards–people I trust. But we can't take her with us in her condition."

Stepping forward, Connor sighed, and his shoulders sank with acceptance. "Agreed. We must part with Layla for now and trust medical professionals and divine providence to deliver her."

Diane spun around on her heels and grabbed the German empath's shoulder for balance. "We're going with her."

The haughty doctor issued a final edict. "Nobody rides in the ambulance except medical personnel."

Again, a potential scream welled within Diane.

Again, Canter laid a soft hand on her as he leaned into her ear and whispered. "Don't react when I say this, because that doctor's a real jerk, but I'll take care of it. Grab Emma and meet me outside the main entrance in five minutes."

Diane's nod was imperceptible to all but the CIA supervisor, who was close enough for her to smell his cologne.

"I'll get you on that ambulance. But be ready to move out on a moment's notice when you get to Fairfax, because that demon knows we've found it, and we need to get moving to Baltimore."

CHAPTER 30

Fatigue crept up Nick's spine as he stepped from the elevator and marched towards the hospital's food court. "I need some coffee."

His husky middle brother's heavy heels clopped against the floor's tiles. "I could eat a house."

"You could always eat a house."

"I'm serious. I've been up since oh-dark-thirty running kamikaze attacks against a demon. A guy can build up an appetite doing that."

"With your bulk you build up an appetite by breathing."

"True." Jake caught up to his brother. "I see sandwiches–a lot of them. You know where I'll be."

Nick wanted the company, and he needed his middle brother's counsel. "Hold on."

A former military man who respected loyalty and hierarchies, Jake obeyed the firstborn sibling and stopped. "What's wrong?"

"I'm coming with you."

"I thought you were getting coffee." Jake nodded at a curving queue across the food court, a respectable oasis of consumerism in an otherwise austere environment which included a coffee shop, a sandwich stand, a grill, a convenience store, and a sprawling array of prepackaged refrigerated goods.

"I will, but I want to keep talking." A veggie burger on a pretzel bun caught Nick's attention. "I might even get something."

"Sure. Come on. It's dinner time."

"You think it's always dinner time."

"Unless it's breakfast or lunch time. Or snack time." Wrapped sandwiches appeared in Jake's hands. "What's on your mind?"

"This whole stinking mess."

"No kidding. My brain hurts too, but what are you thinking about specifically?"

Nick glanced around the court to verify their privacy, and then he lowered his voice. "Whatever we're doing next, I want to leave Joey behind."

The third sandwich Jake balanced in his hand slid off the second's wrapper, but he nudged its trajectory back towards the refrigerated bin. Cellophane crinkling, he tucked the roast beef under his arm, shifted the chicken salad into a free hand, and then reached for the dropped ham and cheese. "He'd hate you forever."

"That's the least of our concerns."

Jake grunted. "Don't underestimate what happens if you piss him off. You've kept him under control for years, but he's a rebel."

"You mean, he's an asshole."

"Yeah." Jake stepped away towards an automated kiosk, scanned his dinner items, and then looked towards his brother. "I'll get that."

Nick extended his veggie burger. "Thanks. I owe you."

Jake paid and returned the burger. "No, you don't. I cash bigger paychecks than I ever dreamed about in the Navy thanks to you. I owe you for this job, though I can't call it work."

"It's work now. It's dangerous."

Jake stepped away, found a vacant table, and sat. He ripped into the roast beef sandwich and bit off a huge bite.

Nick sat and forced his point. "I'm scared."

His mouth full, Jake grunted and then swigged from his water bottle, chewed, and swallowed. "Me, too."

The veggie burger remained untouched as the conversation consumed Nick's focus. "Like never before."

Feeding himself with his usual vigor, Jake bit into a gargantuan chunk of sandwich. His violent mastication slowed as the silence thickened, and then he swallowed. "You're really spooked?"

"And you're not?"

"Guess I haven't thought it through yet."

Nick kept his sandwich at bay. "Then stop stuffing your face for a minute and think it through."

Jake dropped the roast beef onto a napkin. "What's wrong with you? You're spooking me."

"You need to be spooked. You almost died."

As the awareness seeped into his head, Jake inhaled and sighed. "Yeah. I did, didn't I?"

"An autistic man who's barely twenty years old needed wicked black magic to save your ass, and nobody, including Josh, knows if he can do it again."

"He's done it twice now."

"And you want to bet your life on him doing it a third time?"

Jake shook his head and then stuffed the remaining roast beef into his mouth.

"Well?"

"What do you want me to say?"

"Convince me you know what we're tangling with. A demon. A monster with powers we barely understand. He toyed with us like amateurs, he may have killed Layla, and the next time we meet him, we'll be without her."

Jake wiped mustard off his lips. "And you want to keep Joey on the bench, too?"

Content that his brother was listening, Nick took his first bite of the tangy bean and soy patty. "He was just as helpless against the demon as the rest of us."

"We need all the void walkers–fighters–we can get."

"Depends what our plan is. We don't know that yet, and that's weird enough. It's not like Canter. He's trusting Connor a lot."

Half a chicken salad sandwich disappeared into Jake, and then he wiped his mouth. "That's an understatement. He put Connor in charge. Period."

A cloud rolled over Nick's mind, and he needed clarity. He stood. "I'm getting some coffee. You want anything?"

"Get me a latte."

"What size?"

Jake snorted. "Biggest they got."

Nick sorted his thoughts while waiting in line. He wondered if mortals could defeat a demon, what powers Josh hid, and if his most talented sibling was an asset or a liability. Unable to conclude anything while paying for and collecting his drinks, he returned in silence to his brother.

Jake reached for his latte. "Thanks."

Nick sat and slurped his double espresso. The bitterness assaulted his mouth, and he swallowed the fire. "We need to do something."

"No kidding, but we're just grunts in this war."

"I don't think so."

Unwrapping his final sandwich, Jake gave a quizzical look. "I don't think I like your attitude, bro."

"Why not?"

"You've got a rebel edge to you. We're practically a military unit, and we need to follow orders."

"I don't want a lecture on obeying Canter or Connor or whoever. Save it for Joey."

"I'm not wasting any more breath on the asshole, but go ahead. I'm listening." To signal his silent attention, Jake stuffed half the ham and cheese sandwich between his cheeks.

Nick glanced around the food court, leaned forward, and lowered his voice. "We can control animals without entering the void."

Chewing, Jake raised his eyebrows and rolled his finger forward, signaling his brother to continue.

"We can use Layla as our conduit."

Despite the enormity of the bite bulging his cheek, Jake downed it in one swallow. "Seriously?"

"Yeah, but it won't matter if you choke on your sandwich."

Jake caressed his throat. "I'm fine, but Layla's in a coma."

"And we'll use it to our advantage. I think part of her's still connected to the void. If we send our brain waves through her, we can piggyback on her and control some birds to find Solomon."

"It doesn't solve all our problems, but it would help, if you can pull it off."

"I designed the system. I can pull it off."

"Even for three of us at the same time?"

Taking the comment as a challenge, Nick lowered his sandwich onto a napkin. "Two of us. I said Joey's out."

"You said you wanted him out, but you didn't sound convinced."

"I'm convinced. He's out. And I can multiplex a few of us through Layla's mind if I have to."

"Canter isn't going to like leaving Joey out."

"He can be held in reserve. I just don't want him making first contact with the enemy. You saw how that turned out last time."

"Fair enough. I'll support that." Jake decimated the remainder of his final sandwich. "So, you want to use Layla as a firewall?"

"Yeah. More or less."

Jake tipped back his water bottle and then plopped it down. "It's a good idea. You'll have to hook her up in her hospital room. They won't let us take her back to the lab."

"I'll use our road gear."

"And we'll have to be in the room with her."

"I know. It'll work."

"It just might."

On the edge of his vision, Nick saw two men. He glanced in their direction and then gestured for them to sit.

Flanked by the young hunter, Canter sat. "You boys about ready to get back into the battle?"

Nick's heart leapt. "The void?"

On the table's opposite side, Liam sat beside the husky middle brother, creating twin mountains of muscle. "Not yet. Not until we're face to face."

Nick noticed an incongruity. "Where's your dad?"

"He ran off to prepare. He told us to wait for his signal."

"What signal?"

"He said we'd recognize it when it comes."

"Wait where?"

"He said to surround Father Solomon without being detected. Then to wait for his signal."

Seeking his boss' advice, Nick aimed his comment at the CIA supervisor. "I was thinking that we could control animals without entering the void. I could use Layla as a firewall."

Canter frowned. "Show a little respect to your fallen comrade."

Liam stirred. "No. That's a great idea. I'm sure Layla's willing to help. She's a warrior. You should've seen her in Irbil when she took on her son."

Nick was astonished. "She killed her own son?"

"Took him on in mortal combat, but fortunately our angel friend showed up and saved everyone's lives, including her son's."

The Brady Gang continued to impress the firstborn sibling, and he took the opening. "So, you're okay speaking for Layla?"

Liam shrugged. "With Father gone, I'll speak for our family. And I have a basic technical understanding of what you're doing. You're going to run those amplified brainwave signals from your head into Layla's and trust that they'll get passed through her, into the void, and then to your animal?"

"Yes."

"The carrier waves go through the void, carrying the signal, like modulated radio waves. Both directions, to and from the animal?"

Nick respected the young hunter's understanding. "Exactly. You've had some science."

"Enough to know that this could work in theory. But even if you pull it off, you'll still be sending signals through the void. The demon could notice, and that's the whole point of staying out."

Nick had counted on it. "I know. And if the demon notices what we're doing, it might force him to make a choice. He'll either have to release Layla, if he's holding her at all, or he'll have to let us control the animals. But I'm hoping this is subtle enough to avoid his attention."

Liam nodded. "I like it. Even though Father left out details about his plan, I've got a good feeling about this. You should give it a try."

Canter's answered his chiming phone. "It's Stiles. Hold on. Let me get this... Uh huh... No kidding? Okay, text me the address. We'll meet here and travel together. Call me when you get here."

Nick looked at his boss. "Well?"

"We've got something. Father Solomon left a pattern by renting utility vans from hardware stores near his victims. And a witness in a Baltimore Home Depot saw a man who matched his description rent a van, under a false name. Local police are looking for the van now and should find it within hours."

Butterflies erupted in Nick's stomach. "We've got him?"

Canter corrected him. "We think we know his general location, and the police are searching for him. But they'll keep their distance based upon our advice. We need to get up there soon."

"Without Connor?"

Canter nodded. "And without Layla or Josh."

Nick glared at Liam.

"Josh ran off with Father." The young hunter raised his palm. "It wasn't my idea, believe me."

Down three teammates, Nick reassessed his youngest brother's role. "So, we may need everyone, including Joey."

"And including me."

"What about your heart condition?"

Canter shrugged. "Desperate times. If it comes down to it, I'm going in."

Nick judged the plan desperate. "We find Father Solomon, wait out of sight, and then pounce on him when Connor gives a signal?"

Staring at the table while talking, Liam seemed to adjust his vision of events. "We'll assume that Father and Josh are unavailable, until they show up, at which point they'll both be ready to help at full power..."

Nick encouraged him. "That'll be when we can enter the void?"

"Yes. We'll have nothing to hide at that point."

"And we attack with all we've got?"

"Not quite. Father said to immobilize him."

"Your father must have an exorcism in mind."

"I'm sure of it." The hunter's stare remained on the used wrappers. "Attacking with all we've got was a bad idea this morning, and Father instead wants us to harass Father Solomon for the exorcism and not to overextend ourselves again."

Nick narrowed his eyes. "But we're supposed to do nothing until he gives the signal."

"Correct. Then after Father shows up, we'll distract the demon."

"That makes sense." Nick sighed his acceptance. "But I don't know if we can do it, and it puts all the hope on Connor's exorcism." The next question took a few laps around his head before he asked it. "And I suppose he left you in charge?"

Liam nodded. "Good question. Yes, he did. I didn't like it at first, but since we're dealing with a demon, I'm the best guy for it."

Canter nodded his approval.

Nick found the plan imperfect, but he saw no other option. "Fine. You're in charge. But did your father say where he was going?"

"No. But he's as intense as I've ever seen him. I know this sounds like a fool's hope, but I know him, and he's gearing up for something big."

CHAPTER 31

His head spinning with attacking tactics, demonic counter-attacks, and his best interpretation of his father's instructions before the elder hunter's hasty departure, Liam entered Layla's room.

The conscious empaths sat on each side of their comatose sister's bed, and their sad glances signaled the patient's unchanged status.

Liam updated the psychics. "Father left me in charge."

Emma caught the innuendo. "Are the CIA guys okay with that?"

He was ready to accept the burden, but he was unsure if others would follow him in battle. "They said they were. God knows what they really think."

Diane took a different approach to the conversation. "Good. It'll keep you focused."

"What's that supposed to mean?"

"It means you'll be behaving like a hunter again. When did you become a Bible thumper?"

The question dug a pit in his stomach, but it opened a necessary conversation. "Since long before we were married."

Rousing herself from her seat with the inception of a private discussion, Emma excused herself and marched into the hallway.

Diane turned her chair around and sat facing her husband. "You've been reciting a lot of rules and theology lately."

"I've had a good reason."

"A demon."

"Yeah. The rules governing what a demon can or can't do are known only to God, but most of them are known to mankind through the Catholic Church."

She stared at him defiantly. "I don't think the Catholic Church has ever fought a demon in the void."

"I wouldn't know. Only the exorcist knows his own personal experience. Maybe Father works through the void without knowing it when he exorcises demons."

"You say you understand demons, but you've only fought the one in Irbil. That's one less than me, as of this morning."

Liam realized he was trying to win an unwinnable argument. He corrected his tack, approached his wife, and knelt. "Sounds like we make a good team."

Her face softened. "Then stop judging and criticizing."

Unaware of such sins, he reflected upon his behavior since his early morning awakening. He accepted her implication that his body language, word choice, and mannerisms had been harsh all day. He admitted silently that the demon's attack had unnerved him, and he was letting fear pervade his mannerisms. But in his father's absence, he needed to embody leadership, and showing trepidation was unacceptable. "You're right. I'm sorry. I'll do better."

"I hope so. You practically called me an evil witch this morning."

He scanned his memories for evidence of his crime but remembered nothing. "What?"

"In the control room, you said something about ancient religions getting their mystical powers from demons. You made a distinction between preternatural power and supernatural power, which comes only from God."

"I'm still not following."

"Which type of power do you think you married?"

Bullseye. The faith gap between himself and his wife smacked him in the face. "Oh. You think I believe that you're a demon-powered evil witch."

She shrugged.

"No. Your powers are charisms of the Holy Spirit."

"What's a charism?"

"A divine gift. Many saints had them throughout the centuries. You've probably heard of stigmatics who bear the wounds of Christ, but have you heard of people who could bilocate or even fly?"

"Bilocate? Being in two places at the same time?"

"Yes."

"That's cute. If someone could bilocate and fly, they could fly to themselves."

"Don't be that way."

"What way? You're suggesting the impossible."

Liam tapped his childhood training. "I disagree. St Joseph of Cupertino could levitate at will and sometimes by accident during fervent prayer. Saint Alphonsius Liguori and Saint Gerard Majella were known to bilocate, and I'm holding out hope that Sister Maria de Agreda from Spain is proven to have bilocated to America to evangelize Native American tribes."

"I think you read too much speculative fiction."

"Sister Maria's body was found incorrupt when it was dug up over a hundred years ago, three centuries after her death."

"If you believe what you read."

"You need to believe something. And if you believe nothing other than what your five senses can pick up, you've got your head in the sand."

"Whatever." She looked at the patient's tranquil features. "I'm scared. Layla's in trouble, and we're fighting something we don't understand."

Since his wife had killed the theology debate, Liam turned his attention to comforting her. "It's okay to be scared. We've never lost anyone before, and I pray we get her back."

Diane angled her head towards Layla. "She's strong."

"And so are we. Strong enough to win this battle. And now's the time to strike."

Seeming to gather her strength, she lowered her head and fell silent. "I'll strike from here."

Liam stood, dizzying himself. "You mean to stay behind?"

"Me and Emma. When we're cleared to enter the void again,

we'll attack from here. I hope it can be all three of us, with Layla."

The tactic diverged from his father's plan, but Liam judged it acceptable. "Okay."

"Really? You're okay with that?"

"Were you expecting a debate?"

"I don't know what I'm expecting anymore."

"I like it. You, Emma, and Layla if she can fight. You're a team, and no matter what techniques or gadgets the CIA kids can drum up, you're the best in my opinion. You belong together as one. I'll keep Nana with you to watch over you."

"Thanks for understanding. Emma and I were worried."

His father had told him little, leaving gaps in his stated plan that concerned Liam, but he remained strong. "Understandable. We're making plans fast. But I'm sure Father would be okay with it."

Diane offered an unexpected accusation. "You don't think Seth separated us this morning so that we'd be weak?"

"So that you'd get hurt one by one?"

"Yeah?"

"It's an interesting theory, but I don't see the motivation. I also don't see how he'd control that demon."

"He didn't have to. He just needed us to get near him."

"He put all his guys near him, too. Jake and Joe were the closest."

"But they're stronger than us. They can take a beating. It could've been a murder-by-demon trick, where the last humans standing were the brothers."

"Assassination by the CIA?" Liam reconsidered his angle. "Maybe. But I think we're okay." He let the words echo in his head to convince himself.

Three hours later, Liam examined the Grand Cherokee's cargo. His anxiety grew as he missed his father's authoritative and calming presence, and he sought a partner to bear some responsibility. "Hey, Stiles, can you double-check the equipment loadout?"

The middle-aged FBI man stepped to the liftgate and opened the nearest canvas bag. "I'd love to. I can't wait to see how you arm yourselves against a demon."

"You'll be impressed with the plethora of water guns."

"Funny, coming from a guy who knows his firepower." Stiles lifted his phone and thumbed to a memo page to mark the inventory. He whistled while moving aside a Heckler & Koch assault rifle. "This wasn't the one that killed Bin Laden, is it?"

"Now who's funny? Same model, but no. Keep digging."

"Ha! You weren't kidding. What's this?" Stiles lifted a multicolored plastic toy.

"Like I said. It's a water gun. We're bringing a bunch."

Stiles lifted two more toys. "Now I'm confused."

"They're filled with holy water."

"Oh." Stiles set down the water guns and tapped notes in his phone. "Nope. Still confused."

"We're fighting a demon. Demons hate holy water."

"I figured out that much, but what happens if I shoot Solomon with one of these?"

"If he's possessed at the time, the demon will suffer."

"Suffer and fall down, or suffer and still attack me?"

Liam remembered the variations in demonic behaviors. Some beastly responses were deterministic, but others required luck, hope, and prayer to keep the fallen angel from killing those who attempted the exorcism. "I can't predict it completely. Most demons would be distracted enough to beat. But this one? We'll have to see."

"I don't like it, but I'll live with it." Stiles counted the piles and then showed his phone's notes to the young hunter. "We're good?"

Liam matched the numbers against his mental inventory and closed the hatchback. "Yeah. Let's go."

The FBI man's phone chimed, and he lifted it to his cheek. "Stiles... What? Damn it! That's off the lunar cycle... Got it... Yeah, we're on the move."

An ashen face staring at him, Liam braced for unwelcomed news. "That sounded bad."

"A nun was abducted from her prayers this evening, a Sister Marcy. The MO matches our perp."

"That's why you questioned the lunar cycle."

"Yeah. Apparently, he's accelerated that while under pressure from us, as we'd feared, unless he's planning to hold her for the rest of the month."

Liam suspected the worst. "He isn't. He's challenging us to rush to save her and hoping we'll make a mistake."

"What mistakes could we possibly make charging headfirst at an angry demon with water guns?"

Liam appreciated the FBI man's sarcasm, which masked a veneer of fear–the right amount per the hunter's assessment. He walked to the passenger door, slid into the vehicle, and sat. "We're all afraid. This is deadly and dangerous. Trust the plan."

Stiles sat in the driver's seat. "I don't trust the plan a hundred percent, but it's the best we've got." He shifted the SUV into gear. "You buckled up back there?"

Alone in the second row, Canter forced a confident tone. "I'm as ready as anyone can be. Let's go get the poor dumb bastard."

CHAPTER 32

In the corner of the lab, Nick gulped bitterness from a hot cup and admired his work. The helmet, little more than a hardwired skull cap, issued wires like a tarantula groping for its twin. He reached for his iron, dipped its tip in flux, and then hovered a spool of solder over an electronic joint. "Hold it steady."

Seated on a stool beside the firstborn sibling, Jake pressed the exposed copper tip of a black wire against an electrode on a helmet he intended to place upon Layla.

Smoke rising from the joint, Nick completed the modifications. "That'll do it. You get to be the guinea pig."

"Sure." Jake grabbed his helmet from the desk and slid it over his head. "How do I look?"

Nick examined his brother's arrangement. The cap pressed tightly against his skin and appeared oriented with its hidden antennas covering the appropriate spots of his brain. "You're fine."

"Okay. How's the signal?"

Examining the wires from his brother's cap to the circuit breadboard, Nick verified the connections. Output from the husky psychic's helmet went into the board, walked into a multiplexor, passed through several amplifiers, and departed from wires Nick ran to the helmet intended for Layla. An oscilloscope fluttered to life with a sketchy sinusoid representing the wave from a section of Jake's brain. "Looks good here."

"Is it ready? You've been working for hours."

Nick unclipped the scope's leads and reattached them to the wires carrying the wave from a different section of his brother's mind, and another rough sinusoid appeared. "One step at a time."

"You're the expert."

"I designed this system and built the first prototypes." Nick checked wires running from the breadboard to the Persian empath's cap, and his soldered joints showed a solid connection. The final piece, the dormant helmet's output, appeared more like a production-grade product, with its wires merging within insulated wrapping and ending in a serial connection to a laptop computer.

"Well?"

The computer's screen showed Nick the desired sinusoids, encouraging him. "Sweet."

"It's good?"

"It's perfect. Take that off and put on mine."

Jake slipped off his cap and exchanged it for another one that also fed its signals to Layla's helmet. "How's that?"

At the output of Layla's helmet, Nick saw the desired waveforms, but he also noticed a dead channel. "Crap."

"What's wrong?"

"Most of your brainwaves are getting received and retransmitted by Layla's helmet, but one's dead."

"Is it a problem with the multiplexor?"

Nick excused the ignorant question. Although his brother had studied engineering in the Navy, he lacked real-world experience in circuit design. "No. The multiplexor will let us share Layla's helmet on a fifty-fifty duty cycle. That'll make communications with our birds sluggish, but it wouldn't explain a blank signal."

"Huh." Jake leaned over the freshly prototyped system and traced signals with his finger. "Um. Is this supposed to be sticking out?"

Caressing the black cover of a multiplexing integrated circuit, a green wire protruded from the board.

"No. That came out. Stuff that back into pin seven." Nick watched his brother complete the task, and then he glanced at the laptop. All signals were fine. "Perfect."

"Wires pop out all the time. That was the biggest ass ache for me on my senior project at the academy."

"No kidding. It burns everyone on demo rigs and prototypes."

"Don't you want to do this in a better board? Undo this mess and solder these connections into something more permanent?"

"No time. We're up first in this mission, and everyone's counting on us. I'll cake it in conformal coating and call it good."

"Then we're ready?"

"One more test." Nick donned the first helmet and quieted his thoughts. Then he examined the laptop and saw his brainwaves merging with those of his brother. "That's what I wanted. Superposition. Your waves and mine are adding up."

"And that'll work with Layla?"

"In theory, it's a slam dunk. The signals will look like hers within the void, but when they reach the birds, our commands will be unpacked for them. And vice versa coming our way from the birds."

"I hope it works."

"Yeah. But that's all the testing we get." Nick eyed his workspace and decided to bring his tools to the hospital for repairs in case another wire popped free. "You take the prototype. I'll grab everything else."

"To fix whatever needs miracle repairs onsite with bubblegum and duct tape?"

"Exactly. But let's hope it doesn't come to that."

In the comatose psychic's room, Nick walked past the two empaths sitting in spare chairs, and then he lowered himself into his seat next to the patient's head. "You go first."

Unquestioning, Jake pulled his cap onto his head. "I'm ready, but doesn't she have too much hair? Won't it get in the way?"

Nick studied the patient's long black waves. "Crap. I didn't think about that. Let me try it anyway." He slid Layla's helmet over her head, matting as much hair as possible, but thick layers presented resistance to the electromagnetic pathway.

Seated beside him, Diane reached for her sister's helmet and adjusted it. "You're pulling her hair."

"She can't feel it."

"You don't know that!"

"It needs to be tight."

"I get that, but be careful!" Diane leaned back, out of his way. "Is it working?"

The laptop on the food tray showed a jagged sinusoid. "I don't know. Jake, take yours off."

As the husky psychic obeyed, the sinusoid collapsed.

"No. Damn it." Nick accepted his next idea but expected resistance from the others. "We need to give her a buzz cut."

Diane whined. "Don't give her a butch haircut!"

"I'm trying to save lives!" Nick realized too late that he'd raised his voice. He lowered the volume. "Including hers."

Standing, Diane cared for her sister. "No, it's okay. I get it. But I'll handle it. You don't know what you're doing."

"And you do?"

"Not me. Nana. She cut hair before she opened her dress shop."

Half asleep in the corner armchair, the Chaldean grandmother lifted her finger from her cheek. "Sure. I cut her hair. No problem. How short you want it?"

Nick risked his first verbal exchange with the elderly woman whose mobility struggles made her an aberration on the team. "Bald would be best, but if that's too ugly, make it as short as mine."

Lost in the translation, Nana looked to Diane, who repeated Nick's orders in Aramaic.

Nana approved. "Okay. I split the difference. I leave her half an inch. I need clippers, scissors, and a comb."

Diane looked to the German empath seated beside the husky psychic. "Emma, can you get the stuff? I'm sure they have something in the hospital."

"I'm on it." Emma stood and walked into the hallway.

Nick removed the helmet from Layla. "Give me yours, Jake. I'm hiding them under the bed until we need them."

Five minutes later, the German empath returned with the

equipment and with a redheaded nurse trailing her.

The redhead queried the group. "I understand that you want to cut her hair?"

To prevent someone else from revealing confidential information, Nick lied. "Yeah, we do. She'd been complaining about how annoying it was taking care of her long hair, and she wanted to cut it really short. We want to honor her intentions, you know."

The nurse's face softened. "Of course. Let me know when you're done, and I'll have the droppings cleaned for you."

Through his fatigue and frustration, Nick forced a weak smile. "We'll keep it as clean as we can and pick up after ourselves."

"Thank you." The nurse departed.

As Nana stood and hobbled towards the bed, all four psychics moved out of her way, but Diane stopped to help her grandmother organize the cutting equipment on the food tray.

Nick slipped out of the room, strolled down the hallway, and called his boss.

"Yeah, Nick. What's on your mind?"

"Where are you guys?"

"Parked, waiting for your birds."

"You found him?"

Canter oozed cynicism. "Hell, no. He's not making it easy. We found his van parked outside some huge county park, but he's nowhere near it. There's trails all over this park, and he could be anywhere. What's that? Sorry, Stiles is talking. He says the park has over six thousand acres. Shit."

"You're not in Baltimore anymore, are you?"

"No. Father Solomon took off, but a traffic camera picked him up at a crossroads on his way up here. We got here too late to stop him from entering the park, but we think he's on foot now. That'll slow him down."

"You need the birds more than ever now."

"Yeah. Liam's going to throw a couple hovercraft drones at him, but we need all the eyes in the sky we can get. How's your progress on the prototype?"

"Good. Real good." Nick doubled back to the room's entrance and watched Nana cropping the patient's wavy strands. "We're cutting Layla's hair now. It was too much to get a good signal."

"Oh. Well, hopefully she wakes up in time to complain about it before it grows back."

"Yeah. Nana's almost done."

"Nana?"

"Apparently, she made her living as a stylist when she came to America. I'm watching her work, and she knows what she's doing."

"Huh. I thought they let her stay on their team for moral support, but she can handle firearms and scissors."

"Not bad for an old woman."

"Speaking of old, any word from Connor?"

"No. I figure he'll contact Liam first."

"God only knows. His disappearance was weird. Very hushed, very quick. He was talking privately with Liam in the minutes before he left, and then he vanished with Josh. If he doesn't call Liam first, I was thinking Josh might contact Diane with an update."

"Nope. Nothing." Nick stepped through the doorway as the grandmother lowered her hands. "Got to go. It's time to try Layla again." He slid his phone into his pocket, wiggled around chairs, and sat by the patient's cropped head.

As the firstborn brother lifted Layla's cap, Diane intercepted it from his hand. "Let me do it. You'll hurt her again."

"You don't know how it goes on."

Ignoring the protest, Diane slid the helmet over her sister. By luck or empathic intuition, she nailed the orientation. "How's that?"

"Um, perfect, really." Nick checked the laptop and saw a rough sinusoid. "It's working! That's the signal from one of her lobes." He reached for the touchpad and checked Layla's other channels. "She's good. Give it a shot, Jake."

The husky brother donned his helmet, and the laptop showed

an altered form. "How do I look?"

"On the screen, you look beautiful. You're at vastly different frequencies than Layla, but that's expected while you're awake and she's in a coma. Try a return-to-home command."

"I'm not connected to a bird."

"Just think the damned command."

Jake sighed and gazed into space, and jagged lines of higher-frequency information danced along the edges of a larger, skewed sinusoid.

Nick's heart pounded. "I think it'll work. Let's get you a bird."

"I thought I already had one picked out."

"Father Solomon drove too far from Baltimore." Nick lifted his phone and called his boss.

"Yeah, Nick?"

"We're ready for Jake. I need a bird closer to your location."

"Well, alleluia. Hold on. I'll get back to you."

Nick left his phone on the tray beside the laptop.

Curious, Diane pointed at wires running from her sister's cap to the laptop. "You're going to control a bird with that computer?"

"That computer's connected over a virtual private network to one of many transceivers we have spread across major metropolitan areas." Nick accounted for the shifting geography. "But since Father Solomon's running from Baltimore, we'll use Gibson's portable transceiver."

"Oh. I guess that makes sense."

The phone rang, and Nick lifted it. "Canter?"

"I've got you a falcon."

"We need an eagle. This will become a battle."

"Not yet. Start with a falcon. They're easier to manage, and I don't want you wrestling with your bird while you're trying to avoid tracks in the void."

Nick acquiesced to use the smaller raptor, its easier control, and its superior vision for the search. "Fine. What's the location?"

"Twelve miles away, bearing three-two-two. You'll fly to me

on a reciprocal course of one-four-two. I'll text you the coordinates."

"Got it. I'm hanging up." Nick held his phone and waited until the coordinates arrived. He copied and pasted them into a celestial navigation application that showed the sky from the vantage of the falcon's nest. After drawing a line of bearing into the sky on a bearing of one-four-two, he turned the screen to his husky brother. "You see the stars? Got your bead on Orion there?"

"Yup. I know which way to go."

Nick looked at the empath seated by his side. "Please let Connor know that we're going for the birds."

"I'll text Josh. I'm not supposed to bother Connor."

Nick reached into a bag at his feet, rummaged around the soldering iron and the spare wires he'd packed, and found a syringe. After ripping open the wrapping, jamming the needle into a vial of serum, and filling the syringe to the ten-milliliter line, he extended the drug across the hospital bed. "Here you go."

Jake accepted the syringe and injected the serum into his leg.

Seated next to the husky brother, Emma covered her mouth. "Why'd you do that?"

Nick answered. "Did you forget about our serums?"

"I guess so. It looks painful. I don't like it."

Diane compounded the protest. "It's barbaric, really."

Nick clarified. "This is hard for us without serums. We pretty much need them."

Jake's eyes drooped and then closed.

"He's in." Nick checked the laptop. "It looks good. I think he's got control of the bird."

Folding her arms, Diane seemed uncertain about using raptors. "How will you know when he's got control?"

"I see signs of a strong connection in the sine wave here. It's hard to read, but I know what to look for. To be certain, Canter will tell us when the falcon's there."

"Okay. We'll wait for Seth. But how will you know that Jake's not drawing attention to himself in the void?"

"We won't unless the demon reacts, but I'm hoping that doesn't happen until we're slipping handcuffs onto Father Solomon."

"So, as far as you know, it's working?"

"Yeah, I do. But that was the safe part. The dangerous part starts now–for all of us."

CHAPTER 33

As Stiles cut the SUV's engine near a gravel lot's entrance, Liam lifted binoculars and examined the killer's van.

Among the heavy duty trucks scattered across the gravel with empty horse trailers, a lone vehicle stood out for its stark plainness. But the object catching the young hunter's attention was the unexpected black iron block hooked behind the van.

Liam squinted at the towed cargo and identified white propane tanks at its front. "Bloody hell. That's a barbeque grill."

From the back seat, Canter also trained his optics on the criminal's rented van. "A what?"

"Those are propane tanks for a barbeque on wheels."

"Christ! He plans to cook her alive in that thing."

"Not if we stop him." Liam lowered his optics. "I'll send a drone to check it out."

Canter lowered his binoculars. "It's not standard procedure, but there's nothing standard about demon combat. I'm okay with it, but it's your call, Tom."

Deep in silent thought, Stiles nodded. But then he woke from whatever trance consumed him. "I'm dying tonight."

Before Liam could protest, Canter berated the FBI man. "Come on, Tom! You never jinx it like that. What's wrong with you?"

His tone calm, Stiles kept his gaze through the windshield. "It's not a jinx. It's a fact. Somehow, dancing with all this psychic power around me has gifted me this single premonition."

This time, Liam beat Canter to the protest. "What the hell, 'gifted'? You're talking nonsense."

Facing the young hunter, Stiles was the image of peace. "If your wife told you it was your death tonight, would you believe her?"

After mustering the courage, Liam gave the horrible concept a moment of thought. "I would, yes."

"A voice told me that I'm dying tonight. It wasn't malicious. It was peaceful. It was welcoming, like from someone calling me home. I need to call my wife and say goodbye." He clicked open the latch, stepped from the SUV, and closed the door.

Liam turned to the CIA man. "What the hell just happened?"

"I've never seen anything like that. Have you?"

"Never. I mean, I've seen premonitions all the time. I married one. But never anything as... what's the word? Depressing? Futile?"

"I'd call it stupid. You're not giving up on me, too, are you?"

Liam was unsure of Stiles' intention for the evening. But raised as a hunter of preternatural evildoers, he saw no option of turning back. "Hell, no. Can you reach the top hovercraft back there?"

Canter groaned while twisting his torso. "Yeah. Got it." He extended the drone.

Liam grabbed it, turned it on, and connected it to its phone application. With overhead lights casting diffused shadows over the lot, the young hunter turned on the standard camera and the infrared. Checking both video feeds, he saw his face in the phone while he pointed the drone at himself.

"You really know how to use that thing?"

"I'll fly it like I stole it." Liam opened the passenger door and lowered the craft to the gravel. He closed the door and thumbed icons to set the aircraft into manual flight. Watching through the infrared camera, he brought the whirring propellers to life and then flew the drone across the lot.

Under the hunter's skillful control, the drone hovered at the passenger window, revealing empty front seats.

"I'm going to look through the windshield. If he's in there, he'll notice. Get ready."

"What's the definition of 'ready'?"

Unsure, Liam invented his tactics. "Grab a water rifle and lead with that. Don't use firearms if you can help it."

Canter lifted a plastic toy from the trunk. "I'm ready. Go for it."

The drone's vantage point shifted to show the hood and the darkness behind the front row. Again, the van looked empty.

"He's not there."

"You'd see his body heat on night vision, wouldn't you?"

"Yes. And I will when we find him." Liam commanded the drone back to the roof of his SUV. "We need to search this entire park, and we need to hurry."

A dark form raced across Liam's view, slowed, and descended onto the SUV's hood. A black falcon stared at the windshield, spread its wings, and chirped.

"Is that a friend?"

"I think so. Hold on." Canter stepped from the vehicle and walked to the bird. As he extended his finger, the raptor jumped on it, and as the CIA man came to Liam's window, the bird pecked his fingers in an obvious predetermined sequence. "Verified. It's Jake."

Fluttering its wings, the falcon jumped over Liam's lap, landed in the driver's seat, and eyed the young hunter.

"Um. Hi, Jake?"

The bird chirped, bowed, and spread its wings.

Standing by the passenger door, Canter lifted his phone and placed a call. "Yeah, Joey. Tell your genius brother that your other genius brother's inside a falcon and tapped the passcode into my hand.... No, we're not waiting for Nick's eagle. We're going."

Relieved to receive the falcon's help, Liam visualized the search pattern. He unfolded a map from his vest's pocket and opened it in his lap. "Can you give Jake instructions? Will he understand?"

"He'll understand whatever I tell him, but when he's airborne, he's out of touch without the void."

Liam glanced at the bird, who nodded, chirped, and spread its wings. "Void walking's not happening until Father gives the signal."

"I wish he'd hurry."

"It won't matter unless we find Solomon." Liam tapped the map. "The van's here. I'm going to say that Solomon can't sustain faster than six miles an hour."

"I was going to say four. He's got a prisoner with him, and I don't expect they'll be jogging."

Liam conceded. "We'll call it four, then. He got here about ninety minutes before us?"

"Give or take based upon the traffic cam. Call it two hours to be conservative."

"That's an eight-mile radius, but since two hours is conservative, we'll call it seven." Liam did the math. "That's about a hundred and fifty square miles to cover. That's too much."

"And he could be long gone from this park."

"Maybe, but I don't think he brought us here by accident."

"I hope you're right."

Liam recalled the depths of devilry he faced. "He wants to kill us for sport and then finish her off. He's not running. He's not hiding. He's baiting us into a trap."

"Super."

"I'll send my first drone out to seven miles. I'll set it to fly in a tightening spiral. I'll send my second drone out to five miles and have it do the same. The girls will back us up by watching the video feeds. You make Jake search inside a three-mile radius."

"Sounds good." Canter looked at the raptor. "You got that, Jake? A three-mile radius. Don't be an engineer. Be a bird. Plus or minus a mile's fine with your speed and eyesight."

The bird acknowledged.

"Alright, Jake. Remember that we can't contact you through the void. So, look to me and Liam here once in a while for a signal. If we're waving our arms at you, that means to come back for instructions. Got it? Good. Go!"

The falcon hopped onto Liam's lap and then darted through the window into the darkness.

After the raptor whipped by his ear, Canter lowered his head between his shoulders and sighed. "This has been a damned long day. We'll be lucky to survive the night."

With possible demonic despair sullying the lawmen's hearts, Liam suspected preternatural foul play. "That statement suggests demonic oppression."

The CIA man raised his head. "In English, son."

"He's messing with your head–and possibly Tom's, too. He's trying to dishearten you."

"If that's true, then why are you okay?"

"Because I wear the armor of God."

"Well, la-di-dah."

"I'm serious. This isn't a sermon. It's just true. If you strengthen your spiritual defenses with worship and a life aimed at Jesus, you give demons an uphill climb to attack you. Nobody's completely immune, but I'll be the last guy among us to succumb to his tricks."

Canter looked at Liam, glanced away, and then looked back. "Stiles is still on the phone, but he looks way too calm for what I think he's talking about."

"We'll deal with him later. Nothing matters if we can't find Solomon. So, Jake's searching the inner circle, and I'm sending out my drones." Liam stepped from the door and gestured for the CIA man to step back. After his boots hit the gravel, he tapped a circular flight pattern into his phone and commanded the first drone into sky. It whirred to life and took off.

Canter sounded surprised. "Now I see people on horseback."

Liam turned towards a low wooden fence where the silhouettes of three riders passed through a gate as dusk's yielding to darkness signaled the park's daily closing time. "The park has horse trails."

"I just haven't seen a horse since forever. I wonder if the demon's going to kill any horses tonight."

"Focus, Seth. Fight it. You're being attacked with horrible thoughts and distractions." Liam wondered how deeply the demon preyed on his companions.

Canter squinted in pain. "Something's tearing me up from the inside, but…"

"But?"

"You're holding it back. Whatever it is, it's afraid of you."

Liam knew demons were immortal and beyond his capability to destroy. But he could bring about one's suffering. "I can hurt him, but the demon could be making you say that to make me overconfident and throw me off."

Clopping hooves became audible as the three horses trotted towards the SUV and stopped.

Liam reached for his pistol but kept his hand against it. "Hello! Can we help you?"

Ahead of the other equestrians, the middle rider removed his cowboy hat. "I'm teaching my sons to ride, and I own these three horses. But if you'll pardon this bizarre feeling I've got, for some reason I think you need them more than we do."

Liam folded his arms. "Are you serious?"

"About five clicks from here, we met two pedestrians, but they were dressed for riding, and I asked them about their horses. They said they'd given their mounts to two men. I thought it was the strangest thing, until I saw you. For some reason, I get it now. These may be my horses, but I know I must give them to you right here, right now, for your destinies."

Canter was frustrated. "Thanks, but we can't–"

Liam silenced the law man. "We can't thank you enough. We're working on a very important case and may need them to rescue someone from a wanted criminal. If you can wait about ten minutes, we'll know if we need your horses or not."

"That works for us." The lead rider dismounted and gestured for his sons to do the same. He walked to Liam and extended his hand. "Name's Jonathan. Jonathan Simeon."

"Good to meet you, Jonathan. I'm Liam. Can you tell me anything about the two men the other riders saw on the trails?"

CHAPTER 34

Nick called his boss.

"Canter."

"I want to get into the eagle and help with the search."

"Good. We need all the help we can get."

"Did you forget that'll put Jake on a half duty cycle? His control will become sluggish."

"Sorry. I forgot. I'm not thinking straight."

"You sound tense."

Canter sighed. "Liam thinks the demon's trying to oppress me and Stiles. We're both being affected, but Liam seems to be immune. He'll help us fight it. Don't you worry about me. You've got enough to worry about."

"True. Anything from Connor yet?"

"No. You?"

"Nothing. So, are you okay if I take the eagle?"

"You're leaving Joey to run things there."

Nick considered his youngest brother's recent behavior acceptable as the shame recalibrated his attitude. "He can handle it. He may be an ass, but I think he learned his lesson. Plus, he's got Nana to back him up."

Both conscious empaths were curled in their chairs staring at their phones, each lady searching a distant drone's feed for Solomon while they awaited their chance to enter the void.

"Fine, then. Remember to look at me periodically for comms. Waving arms means to come talk to me, since I can't talk to you without the void."

"Roger that. I'm going in." Nick hung up and then put on his electromagnet cap.

Seated beside him, Diane checked his helmet. "It's not very

stylish, but what it does is pretty cool."

"Um, thanks."

"Sure. Are you going to be just like him?" Diane pointed at Jake.

"You mean out cold in my seat? Yep. Joey can handle talking to Canter while I'm gone."

Pacing in front of the seated grandmother, Joe appeared nervous. "I screwed up bad, but I'm going to make it right. You can count on me from now on."

"I know I can count on you, little brother." Nick lifted a syringe from his bag, filled with serum, and injected it into his thigh. "Good night everyone, and goodbye. Wish me happy hunting."

Although forced, Diane's voice was cheery. "Happy..."

Nick's awareness materialized within the eagle. The raptor soared through the high altitudes, seeking food, and the first-born sibling sensed its hunger.

"Wait for food."

The bird accepted the command and raised its gaze. The stars showed the raptor flying in the wrong direction.

"Turn right... now steady." Sharing the pipeline through Layla with his brother's falcon slowed the back-and-forth signals, and Nick likened the sensation to driving a high-performance sports car on black ice. "Accelerate."

The eagle pumped its wings, and jagged mountaintops appeared as black lines on the horizon. Within minutes, the park appeared below, and the raptor's sensitive eyes found the Jeep.

"Descend. Land on hood."

After a fast diving stoop, the bird leveled and then entered a spiraled descent to the Jeep. It extended its talons to a roof rack, landed, and perched itself on the crossbeam.

Nick had wanted the hood, but he accepted the roof, given the sluggishness of his multi-plexed control.

Canter extended his finger towards the bird's beak.

"Jump to finger. Peck thumb. Peck middle finger. Peck middle finger again. Peck thumb. Peck middle finger."

"Good to see you, Nick. We've got full coverage with the search pattern. So, you're free to look wherever you want."

"Bow head, extend wings, chirp."

"Okay, good. Get out of here, but remember to look at me whenever you can for comms."

Nick took off but heard a loud bellow rise from the hunter.

"Stop! Come back!"

Spreading the majestic bird's wings, Nick hit a sharp turn and brought the raptor to Liam's feet.

Crouching, Liam radiated hope. "You need to see this, Nick. You, too, guys."

The lawmen squatted next to the hunter and examined the map.

"Take a look here, especially you, Nick." Liam tapped the sheet. "This is an old blast furnace, right here in this park."

The discovery brought back Stiles into law enforcing mode. "Catoctin Furnace. It's a historical site, but the furnace has been idle forever."

Liam pressed for his discovery to have meaning. "But Solomon could burn her in there, if he gathered wood and started a fire."

"Sure, but he could do that anywhere."

"He needs privacy to do this. He needs privacy to torture her before he kills her. I imagine this furnace is inside a brick building that would hide him?"

Stiles shrugged. "Yeah. Close enough. One wall's open, but it's otherwise secluded. That's a good theory."

Canter protested. "How do you know?"

Stiles pointed. "There's a picture on that historical marker right there. I saw it earlier while I was... saying goodbye to my wife."

"Try the furnace, Nick. If it doesn't turn up anything, then head high and search wherever you want." Canter turned his head to the map. "You'll need to fly on bearing zero-three-two for about a mile and a half." He stood and extended his arm. "It's that way."

Nick gave the affirmation. "Bow head, extend wings, chirp." But then he noticed three strangers in riding gear standing with idled mounts. He aimed his beak at them and chirped three times.

Everyone stared at him.

Again, he chirped three times.

"Oh, shit. That's for me." Canter still sounded anxious. "Three chirps is an interrogative. Are you asking who those men are?"

"Bow head, extend wings, chirp."

"Those men offered to lend us their horses. But we need to find Solomon first. Check out the furnace. Go!"

Nick rose into the sky and flew low but fast in the prescribed direction. Within seconds, he spied his target and examined the old building for vantage points.

With the open wall, the building presented insufficient hiding places. So, Nick landed the eagle on a branch facing the workspace in front of the historic furnace, and motion caught his eyes.

In covered torchlight, a silhouette matching Father Solomon's dimensions hovered over a human-shaped silhouette on a table.

Success. Nick ordered the eagle back to the Jeep.

But glimmering steel reflected the moonlight as Father Solomon raised his arm. His words were audible in the eagle's sensitive hearing. "Will you not renounce your god? Reject your faith, and I will release you unharmed."

Nick made his eagle stay the extra seconds to observe.

"No? A shame, but expected." The knife came down, and the victim screamed. Solomon lifted the severed hand and then held the torch's flame to the wound to cauterize it. The nun screamed again.

"Back to Canter. Go! Full speed."

Exerting itself, the eagle sprinted the distance and landed on the gravel at the men's feet.

Surprising the firstborn sibling, Liam crouched in front of his beak. "Did you find Solomon?"

"Bow head, extend wings, chirp."

"Was he at the furnace?"

"Bow head, extend wings, chirp."

"Great. Was Sister Marcy with him?"

"Bow head, extend wings, chirp."

"Is there anything else you need to tell us before we go?"

Nick had hoped for the question, and he respected the hunter for thinking of it. He assumed Liam led the inquiry while Canter wrestled with whatever figurative and literal demons assaulted him. "Bow head, extend wings, chirp."

Liam revealed the limits of his avian interrogation skills. "I don't know how to get anything from him but yes-no answers."

Canter's ongoing struggle against anxiety was evident in his voice. "It's pretty much yes-no unless you want to draw an alphabet chart in the dirt."

"Not yet. Does Solomon have firearms?"

This time, Nick ordered something different. "Raise wingtips. Look up."

"That's his 'I don't know' response. He probably didn't get close enough to see."

Liam continued. "Was anyone else with them?"

"Look left. Look right. Look left. Look right."

"That's a 'no'."

"Thanks, Seth, but I figured that one out on my own." The hunter looked to the ground. "But I'm stumped on what to ask next. You guys got any ideas?"

The lawmen shook their heads.

Facing the impasse, Nick drew letters in the sand. With the sluggish control of sharing the bandwidth with Jake's falcon, he moved slowly, commanding talons to reposition the bird while he scratched lines with its beak.

Liam announced the letters as they formed. "A... M... B... U..."

Stiles guessed. "Ambulance!"

"Bow head, extend wings, chirp."

"He said 'yes'." Liam looked into the eagle's eyes. "He wants us to get an ambulance now. Is that right, Nick?"

"Bow head, extend wings, chirp."

Liam scowled. "That doesn't show much faith in us."

"Look left. Look right. Look left. Look right."

"No. What does 'no' mean? No, it does not, not show much faith in us? God help me. I'm interpreting double negatives with a bird." He looked up for translation support, but Canter was wringing his hands. "Maybe… someone else is already hurt?"

Nick appreciated the attentive audience. "Bow head, extend wings, chirp."

"Sister Marcy's already hurt?"

"Bow head, extend wings, chirp."

"Shit. He's already cutting her up?"

"Bow head, extend wings, chirp."

Overhearing the exchange, Stiles announced his decision. "I'll call for an ambulance. I'll have them bring ice to preserve her severed body parts."

Liam stood. "And we need the horses to get there. Shit. We're charging into a trap. We know it, and so does he. This is completely against Father's instructions, but we have no choice. Let's grab everything we can carry and get on with it."

CHAPTER 35

As the lawmen wrestled despair and anxiety, Liam took charge of the three-man, three-horse team. He stuck buds into his ears and tested their communications. "Seth? Can you hear me?"

Canter's voice issued from the hunter's phone, through the wired headset, and out the buds. "Loud and clear. Can you hear me?"

"I hear you. Keep the line open. Tom, are you there?"

Though resigned to his death, Stiles remained functional. His connection was strong. "I hear you just fine, Liam."

"You guys ever ride before?"

Canter and Stiles shook their heads.

"It's been a few years for me, but Father taught me how to hunt on horseback. Your horses will move fast, but they'll follow mine. You guys have one job, and that's to hold on." Liam climbed his steed, threw his leg over its far side, and sank into the saddle. His groin tightened against the strain. "Easy, boy."

Aided by the former owners, the lawmen mounted their horses to neighing protests.

As he eyed the anxious animals, Liam felt a strange and temporary lordship over them, like they were on divine loan to him. "Steady! Follow me, and don't buck!"

The horses behind him quieted.

Liam found the whip by his hand, lifted it, and cracked it down. "Yah!" The horse broke into a gallop, jerking the hunter's arm and hips and smacking his teeth together. After several strides, he slowed the horse to a trot and looked over his shoulder.

Behind him, the lawmen clutched their reins and crouched

for their lives atop their trotting steeds.

As he passed through the gate into the main path, Liam nudged his horse onto the beaten pathway. With the map memorized and the trail marked with points of interest, he was confident in his direction.

Something unnatural, an entity on the edge of the young hunter's awareness, revealed to him its friendly intervention in guiding the horses.

As his steed accelerated, wind tickled Liam's cheeks. He fell to one side but then found his balance, his stale equestrian skills returning. Another rearward glance showed the lawmen keeping pace, which confirmed for the hunter the presence of a foreign spirit guiding the novice riders and their mounts.

The historic worksite rose between the trees, and torchlight cast a blockish shadow onto the trampled earth outside the furnace's open wall. A weaker shadow arose and moved in a long downward arc, followed by a woman's horrific shriek of pain.

Seeking the light source, Liam looked under the roof and saw Solomon's silhouette hovering over his restrained victim. The shadows twisted as the priest lifted his torch's flame from the cauterized wound. "Bloody hell. He just cut off her hand!"

Though beyond earshot, Father Solomon snapped his head in the young hunter's direction. Red auras rose from his eyes and then disappeared as the priest swept his arm across his body.

Unsure how to interpret the demoniac's movement, Liam got his answer when he heard men shrieking in his ear.

Canter flew across his field of view to the right, hit the dirt, and rolled. To the left, Stiles finished his aerial summersault with a ballistic trajectory hurling him at a dark rock outcropping. Both horses went limp before they hit the ground.

Wondering why the demonic gesture had spared him, Liam stopped his steed. He kept his eyes on Solomon, who glared back while the hunter checked if his partners remained with him. "Seth? Tom? Talk to me."

Groaning, Canter sounded hurt. "I'm here."

"What happened?"

"Damned horse just threw me. Ah, shit. It's on the ground behind me. Looks dead as a doornail."

Liam eyed the other lawman. "Same thing happened to Tom. But he's not talking. Tom? Tom? No. Nothing."

"Sorry about Tom, but I've got my own problems. My leg's broken pretty bad."

As he dismounted, Liam adjusted his plan, or his lack thereof. "Can you move?"

"Yeah. I think so."

"Can you hide in the tree line to the left? It'll give you a clear field of fire."

"Yeah. I think so. I'll need a couple minutes."

"I'll distract him. Check on Tom on your way there."

"Roger that."

Keeping his gaze on Solomon's dark and unexpectedly unmoving form, Liam reached behind his back for his assault rifle. Its grip felt familiar and true. But as he remembered that Father Solomon may be worthy of rescue, the young hunter recalled his invented tactics, released the weapon, and grabbed his water gun.

Alone, he stood facing the beast. A barb of stark terror pierced him, and he steeled his will before lifting his boot off the fallen pine needles. He whispered to himself. "Father, where are you?"

Solomon's voice was haughty but human, complicating the discernment between the man and the demon as the sentiment's source. "Your father is not here. Your companions cannot help you. Do you believe that you can stop me by yourself?"

Unsure if he should answer, Liam scoured his memory for the rules of dealing with demons. He was tempted to enter verbal combat, but the dangers of debating a wickedly superior intellect stopped him. Instead of talking, he reached under his bulletproof vest and revealed the cross hanging from his necklace.

Sarcasm dripped from Solomon's lips. "A crucifix. Please, no." He flipped up and brandished his own cross from under his chin.

Although exposed as an easy target, Liam crouched and crept towards the torch and the priest holding it.

"A water gun? Do you intend to defeat me with holy water?"

Again, Liam held his silence, despite his fear and uncertainty.

Canter's hoarse voice interrupted the hunter's standoff. "Liam? You copy?"

"Yeah."

"Tom's dead."

Although the FBI man was a new member, the team's first death stung. "How? Can you see a cause of death?"

His features twisting in the torchlight, Solomon intercepted the question. "Oh, I'm afraid he broke his neck. When I crushed your horses' hearts, they fell rather abruptly. Equestrian accidents can be quite violent."

Liam reached the stone floor and stepped to the central table.

Below him, the restrained and gagged Sister Marcy squirmed and cried. Bloody, cauterized stumps capped each wrist where her hands had been detached. Upon seeing her champion, the nun broke into uncontrolled weeping.

Liam raised the water gun for Solomon's viewing. He walked around the table, stopped a yard from the killer, and pointed the plastic nozzle at his face. "You're going to depart from the priest before you harm this woman of Christ further."

"No."

"Yes." Liam squeezed the trigger, and holy water peppered the priest's face.

The demon screamed, and the beast's eyes glowed red. Then, the priest's face stretched into a hawkish shape, the underlying bones crunching and reshaping themselves as they moved under his skin.

Liam lowered his water gun as he cringed. "Disgusting."

"Silence!" Solomon thrust his knife towards the hunter's throat.

Redirecting the attack, Liam dropped his toy. Before the water gun hit the ground, he stepped aside, caught the assailant's arm, and put the demoniac's wrist into a joint lock behind his back. With control over Father Solomon's frame, he pushed the murderer against the work area's far stone wall.

Solomon hit the façade, and he coughed as the impact emptied his lungs.

With the serial killer pinned against the unmoving surface, Liam dared to hope he'd ended the ordeal.

The force bursting from Solomon corrected the hunter's optimism. Despite impossible leverage, the priest's joint-locked arm smacked the bulletproof vest, knocked the air from the hunter's lungs, and toppled the would-be rescuer backwards over the nun.

As the helpless woman groaned under his weight, Liam strained his abdomen to curl his torso upright. Returned to his feet, he squared off against the priest, who faced him.

Solomon's facial bones had retaken their normal shape, causing the hunter to stare an extra beat.

Too slowly, Liam saw the grounded water gun. He stooped and reached for it.

Solomon's heel crashed down on the plastic toy's barrel, cracking it. "No. Holy water hurts." He smirked and then backhanded the hunter's cheek.

Liam whipped his jaw with the blow to soften its impact, and then he panicked. His father handled demons, and without paternal guidance, the young hunter wavered. With one thought, he wanted to kill Father Solomon. With the next, he wanted to attempt an exorcism. Then still another idea called for him to wrestle the serial killer into submission and await the proper exorcist.

But how long to wait? Liam felt helpless while his father made his private preparations for a battle that had already started.

A muzzle flash preceded the crack of thunder echoing off the work areas surfaces. Dust flew from a projectile's impact against the stone wall behind Solomon.

Liam glared at the priest.

The demon returned the gesture. "Your colleague has good aim, but I will dodge every bullet." A second shot whizzed by the possessed man, but he twisted his torso and canted his head to avoid damage. He chuckled and turned his cheek to show the hunter the scrape the grazing bullet had left under his ear. "He's wasting bullets."

Liam kept his eyes on the priest while addressing his partner. "Stand down, Seth. He's dodging your shots."

"Well, that's a relief. I thought my vision was going."

"Did you hear me? He's dodging them. He just used his little pinky to toss me, and now he's showing off how much faster he is than your bullets."

"Don't bitch to me about it! I don't know demons. I thought I should kill him after he tried to put a knife through you, but now I'm afraid I just pissed him off."

"Apparently, I haven't learned as much as I thought from Father."

"Yeah. Where the hell is your damned daddy?"

As the possessed priest thrust his knife towards the gap above the hunter's armor and below his jaw, Liam predicted the motion and sidestepped the blade. Ducking, he lowered his center of gravity, disarmed his assailant, and then pushed his shoulder into the overextended priest.

The wrestling duo toppled onto the horrified nun and then fell to the floor next to the fallen knife.

With a size, weight, and skill advantage, Liam used his momentum to pin the demoniac's chest to the floor with both arms barred behind his back. "Seth. Hurry."

"Hurry where? I can't see shit!"

"I've got him pinned to the ground. Come here and free her. I don't know how long I can hold him."

"Did you forget about my shattered leg?"

The priest overpowered his captor's weight, sliding a leg forward.

Liam felt the resistance, the skillful shifting of weight, and the unnatural strength rising within his prisoner. "Come on, Seth."

His second leg forward, the demoniac hunched himself and lifted his haunches.

Adjusting, Liam dug his boot heels into the priest's thighs and arched his back. The counterpressure stalled Solomon's escape, but the hunter considered his predicament a degrading stalemate. "I could really use some help about now."

"Damn it, I'm coming. Shit! Ouch! You try this with a busted leg and–son of a..."

"Seth?"

"Yeah. I'm here. That hurt like hell."

Liam knew he was taxing his injured partner, but Solomon had wiggled a wrist halfway free, and time was running out. "How many more seconds?"

"Seconds? You're an optimist, son. I'm still at least a minute out."

Sweat lubricated his victim's fingers, and Liam held just two fingers of the priest's escaping hand. "I've got about ten seconds."

"Until what?"

Frustrated, Liam yelled loud enough for his partner to hear without the telephones. "Until Father can get here and nail this bloody demon. Otherwise, we're screwed."

"I don't see your father, Liam. It's just you and me. You got a plan B?"

"Yeah. Come shoot the jackass in the head. Let's watch him dodge a bullet from inches away."

"Roger. I'm trying. I'm forty seconds out."

Solomon yanked his hand free and then reached backwards for the hunter's hair.

Liam blocked the grab but needed to elevate some of his bulk from the priest to do so.

The sly demon bumped and wiggled the possessed priest at perfect moments to buck and slide from under the larger man.

"This is taking longer than I thought." Canter sounded exhausted and frightened. "I need another forty seconds. Liam? Liam? Shit. Should we call the women into the void?"

The question shocked Liam's attention from his wrestling match, and he barked his answer between grunts. "No. Don't get them killed, too."

"Damn it, Liam. They're not dying today. You're not dying today."

Bracing his freed arm against the ground, the priest reared with lighting speed, knocking the hunter back with super-human force.

Liam heard the back of his helmet thud the stone wall before losing consciousness.

When he awoke disoriented, he was seated on the floor with his back against the wall. He tried to caress his head wound, but his hands were bound behind him, and his feet were tied.

Beside him, Canter posed in a similar position but with his untied broken leg angled to the side. "Sorry."

"About what?"

Stepping from the shadows, the priest brandished his blade. "He's sorry for failing you–just like your friends, wife, and father."

Gathering his bearings, Liam realized his predicament. Fail-ure. He wanted to show defiance, but the demon's victory weak-ened his spirit. "Father has failed?"

"He abandoned you. As has your brother-in-law."

"No. They'd never quit."

"Would I have kept you alive if there were any chance of someone helping you? No. Of course, not."

Resigned, Liam spat his anger. "Get it over with. Kill us."

Canter nodded. "Damned right. We're not afraid to die."

Solomon smirked. "First, you watch horror. Then, you feel horror. Then, you die." He lifted his shimming knife above the squirming nun's exposed foot.

Liam's heart pounded, and he screamed as the blade arced to-wards the woman's flesh. "No!"

A dark flash streaked into the work area and knocked the knife from the priest's hand.

Canter yelped. "Way to go, Jake! Come on, Nick. Get him!"

The second streak was slower and larger when it spread its wings in front of the serial killer. The eagle stayed in the priest's face, assailing it with shrieks and talons.

After circling back, the smaller original flash joined its larger cousin in combatting the demoniac.

Unsure how a falcon and an eagle could defeat a possessed priest who could overcome knives and bullets, Liam thought about escaping. "Work on your bonds!"

"What do you think I've been doing? Apparently, demons tie mean knots."

A glance revealed a stalemate between the birds and the nimble-handed, parrying priest. There would be no avian savior, but the raptors were buying time.

But Liam struggled to use it.

With his head aching from impacting the wall, he struggled to link sequential thoughts. He tried to force his mind into gear, but the fog of battle, the demon's spiritual oppression, and his innate fear thwarted him. He began silent prayers and prepared for death.

Then hope sprang.

Connor's voice thundered from the shadows beyond the torchlight. "Our Father who art in heaven, hallowed be thy name!"

CHAPTER 36

Diane answered her phone. "Josh?"

Alarming her, her brother issued an order. "Connor gave the signal. Enter the void and distract the beast."

"I will. Is everyone okay?"

"Stiles is dead. The others are in jeopardy."

Her brother's confidence and bluntness convinced Diane that he was channeling a greater power, but the confirmed casualty concerned her. She wanted to ask about her husband, but she accepted her brother's terse answer. "I'm sorry about Stiles. Emma and I will go in now."

"Yes. Hurry." Josh hung up.

Emma's eyes were wide. "Is it time?"

"Yeah. Daggers!" Diane reached into her purse and extracted her blade. Freeing it from its wrapping, she welcomed its touch. The bronze felt solid and warm as she lowered it to her lap. She then fished out Layla's knife, unwrapped it, and slid it between the comatose empath's crossed fingers.

Her face a mix of fear and excitement, Emma held her dagger upwards and placed her free hand on Layla's skin. She then extended her dagger across the bed.

After placing her fist and weapon on Layla's fingers, Diane accepted the German empath's hand over the bed. Then she pulled back her hand from the comatose empath and rethought the approach. "We can't bring Layla with us. Whatever her condition is, Nick and Jake need her right now. They're using her brain waves."

Emma lifted her hand from her Persian sister. "You're right."

Before the empaths could depart, Joe shared his concerns. "You're really going into the void?"

Diane looked up at him. "That's what we do."

"Even after what happened this morning?"

"Connor gave the signal. He needs us."

Joe looked at the laptops on the food tray, which he monitored from his stance at the patient's feet. "But I won't be able to watch over you. I can't watch my brothers because of the hops through Layla, and that sucks. I should be available for them."

Seated next to Diane and Emma, the other brothers held their links with their birds, but the jury-rigged route through Layla's helmet sifted out information about their statuses.

"We'll be fine."

"I don't like it."

Nervous about reengaging the demon, Diane wanted to get on with the confrontation, but she agreed with the youngest brother about establishing a communication line to the void walkers. "If I can get one or both of your brothers to agree, they can park their birds somewhere and come back to you. Then they can go back in without using Layla."

Joe perked up. "Yeah! Great idea."

"Now that I think of it, we should do that first to free Layla to help us. Otherwise, your brothers will still need her."

Satisfied with the Chaldean empath's proposal, Joe voiced his final concern. "Nobody asked me to go in, did they?"

As her husband had explained Connor's plan, Diane considered Joe indefinitely banished from the void, pending the outcome of the battle. "No. You're not going in. We need you to watch us."

Although the grandmother sat in a corner chair and was watching everyone, Joe seemed relieved to accept his role as the mission's official sidelined observer. "Sure, I will. I'll watch over you as much as possible." He scrunched his face in thought. "Hold on. You can't contact them without helmets while they're inside the birds. I'll have to get Canter to help."

Diane considered the complexity and agreed. "Yeah. You're right. Can you get a hold of him?"

"I'm calling him now." Joe's face flushed when he heard his

boss' voice. "Can you hear me… your hands are tied? How'd you answer my call? Oh. Voice command."

A pit formed in Diane's stomach. "His hands are tied?"

Ignoring her, Joe continued his call. "Diane and Emma are going into the void, but we need one of my brothers to rearrange the helmet situation. That's fine… We're hurrying." The youngest brother lowered his phone. "He said he and Liam are tied up."

Diane called out. "Is he okay?"

"I assume you mean your husband, but both of them are fine, for now. Connor's got the demon's attention."

Across the bed, Jake's eyes fluttered open. "Whoa. Shit."

Impressing the Chaldean empath, Joe showed a glimpse of leadership. His normally aloof demeanor shifted to one of businesslike care. "Look at me, Jake."

The husky middle brother turned his head.

"You just returned from a falcon to a hospital room with me, Nick, and our new psychic friends. Do you know where you are?"

"Yeah. Canter yelled at me to come back and hook up through my own helmet. I need to get back in there."

Joe scurried to a bag resting on a windowsill and pulled out a skull cap. He stepped back to the laptops and tossed it. "Here."

Jake slid off the cap he shared with the patient and slipped into his solitary helmet. He then handed the connector end to the German empath. "Plug that into the laptop."

"Which one?"

"The one where Layla's is plugged in. There's a free USB slot." Jake pointed to the connection that would relay his brainwaves through the void, to Canter's field transmitter mounted in the trunk of a parked Jeep, and into his waiting falcon.

After the German empath complied, Joe tapped the keyboard. "You're connected to Canter's transmitter."

"I'll tell Nick to come back, and then I'll get right back into the demon's face."

Diane faced the husky brother. "How can you talk to Nick?"

Jake smirked. "We've been doing this for years. We've got

ways to communicate bird to bird."

Adapting to his coordinator role, Joe snapped. "Get back in there. Do you need more serum?"

"No. I'm still groggy enough." Jake leaned back into his chair and closed his eyes. He stirred and wiggled for a few seconds before calming himself and falling still.

Diane looked to Emma. "I can't wait anymore."

"You want to go in without Layla?"

"Yes. Liam's out there. It's our turn now."

The German empath glanced at Joe for a confirming nod. "See you in there."

"I'll go first. You follow me in immediately."

"Okay. Go ahead."

Diane's awareness materialized within the starry world, and her initial impressions suggested a lingering paranoia. Active void walkers were few, and the movement of light sources was subdued during the demon's heightened activity.

Emma appeared beside her as an azure body. "Diane?"

"I'm here. I see you."

"I don't see anyone."

"It's gotten even more quiet in here."

"It's creepy. We're practically alone."

"But we're not alone. Let's find our friends." Diane scanned the dark canopy in the direction of Cunningham Falls State Park. In the void, the huge expanse of protected land was a strobe of interlaced auras. The Chaldean empath couldn't discern one light source from another, but their clustered glows offered a destination. "Over there."

Acting on the suggestion, Emma thrust herself forward.

"Wait for me." Diane caught her colleague and grabbed her ethereal hand. "We're keeping our minds separated until we unite with Layla. But we're stronger together. Stay close."

As the battle came into view, Diane saw six familiar auras in which blues, violets, and azure hues swirled slowly, marking her friends. Centered among her colleagues, a dark blob of bruise-like and sanguine colors marked the beast.

Two sources of light were stationary on one side of the demon. Two different sources were unmoving on the beast's other side. Two final friends danced around the priest's head so frantically that Diane couldn't discern her enemy's face from his nape.

But she recognized her adversary. "I see the demon!"

"Me too. What now?"

Scenarios had churned through Diane's mind for hours, and she'd discussed the good ones with the German empath. "You remember me saying that we could harass his mind?"

"Yes. I like that one."

The glowing beast grew rapidly larger as the psychic duo drifted towards the battle. "It's going to take a lot of energy. We need to distract him for up to an hour in reality. That's going to feel like forever in here. Pace yourself."

"I know. I'm ready."

"Nick and Jake will harass him from the outside. We'll mess with him from the inside. No matter what, don't stop, and yell if you get in trouble. Here goes..."

Diane aimed her awareness towards the beast and forced herself into the priest's mind.

Abject horror consumed her.

She saw through the priest's eyes, heard through his ears, and smelled the woods through his nose. But inside him, her immaterial body burned, and sharp objects tore at her ethereal flesh. Trying to bear the pain, she redoubled her resolve to stay, but the agony overwhelmed her, and she retreated.

Beside her, Emma's glowing face revealed terror. "I was in him. Now I'm not."

"Me neither. It was like he's being burned and carved alive inside his own body. Right? That's what I noticed."

"Me too. Burning and cutting. It's horrible. You saw through his eyes, too, right?"

"Yeah." Diane recalled the quick snapshot she'd seen before the pain had evicted her. "Connor and Josh were there on horses. I don't know why they had horses, but I bet Connor wants to get started on an exorcism and needs us to distract Father Solomon."

"But we can't do that. I can't take that burning and cutting."

As her mind calmed, she understood her predicament. "Demons. Liam told me that multiple demons usually possess a body. Those were lesser demons attacking us."

"That's a good thing. That means we're distracting them."

Diane despaired. "Only if we can sustain it, which we can't."

Jake surprised the empaths. "Hello, ladies! Did you miss me?"

"You gave up on the bird?"

"I got called back. Canter saw the priest drop his arms and go catatonic for a couple seconds. We figured that was you and Emma stopping him from the inside. So, I came here to join you."

Diane welcomed the brother. "We think there are multiple demons inside him, and they're ganging up on us when we get in. They're burning and cutting us. The pain was too much, and we had to run."

"I can't make us fireproof, but I can make constructs that will give us extra time against heat and cuts. But first, your daggers." Jake gazed at his rolling hands as he drew twirling light to them and weaved the weapons as if pulling taffy. He handed out the luminous daggers and then weaved a garment "Here. See if you like this." He tossed the armored proximity suit at the Chaldean empath.

After tucking her void-dagger into her void-jeans, Diane reached out to catch the suit, but it slipped by her hand and enveloped her glowing form. "I don't even feel it."

"Nor should you. Try it in there while I make one for Emma."

"Okay." Without resistance, Diane slipped back into the priest's mind. This time, the flames invoked a distant but rising pain over the fuzzy contours of her body, and she noticed the reddish and purple auras twisting into claws and talons as they poked, sliced, and gouged her. But the suit deflected the attacks–initially.

Angered, demons within Solomon's head howled.

Diane smirked and pumped her feet, trying to reposition herself anywhere within the priest's mind, see what she could see, and become a general nuisance for the unwelcomed spirits.

The demons adjusted their tactics and redirected the flames and puncture attacks into her moving body. With scant room for her maneuvering inside the demoniac's head, they overwhelmed her.

Within minutes, the heat overwhelmed her defenses, and Diane withdrew.

Back in the void, above the park, Emma wore a similar suit. "It must have worked well."

"It did. I ran around and screwed with them. They didn't like it!"

Emma was enthused. "Me next!"

"No. Me next, after I repair Diane's suit." Jake wore his own version of the protective construct. "I need to see for myself and let Joey know."

Diane nodded. "Okay. But do you think we have a chance?"

Jake smirked. "Per my estimate, you just spent more than three void minutes in there. That makes a difference in reality. If we take turns doing it, we can stall this guy."

"That doesn't mean Connor's exorcism will work."

"Agreed. We're doing our part, but he needs to bring this home."

CHAPTER 37

Nick flapped his wings and pecked Father Solomon's nose. The demoniac swatted the eagle away, but the firstborn sibling recovered and pumped himself back into the enemy's face.

On the next pass, the priest's face froze and his flailing arms fell to his side.

Nick hesitated and then aimed his beak at his boss.

Canter was talking to the young hunter seated and restrained beside him.

Needing guidance, Nick chirped.

Hearing the hail, Canter craned his neck towards the psychic and shot glances at the combatants within the work area. "When Solomon turns into a statute, that's thanks to the ladies and your brother. They're in his head."

Father Solomon came to life, growled, and smacked the unwary eagle.

Nick tumbled against the wall and then fell to the ground. He checked his wings for damage, but despite a few lost feathers, the resilient and pliant bones were fine. Control of the raptor had accelerated with his brother's departure from the falcon, but the firstborn sibling noticed a lingering delay through Layla's helmet. Feeling his mental exhaustion and the raptor's physical fatigue, he looked again to his boss.

Canter clarified his latest update. "Jake's in the void with the ladies helping them invade his head."

Aiming the bird's face upward, Nick watched Connor guide a horse to the table and its restrained nun, followed by Josh, who sat tall in the saddle of his borrowed steed. Unsure if his eagle eyes tricked him, he thought Connor appeared entranced, repeating incessant prayers aloud while Josh seemed hyperaware and regal.

Josh stopped short of the work area's roof and remained on the table's far side. His torchlit frame re-radiated and multiplied the light in the darkness, adding a glimmer of gold to its hues.

Connor dismounted and walked between the priest and the long-ago retired furnace. His eyes were narrow as he recited the Athanasian Creed. "For there is one Person of the Father; another of the Son; and another of the Holy Ghost. But the Godhead..."

Solomon turned and squared off with his would-be exorcist. "You attack from within and without. But you cannot–". The priest went comatose.

Connor reached for the stole around his neck, stepped forward, and lifted it to the priest's forehead. He signed the cross and then lowered his stole.

Before the exorcist could return his arm to his side, Solomon grabbed it. "You cannot win."

Nick spread his wings to pump to Connor's aid, but his boss barked.

"No, Nick! Get back to Joey and get Layla off your jury-rigged helmet. Then get back into your eagle the right way."

Obeying, Nick extracted himself from the bird. The journey to reality was slower than usual, and he blamed the extra hop through Layla's head. But he reached his body and opened his eyes.

Unconscious people surrounded him. Layla lay before him, while across the bed next to Emma sat his brother. Beside him, sat the entranced Diane.

The only awake people were the grandmother and Joe. "Nick?"

"Yeah."

"You just returned from an eagle to a hospital room with me, Nick, and the three psychic ladies. Do you know where you are?"

"I'm in the hospital, but not for long."

"Correct." Joe scurried to a bag, grabbed a proper skull cap, and lobbed it. "Here."

Nick caught it, wiggled out of the jury-rigged contraption, and shifted to his helmet. "Any words of advice?"

"Protect Connor during the exorcism. Jake, Diane, and Emma can only strike in short bursts. You need to strike, dance, and dodge like a boxer as Solomon shifts between awake and asleep."

"I'll do my best. I don't need any serum." Nick closed his eyes and tried to relax, but the void eluded him. "Forget that. I need another ten milligrams."

Joe prepared a syringe and handed it to him.

"Thanks." Nick injected the fluid into his thigh. Moments later, he reappeared within the eagle, which stood quietly on the ground beside his boss. He looked up and chirped.

"You in there, Nick?"

Nick bowed his head, spread his wings, and chirped.

"Are you direct through your helmet?"

Again, Nick gave the affirmation.

"Good. Now untie me, for crying out loud."

Glancing upward, Nick saw Connor praying over the compliant priest. Seizing the opportunity, he stepped behind his boss and examined the zip tie binding his wrists. With a determined bite, the eagle's beak snapped the plastic.

Canter grabbed Nick, clasping his wings while lifting him to his face. "Protect Connor, but don't hurt Solomon. We're rescuing him, too. I'll free Liam, and we'll get Sister Marcy to the ambulance." He tossed the raptor at the priest.

The priest came to life, signaling another changing of the guard. As he thrust each psychic from his mind, he enjoyed several seconds of freedom to thwart and harass the exorcist. "All this effort to get to me? I knew you were foolish, Brady, but this is ridiculous." He extended his hand to slap the elder hunter.

Nick pumped to alter his ballistic path, and he undercut the blow, interrupting it.

Feathers flew, but the hunter ignored the glancing strike against his face. "In the name of Jesus Christ, tell me your name." He pulled a vial of holy water from his garments and sprinkled the subject.

The priest grimaced and moaned as water hit his face. "You think you know my name. But you want me to say it to gain power over me. You should know better."

"In the name of Jesus Christ, tell me if you are held in him by necromancy, by evil signs or amulets."

"I'm held in him because I want..." Solomon went comatose.

Seeking a clue of his next move, Nick landed on the priest's head and looked to his comrade's faces.

Like a robo-exorcist, Connor continued his praying.

Seated tall on the steed, observing the confrontation like a judge, Josh appeared to have undergone a transformation from a shy autistic man to a golden-hued overlord.

Behind the demoniac, Liam helped the CIA supervisor stand on his good leg. "Help me untie Sister Marcy. You'll take her to the ambulance on my horse. Remember to bag up her hands."

Seth hobbled towards the nun. "Roger that."

The young hunter pointed at the eagle's beak. "Is that Nick?"

"Yeah. He's direct through his helmet now."

"Stay on his head, Nick. Pull his hair and use his hair as reigns for a bull ride. Peck his ears and nose from there."

Liking the young hunter's advice, Nick gave the affirmation gesture and chirp, and then he dug his talons into tufts.

The priest awoke, but the commotion beside him distracted him from the exorcist. He looked to his left. "You may rescue her tonight, but she is still mine. You cannot protect her forever." Keeping his feet planted, Solomon whipped his left arm at the young hunter, who was reaching for the bonds at the nun's closest foot.

The superhuman speed and strength surprised Liam, who howled as bones in his forearm cracked.

Nick pumped his wings and yanked the tufts like guy wires.

Seeing the dilemma, Connor continued his praying but also doused the energumen with holy water.

Screaming, the priest released the young hunter's broken arm and reached for the bird.

Nick let go of the hair and flew above his enemy's reach. His wingtips hit the roof as he evaded the demoniac's groping fingers.

Solomon went silent again.

Nick descended to his hair, grabbed tufts, and awaited the next round of combat.

Connor continued his recitation. "In the name of Jesus Christ, tell me the sign of your departure, so that I'll know when you have left God's servant."

Sister Marcy cried in pain, horror, and hope as the young hunter helped her and the limping CIA supervisor to a horse. "My hands."

Liam consoled her. "We bagged them up. We've got an ambulance in the parking lot and microsurgeon waiting for you at the hospital. Get out of here while you still can." He helped Canter and then the nun to the back of his horse.

Sister Marcy looked over her shoulder and locked her gaze onto the mounted autistic man. "Forgive me. My crisis of faith is over. God's angel has spared me."

Josh gave her a slow nod.

She faced forward abruptly.

Holding the reigns in one hand and the nun in the other, Canter dangled his broken leg over the saddle's side. With his good leg, he kicked the animal, and it trotted away.

Cradling his broken bones, Liam kicked the knife from Solomon's limp hand and then marched to his father. "What more can I do, Father?"

From his mount, Josh intercepted the question with a deep voice that carried impossible authority. "He cannot speak beyond the exorcism."

"Is it working?"

"It is too soon to know."

Solomon became animated again and reached for Nick. "Your best efforts are mere annoyances. You can save Sister Marcy today, but I will abduct her again and finish this, after I finish all of you."

Again, Nick climbed free from harm.

When the priest went quiet again, Liam surprised the first-born sibling by bending over the table and scratching lines in the dust. "Look here, Nick."

Nick landed on the table and saw the alphabet chart.

"Josh and Father are in some other state of mind. That makes you the only human I can talk to out here. I want us to communicate."

With the opening, an idea rushed into Nick's mind. He scratched a line beside the chart, tapped three letters, and then tapped the line.

"C... A... N... and then a line. What's that line?"

Subconsciously, Nick despaired and sent a "slumped shoulders" order to the eagle. He then repeated the first three letters and the line, and then he added two more letters.

"C... A... N... line... I... T... Got it. 'Can it'. The line is a space between words.

Nick gave the bobbing affirmation and then pecked his question.

Liam recited it out loud. "Can it work with team in his head?" He looked at the eagle. "It? You mean the exorcism?"

Nick signaled the confirmation.

"That's a great question. If it can't, we're screwed. I'll ask your brother and find out."

CHAPTER 38

Liam called Joe. "Hi, Joe?"

"Hey. Is this Liam?"

"Yeah. It's me. I thought we'd share a situation report. Seth just extracted Sister Marcy to the ambulance, but I think we've got a standoff between Father and the demon."

"What's that mean?"

As the demoniac awoke and taunted his father, the eagle taunted the taunter, and the process repeated. "I don't know enough about exorcisms to say, but this looks like it's going nowhere."

"Where do exorcisms normally go?"

"Good question. This may be normal, but I've got a bad feeling. I expected something more definitive from Father."

"If you don't know, I sure don't. Your dad's the expert."

Seeking a sanity check, Liam recalled his father's teachings out loud. "He said these normally take multiple sessions and weeks or months to complete. So, why are we trying to power through a legendary grade demon in one night?"

"We didn't have any choice. We had to save Sister Marcy."

As Father Solomon went limp again, the young hunter recalled his prior demonic battle. In the Iraqi wild, a demon had been defeating Connor until Josh had channeled an angel to the confrontation. Now, Josh and his divine puppet master let the exorcist struggle through tonight's session. But the session reached its halfway point without a setback, and Liam tried to set aside his doubts. "You're right. He cut off her hands, but she's safe now."

"Are you safe?"

Liam found the question insightful for the team's previously aloof member. "I don't know." Beside him, his father continued his prayers and commands to the demoniac. Over his shoulder, whoever resided in Josh's body kept the steed steady and oversaw the exorcism. Though he found the setting strange, he couldn't point to a flaw. "I guess I'm fine. Father and Josh may have this under control after all. Maybe I'm just paranoid."

"After what we've been through, there's no such thing."

The agreement helped Liam's sanity check. "Good point."

"Do you know where Josh and your dad went?"

"Father said he to await his signal while he prepared. That was all. I'd say he gave the signal for certain when he and Josh showed up on horseback."

"That's what Canter said. I guess it was an impressive entrance."

"It was, but the outcome's still far from known." Liam wanted an update. "Have you heard from the void?"

"Just reports from Jake when he can make it to a communications conduit. They're taking turns attacking. He says it hurts a lot, but they can keep it up."

"And it's working, from what I can see on our end. Solomon's going limp and helpless every minute or so, and then he's waking up half a minute later."

"That sounds like how we planned it out."

Solomon became reanimated. "Pull my hair. Peck my face. Invade this meat suit's mind. Try all your tricks, but you must know that exorcising me is hopeless."

In the third and final iteration of commands, Connor continued to his next order. "In the name of Jesus Christ, tell me the sign of your departure, so that I'll know when you have left God's servant."

Seeing an opening during which Nick placed the eagle beyond reach, Solomon reached into his tunic, withdrew a hidden blade, and thrust it towards the exorcist's exposed neck.

Atop his horse, Josh addressed the demon, and his eyes glowed with a violet glint. "Stay your devilry." The priest's hand opened, the knife slipped from his grip, and the edge bounced off Connor's armored vest.

Red eyes of ire rose from the demoniac, and he shot a ruthless glare to the rider. "You?"

Meeting the enemy's stare, Josh said nothing.

The beast possessing Solomon sounded scared. "How can it be? I should have sensed you coming."

Josh lowered his gaze to Connor. "The Lord's servant prays."

"His prayers hid you from me?"

"You know our laws."

Solomon's eyes narrowed. "The laws of our so-called Father. So, you hid behind a praying meat suit to lure me here. Well played. But those same laws you skirted also prevent you from harming me."

Josh lifted his gaze. "I cannot. But the Lord's servant can."

Connor whipped holy water onto the energumen's face.

Solomon screamed but went limp before emptying his lungs.

An idea sprang into Liam's head. He kicked away the fallen knife and then reached into his vest for his handcuffs. Extracting them proved difficult one handed, but he succeeded. He closed the clicking metallic teeth around his wrists and secured his hands behind his back.

Solomon woke up, and the stainless steel shackles turned bright orange, smoked, and melted off his skin.

Undeterred, Connor continued the session. "In the name of Jesus Christ, tell me your number."

Liam looked to Josh for guidance. "What can I do?"

No response.

The young hunter raised his voice. "Can't I do anything to help?"

Again, no response.

"Josh! Are you in there? I need help."

As the possessed priest fell once more into a standing sleep, the exorcist's readings became a background drone. "In the name of Jesus Christ, tell me why you entered God's servant."

Frustrated, Liam felt his adrenaline falling, and the pain in his arm rose. "Damn it, Josh. I don't know what to do."

Again, the rider ignored him.

"I'm begging you, Josh, or whoever you are. I recognize you as a servant of the Lord, and I seek your counsel."

"Stand by your father."

Surprised, Liam realized the advice was more than wise counsel. It was an order. He stepped to the right hand of the exorcist and faced the demon.

"Read with him."

Again obeying Josh, Liam lowered his head and read from the book resting on his father's forearm. His voice merged with the exorcist's. "Depart, then, impious one, depart, accursed one, depart with all your deceits, for God has willed that man should be His temple. Why do you still linger here? Give honor to God the Father almighty, before whom every knee must bow…"

Solomon glared but kept his hands at his sides and said nothing. Halting its attack, the confused eagle stood on his head.

With his father, Liam continued the session. "You might delude man, but God you cannot mock. It is He who casts you out, from whose sight nothing is hidden. It is He who repels you, to whose might all things are subject. It is He who expels you, He who has prepared everlasting hellfire for you…"

Solomon's eyes glazed over again, and he was gone.

Connor finished his recitation. "Amen."

Liam assisted. "Amen. Father?"

For the first time since his hasty departure for his preparations, Connor spoke to his son. But he kept his eyes on the enemy as he shut his tome and handed it to the young hunter. "Hold this."

"Okay. Now what? That's the end of the session."

"Not quite." Connor stepped to the energumen as he awoke from the latest pass of a psychic harassing his mind. "I have one more command."

Solomon's energy had waned, but his attitude was resolute, and his eyes burned red. "You have exhausted the commands of the rite. You have failed. It was destined."

Connor stopped inches from the possessed priest's face and

clasped his shoulders as he drifted away again. "I've consumed nothing but holy water and Eucharist since learning your name, and I've repeated a litany of prayers incessantly to prepare."

"Father? You're acting outside the bounds of the rite."

"I know, lad. I must. For, you see, this kind does not go out except by prayer and fasting."

"Matthew seventeen, verse twenty-one."

"Mark nine, twenty-nine was what I had in mind, but yes, those verses allude to the same thing, the same kind of demon."

"A fallen seraph or cherub?"

"I'm afraid so."

Solomon awoke again. "You wretched creatures cannot know the difference. Why argue? Seraph, Cherub, Thrones... even the lowliest among us is too great for all of your kind combined."

"He's right, Father. That's like battling something powerful enough to smite the entire planet. We have no business doing this on our own."

As the beast slept again, Connor looked over his shoulder. "That's why Josh and I solicited help from one even stronger."

Josh met Connor's gaze but then shifted his violet eyes to Liam. "When your father falls, leave him here."

The influx of surprises shocked Liam. He thought a top-choir angel was inside Josh, watching his father exorcise a fallen beast of the same choir while making plans for his father to die. "What?"

Connor answered. "I must fall."

"What? No!" Liam dumped the tome on the table and reached for his father.

Solomon awoke. "This is your plan? Fail at an exorcism and then taunt me with idle threats?"

"No. That's not a plan. This is." Connor glared at the demon and stated its name.

Scrunching the priest's face, the demon tried to hide his pain. "I was waiting for you to try that. But you will never hear me say my name. You think you know it. You will never be certain."

"Joe Slate told me." Connor said the demon's name again.

Steeled against hearing the name, the demon was less shaken. "Depart from me while you still can, Brady."

As the priest slept again, Connor addressed his son. "Tell the team to leave Father Solomon and the demon alone. No more distractions. I need his full attention."

Liam reached with his good hand to the pocket with his phone and made the call. "Joe?"

"I'm here."

"It's Liam again. Tell them to stop. Father needs Solomon's full attention."

"You're sure?"

"I'm sure."

"Consider it done."

Solomon remained awake, unrestrained, and terrifying. "No more mosquitos in my meat suit's mind? Did you finally quit, Brady?"

Connor said the demon's name a third time and then raised his voice. "In the name of Jesus Christ, enter me."

"Father! No!"

Solomon's eyes became fiery orbs. "You cannot command that!"

"In the name of Jesus Christ, enter me."

"I refuse. You cannot." Solomon looked to the mounted rider for justice. "This cannot be."

"The Lord's servant has prayed for it."

In a final command, Connor screamed. "In the name of Jesus Christ, enter me!"

Together, Solomon and Connor collapsed to the ground.

Liam darted to the exorcist's side. "Father?"

"Bind my hands and gag me."

"Why?"

"Trust me."

"Okay." The young hunter found his backup handcuffs. "My arm's broken. I need help gagging you. Can you help?"

"I don't know how much longer I can control myself. I feel that beast in me."

"Never mind, then. Roll to your stomach." He shackled his father's hands behind his back, and then he looked to the eagle. "Nick, grab the cloth he used to gag me."

The eagle flapped its wings, moved to the wall, and curled its talons around the cloth. It then flew to the young hunter's side.

"Help me tie this." One handed, Liam slipped the fabric into his father's mouth and folded the ends behind his neck. He lifted an end to the bird's beak. "Bite and hold."

Stabilizing the bond, the eagle showed its strength.

Liam interlaced the ends and tightened the first knot. He then doubled the loop, yanking the eagle off balance and forcing it to flap and recover. "Sorry, buddy."

Pushing to his knees on the dusty floor, the priest groaned.

"Is that you, Father Solomon?"

The priest whimpered. "Yes. I deserve death."

"You were possessed."

Solomon reached for his buttocks and leg and caressed the bullet wounds Liam had given him in the cathedral. "No. It's my fault. It's all my fault. My daughters."

Liam looked to the rider for guidance. "What's next? I assume you saw this coming."

A soft violet glow issued from Josh's eyes. "Take Solomon into civil custody. Place your father on my steed."

The young hunter lifted his father's shoulders and helped him to his feet. "Are you still you?"

Connor grunted and nodded.

Liam pulled the gag under his father's chin. "Yes. The angel within Josh is keeping the beast within me at bay, for now."

"Should I free your hands?"

"No. I must be retrained. Josh will see to it from here."

"Can you get on the horse?"

"You'll have to help."

"I have one hand."

"He has two. Use him, and gag me again." Connor nodded at Father Solomon, who remained on all fours.

Liam barked. "Quit sniveling and get up here."

"I killed them all."

"Sister Marcy survived. She might even get her hands back."

The news enlivened the serial killer, and he staggered to his feet. Liam stepped back as his former enemy found his balance and walked to the horse.

"Help him up. I only have one hand."

"I'm sorry about that."

"You remember?"

"I remember too much." Solomon stuck his shoulder under Connor's buttocks and pressed his hands against the elder hunter's back while lifting him.

Liam extended his healthy hand to stabilize the effort.

Without a word, Josh set the horse in motion and carried away Connor and his possessing demon.

CHAPTER 39

Diane drifted beside the German empath. "Where's Jake?"

"He should be out now."

"Should we go in after him?"

Jake's bluish glowing form materialized beside the ladies. "He's not resisting anymore. The demons are gone."

Diane dared to hope. "Connor did it?"

"Maybe. I'll ask my brother." Jake propelled himself towards the nearest communications conduit and disappeared into the distance.

Moments later, green lines rolled across the horizon as Joe turned on the grid coordinate system.

"That's a good sign."

Emma nodded. "Yeah."

Jake reappeared. "It's over. Connor did it."

Diane was exhausted. "Thank God. I didn't know how much longer I could have kept that up."

"Me neither. That was tough, but we did it."

Feeling a kinship with her former enemy, Diane considered Jake tenacious in battle. "Yeah. We did."

"Let's get your friend. Joey turned on the grid, in case it helps."

Diane's thoughts shifted to Layla. "I don't know what to do. I don't know where she is."

"Where'd you last see her?"

"I pushed her down Seth's Door Four before her coma, just before I got my ass kicked by a demon."

"We all were getting our assess kicked. Alright, then. Follow me." Jake glided towards the communications conduit where the Chaldean empath had last seen the metaphysical Layla.

Diane checked with her German colleague. "What do you

think?"

"I doubt we'll find her there, but I don't have a better idea."

"Let's follow him."

"Why not? It can't hurt." Emma studied her colleague's belly.

The gesture made Diane insecure. "What's wrong? Did I get fat?"

"Don't be silly. Of course, not. I didn't see it before, but there's a small light inside you. Look!"

Diane glanced downward at an orb of brightness within her. "I've never seen that before."

"Oh, my God. You're pregnant!"

Diane didn't feel pregnant, but with her attention focused outward since her wedding night, she'd ignored her inner self and accepted the possibility. "Okay. I'll take a pregnancy test when we get back."

"What? You don't know?"

"If I am, it's still early."

"You're an empath. You know!"

"Not in here, I don't, or I'm too dense to notice."

"You're not dense."

"Doesn't matter. I can't tell in here, and the sooner I get back to reality, I'll know. Let's go." Leading Emma, Diane caught up with the husky brother and slowed beside him at the conduit's event horizon.

But when they joined Jake, the three psychics were alone. "Sorry, ladies. She's not here."

"She could be anywhere." Diane reconsidered the Persian empath's fate. "I don't think she's in the void anymore."

"We could search for her. Patrolling this place tedious, but we can cover a lot of ground with the three of us, and we have good search patterns."

Emma groaned.

Diane agreed with the German empath's sentiment. "If she was in here, I think we'd feel it. But we don't. And if you're both as tired as me, you need to rest."

Jake grabbed the ethereal hands of both ladies. "I was hoping one of you would admit it first. I'm exhausted, and we have forever to find Layla. So, let's go back now." He dragged his colleagues across the void to the conduit nearest the hospital.

Diane let the brother whisk her to reality, and then she awoke in her seat by the hospital bed.

Peaceful, Layla appeared asleep, remaining insentient since the battle against the demon.

Meeting the eyes of her awakened colleagues, Diane faced Jake and Emma across the bed and then saw the firstborn sibling at the sink filling a plastic cup from the tap.

His hair matted with sweat, Nick gulped water and then addressed the Chaldean empath. "Liam's waiting for you to answer his text."

"Huh?"

"Before I extracted from the eagle, he told me he was sending you a text. He told me to nudge you in case you missed it."

Diane put away her dagger and checked her phone.

Her husband had asked her to meet him at the Cathedral of St. Matthew the Apostle.

"Did he say what was happening?"

"No, but I saw everything. Connor commanded the demon to enter him. Then he and Solomon fell to the ground. Then Solomon was all of a sudden compliant and helping Liam put Connor onto the horse with Josh. Liam had Connor in handcuffs and a gag. Then they rode off."

"Who rode off?"

"Josh and Connor. Before he took Solomon into custody, Liam told me to make sure you check your texts."

"That's it?"

"Well, I checked the parking lot before I extracted myself. There was a cop car there and a second ambulance for Canter and Liam."

Diane's adrenaline spiked. "What's wrong with Liam?"

"Oh, right. You missed it. Solomon broke his arm."

"Is he okay?"

"He's fine. He handed Solomon to the cops. Then I came back

here and waited. I only got back a few minutes before you did."

"Okay, thanks." She called her husband and lifted her phone to her ear.

Liam sounded tired and tense. "Diane?"

"What's wrong? You're stressed out."

"I didn't know it was obvious. Yeah, I'm a little tense. Father took the demon into himself and then Josh took him away. He said to meet him at the cathedral."

The concepts confused Diane. "Josh isn't Josh, then."

"No way. If you'd seen him, you'd get it. There's an angel inside him. And Father isn't Father."

"I see why you're stressed, but stressing won't help."

"I'm working on calming myself. Don't worry about me."

Diane knew she'd keep worrying about him. "Where are you?"

"Driving to the cathedral. I don't know what else to do except obey Josh."

"I thought you were in an ambulance."

"For a broken arm? It can wait until I know Father's okay. Gather the gang and meet me at the cathedral."

"I can't leave Layla alone."

"Keep Nana there. She doesn't need to see Connor in this condition."

An hour later, the Uber driver stopped in front of the Cathedral of St. Matthew the Apostle. The German empath stepped from the car, and Diane followed her towards the vertical columns holding up the decorative red brick molding. "The others are already here."

On the stairs, Emma stopped. "No sign of Josh or Connor yet."

With dawn's crepuscular rays bathing her team, Diane counted the people. Her husband and the three siblings stood at the cathedral's entrance. Absent but accounted for, Canter was getting his leg set, Tom Stiles was dead, and Nana was with Layla in the hospital. Diane trotted to her husband and hugged him.

Reflexively, Liam lifted his splinted arm but embraced his

wife with his other hand.

Diane stepped back and examined the injury. The field splint was sturdy and closed with Velcro. "You're hurt."

"It hardly hurts. I've had worse."

"I know. You took a bullet for me the day we met."

"Two bullets."

"Whatever. Where's Josh and Connor?"

The silently darting eyes revealed an air of anticipation hovering over the group as they waited for her father-in-law and brother. Liam shrugged. "I wish I knew. Josh said to wait here."

Diane checked her phone and counted three unanswered texts and two unreturned calls to her brother. "I don't think he wants to be found yet."

"I don't like this."

She scowled. "Neither do I! Josh is my brother, and Connor's important to me, too."

"I know. I just can't remember him being so helpless."

Diane realized her husband was combatting exhaustion, mentally and physically. "We can keep someone here to watch for them. You might be better off going inside and resting."

"I'm not–" Liam looked to the street as a Lyft vehicle pulled up to the sidewalk. Josh stepped from the rear seat, and then Connor followed, his wrists cuffed behind his back. "That's Father!"

As the car departed, Josh withdrew the gag from his pocket and lowered it over his father-in-law's head. He grabbed the elder hunter's shackled hands and pushed him towards the building.

Connor looked at the cathedral, his eyes wide, and he howled into his gag. Though he could physically overpower his thin son-in-law, he made no attempt. Instead, he trembled and wiggled as if divinely restrained from head to toe.

The angel within Josh addressed his audience. "I restrain him, but I cannot carry him. Liam! Leonard! Come!"

Obeying, the husky men bounded down the stairs and stationed themselves on each side of the exorcist-turned-demoniac. With his arm in a field splint, Liam placed his uninjured side beside his father.

Josh stepped forward. "To the altar."

Connor writhed and howled as the muscular men manhandled him into the holy place.

Following her brother, Diane led the entourage into the sanctuary, which early arrivals to morning services inhabited. The rising sun illuminated the stained glass windows, and a white-haired man in a red choir dress prayed in the front pew.

The praying man stood as he heard the commotion, revealing himself as the archbishop. "Welcome, all." He shifted his gaze to the young hunter. "You were accurate in your description on the phone. I've heard of such possessions, but I've never seen one myself."

Liam grunted as his father tried to jostle him. "Father's a devout servant of the Lord. This shouldn't be happening."

The archbishop locked eyes with Josh. "But it is happening. Perhaps this young... man can explain it further."

His eyes casting a violet glint, Josh met the clergyman's stare. "Build a holding cell in your basement below this altar. Ward each surface with sacramentals blessed in honor of Saint Joseph, Terror of Demons. Hold Connor within it."

The archbishop canted his head. "Who are you?"

"I serve the Lord."

"I believe you. I know in my heart that I must obey you, but I have many questions."

"All will be revealed."

"How much time do I have to build this cell?"

"Three days. I will guard him while you work."

"You guard him? You keep the demon within him?"

Josh nodded.

"How long must I hold him in the cell?"

"All will be revealed."

"This is all so abnormal. But it is proper. It is holy. I'll give you a spare office to wait during construction."

"Take us to the office."

After digesting the command, the clergyman turned on his heels and led the husky men and Josh forward with their prisoner.

Diane waited in silence while the men escorted her father-in-law to a de facto divine jail.

Emma leaned into her ear. "Wild."

"Some honeymoon."

"I'd almost forgotten. You're still owed one of those."

"And I'll have it, eventually."

"Are you going to tell Liam?"

Diane frowned and switched her thoughts to the new topic. "About being pregnant?"

"Yeah."

Diane wanted to, but after seeing her husband's frustration, she reconsidered. "Not yet. He just lost his father. Let him get Connor back first."

"What if he doesn't get him back? Nobody said anything about a plan to save him."

Diane reflected upon her mission and her life. Her adopted psychic sister was in a coma, her beloved father-in-law fought for his life against a top-choir demon, her husband shouldered a world of responsibility and worry, former mortal enemies were her new allies, and she was hiding her first pregnancy. "I don't want to lose him either. It would devastate Liam. It would devastate me."

"I guess this is a hero's life. It's hard. Sacrifices."

Knowing she'd go mad otherwise, Diane accepted her role as a hero. She'd helped her colleagues save Sister Marcy and take the possessed Father Solomon into custody. She was doing good in the world, but the cost weighed upon her.

His eyes moist, Liam appeared in front of her. "I couldn't watch him like that. It's not him anymore. It's an animal."

Diane hugged her husband, as much for her sake as his. "We'll get through this. We'll save him. We'll save Layla, too."

"And we'll bring the dead back to life? We let Stiles and Sister

Jane die. We can't always undo all our failures."

Diane stepped back and eyed her husband. "But we can accept our failures and move on. We can't let fear stop us. We have work to do, together. Is my husband with me?"

He looked away. "My life's turning out a lot differently than I'd ever dreamed."

"I was never part of your dreams growing up. So, are you calling me a nightmare?"

Slowly, he returned his attention to her. "What?"

"Am I your worst nightmare?"

He snorted. "No, silly. Being without you would be a nightmare worse than serial killers and demons combined. I need you by my side, and I'm with you, Misses Brady, no matter what's next."

THE END

About the Author

After graduating from the Naval Academy in 1991, John Monteith served on a nuclear ballistic missile submarine and as a top-rated instructor of combat tactics at the U.S. Naval Submarine School. He now works as an engineer when not writing.

WRAITH HUNTER CHRONICLES:

PROPHECY OF ASHES (2018)
PROPHECY OF BLOOD (2018)
PROPHECY OF CHAOS (2018)
PROPHECY OF DUST (2018)
Prophecy of Eden (2019)

ROGUE SUBMARINE SERIES:

ROGUE AVENGER (2005)
ROGUE BETRAYER (2007)
ROGUE CRUSADER (2010)
ROGUE DEFENDER (2013)
ROGUE ENFORCER (2014)
ROGUE FORTRESS (2015)
ROGUE GOLIATH (2015)
ROGUE HUNTER (2016)
ROGUE INVADER (2017)
ROGUE JUSTICE (2017)
ROGUE KINGDOM (2018)
ROGUE LIBERATOR (2019)

PROPHECY OF EDEN

www.ingramcontent.com/pod-product-compliance
Lightning Source LLC
Chambersburg PA
CBHW030240200626
46816CB00002BA/445